LUMEN LEGENDS

THE GIFT AND THE DEFENDER

LUMEN LEGENDS, BOOK I

TYREL BRAMWELL

GRAIL QUEST BOOKS ✝ BANGOR

PUBLISHER
Josh Radke

EDITOR
Eric Postma

COVER ART & DESIGN
Ed Riojas
www.edriojasartist.com

LUMEN LEGENDS: THE GIFT AND THE DEFENDER

PUBLICATION HISTORY
Paperback edition / December 2016
ISBN: 978-0-9835488-4-3

PRINTED IN THE UNITED STATES OF AMERICA
1 3 5 7 9 0 8 6 4 2

In memory of Dan, who suffered yet remained steadfast in His victory

In the battle of good versus evil, the two forces use different tactics. Those on the side of good fight boldly in the light, their maneuvers exposed for all to see. Evil, on the other hand, attacks under the shroud of darkness, concealing its horrific actions until the moment is right to strike.

Prologue

The battered soldier lit a fire and leaned back on his heels as it crackled to life. He watched the flames grow. A moment later his eyes shifted from the orange glow of the fire to the men. They were tired, dirty, and hungry, as they lumbered about the camp. One of them joined the soldier at the fire to warm himself.

"Look at that," the man said, nodding in the direction of a particular tent. Five Royal Commanders were laughing as they entered. "What is there to laugh about?"

"When you live as they do I suppose all this looks like a joke," replied the fire starter, referring to the battle-fatigued conditions of the camp.

"Come now, do you actually believe that?" came another voice.

"Why not? They live in luxury at our expense. It must be funny for them to consider the fools outside their tents. We leave our homes to come out here, live in squalor, fight, and die. All the while, they sit in their lavish tents—that we pitch—sipping wine and stuffing their faces with roasted pork. How is that not the funniest joke they have ever heard?" He rubbed his hands together and then opened his palms to the warmth of the fire.

The conversation continued as more groundsmen were drawn to the heat. There were fires like this one all throughout the camp, each one outfitted with disgruntled groundsmen.

"What is wrong with you, fleabags?" blurted one of the royal officers as he stomped toward a fire.

"What is the matter, sir?" asked an older man.

"You. You are the matter," replied the nobleman as he pushed the man to the ground. "You call yourselves Lumenites. Real Lumenites know how to fight. Real Lumenites would not be getting their backside handed to them over and over again by the Malum." As the nobleman spoke he circled the fire, shoving any groundsman he chose until no one but himself was within reach of the fire's warmth. "Why should you get to warm yourselves by the fire? Why? Do you deserve comfort?" No one dared answer.

He continued, "You all should be ashamed to call yourselves men, let alone groundsmen. How does it feel, sitting by the fire, warming yourselves, when your brothers are dead, their bodies never to feel warmth again? You are pathetic."

A groundsman made eye contact with the nobleman and before he knew what happened he was doubled over on the ground, coughing from a blow to his stomach.

"I cannot stand to see you anymore. Go! All of you. Get out of my sight." He flung an arm into the air as if to chase away a pest and then grabbed a nearby bucket and dumped it on the fire.

The older man who had been pushed down carefully approached his superior. "Sir, may I…"

"No, you may not," barked the royal officer. "What part of get out of my sight do you not understand? Go!"

The groundsmen, used to this treatment, turned from the nobleman to make their way to the other fires. Some of them found themselves at a fire where three men were in the middle of discussing whether or not they were the punchline of a joke. They stepped near the flame, directed their attention toward a tent filled with exuberant laughter, and then one by one offered their thoughts.

Chapter One

Startled by someone shouting his name, Michaelis grabbed his sword and rolled off his straw bed. Not yet accustomed to military life, he moved sluggishly. The other groundsmen were already awake and out of their tents.

He stepped out into the cold night, the wind stinging his cheeks. With no moon in sight, darkness concealed the urgency of the moment. Lit torches moved all over the camp, gathering toward the east.

"Come on, they are already here, hurry!"

Troops stumbled to get to the forming line at the edge of camp, their cumbersome armor clanking about. Groundsmen were not professional soldiers, but average men. Their armor for the most part was ragtag, consisting of leather chunks sewn together and scraps of metal shaped to cover as much of the body as possible, hindering the men more than helping them. Unfortunately the only fighters afforded the privilege of effective equipment were royalty. The groundsmen's level of training coincided with their shabby armor. They never acquired the experience necessary to become good warriors because most who fought, died. The majority of their combat skills came from fighting fellow country-men at fairs and festivals in sport; facing an enemy in conflict was entirely different.

Every battle required new recruits, a fact that was wearing thin among the villages forced to make the sacrifice: losing farmers, blacksmiths, mill workers, and carpenters every time the king called. The men had families: wives, daughters, and sons alongside whom they inevitably ended up fighting. The time between conflicts grew shorter every day. Survivors would return, having only enough time to bury the dead before leaving again, a new group of survivors returning home to bury them. The evil they faced was relentless, never showing mercy.

Just as Michaelis approached the battle line, the warning horn blew. However, the opposing force crashing through the assembled men cut the sound short. Instantly, the agonizing screams of grown men pierced the night air. Metal on metal was the only noise drowning out cries of pain. Ranks had barely begun forming prior to the attack. Predominantly new soldiers, the groundsmen's lack of organization engendered panic among them. The enemy seized advantage of the inexperience without hesitation, coming in from all directions. Michaelis and his comrades had no clear front to defend.

"For the kingdom! For Lumen!" Sounding the battle cry, a soldier ran past Michaelis, frantically swinging his sword. The echo of his words had not yet dimmed as a hideous creature cut him down.

The enemy Michaelis fought was the same one his people had been opposing for centuries, although lately the evil foe embraced frighteningly brutal tactics. The Malum tossed away the law of arms as they found new, unorthodox and very effective techniques. The current war began when the Malum started attacking Lumen's primary trade route, but it became obvious that there was a new cause behind the bloodshed. It was about more than controlling land. The Malum destroyed everything.

An unusual breed of human, the Malum did not look unlike a normal man, but displayed mannerisms unquestionably different. Hunching over as low as physically possible when they moved, they let their arms dangle, nearly touching the ground with their fingertips. Full of conviction and truly fierce fighters, the Malum bounded around like cats descending a mountain, leaping from one ledge to the next. Their clothes were made of animal skins, primitive in comparison to the Lumenites' attire. As in any culture, some of them wore articles of clothing more elaborate than others. Some had on piecemeal garments, made up of a bizarre collection of rodent furs; others donned skins that were big enough to cover them from head to toe, those of lions, goats, or bears. Many wore grisly apparel made from the skin of Lumen soldiers whom they had defeated in previous battles, or of men from other kingdoms that they had conquered. Easily recognizable, these Malum men utilized this battle dress as an effective demoralizer.

On their faces they bore scars, artistic marks from ritualistic ceremonies. Their armor was light and flexible, allowing them to move with remarkable agility. Many of them carried only small curved daggers, wielded so smoothly that the blades appeared to be an extension of their natural body. Other warriors used a weapon unique to the Malum, an extremely thin piece of rope which easily cut through the flesh of a man. The rope was odd, shining in certain angles of light. Dreaded by all, this weapon was emblematic of how the Malum fought.

Uniquely, and with horrifying skill, as only they possessed, they would whip the rope in front of them, slashing their opponent before he was within a sword's length. The weapon was extremely versatile. Some used it to slice the ankles off their enemies, leaving them writhing on the ground to either bleed to death or be killed by another Malum fighter. The more brutal of these rope masters would wrap the device around the neck of their enemy, holding each end with opposite hands, decapitating the soldier with a quick pull. The Malum had no remorse. They utilized fear and malice as much as any handcrafted weapon to defeat their enemy. Seldom did they give any sign of their approach. That a warning had come tonight was unusual.

Although their advances were secretive, no mystery cloaked where this evil army came from. East of the Kingdom of Lumen there was a massive mountain range covered with snow-packed peaks and dim rock-piled valleys that were so low they were thought to dip into hell itself. These mountains were the Malum's playground. To anyone from outside the mountain range the area was forbidding. The barren land was void of vegetation, reeked of death, and had nothing to offer but harsh climates and brutal temperatures.

Shadows created by fallen rocks paraded about the mountains, ever changing with the shifting sunlight. Lumenite lore depicted the shadows as demons, or according to some tales, the spirits of deceased conjurers: Lumenite villagers exiled from their people due to their refusal to stop meddling in the spirit world, pursuing supernatural powers and guidance from demons through bizarre rituals.

In reality, none of the villagers knew much about the Malum Mountains. Only foolish knights-errant dared tempt their fate in the realm claimed by the Malum. The mountains provided perfect protection from any invasion, allowing their inhabitants plenty of time to prepare a defense against intruders. If a force survived the strenuous trek into the mountain range, they would undoubtedly be exhausted, hungry, and demoralized by the time they encountered the Malum.

Acerbus rested deep within the Malum Mountains. It was the stronghold of the Malum emperor, Bebbel-uk. From there he gave his orders, from there he reaped his rewards, and from there he became obsessed with conquering all of Lumen. Bebbel-uk was inconceivably evil. Only the one whom he fervently served, a woman whose unnatural beauty enslaved the hearts of the men she chose as her own, out-performed the cruelty within his heart.

Michaelis ran forward, dragging his weapon behind him. The weight of the sword was heavy in his hand, his arms not yet strong enough to swing the blade comfortably. The steel was of poor quality and the size was not well suited for the young man. What he wielded was a greatsword, a tool designed more for sport than war, typically carried by a well-trained and experienced knight. Only by dumb luck did Michaelis connect with the Malum creature who jumped in front of him. The force of the massive weapon drove the monstrous warrior's limp body down to the ground. This was his first encounter on the battlefield. A gasp of shock bellowed from his lips, releasing a wisp of air from his lungs. Before the reality of his actions could fully sink in a voice called from behind him.

"Boy! No time to celebrate. We have to go!" Speaking with the resolution of a warfront veteran, a Lumenite soldier impatiently waved for Michaelis to follow him. Under his cloak a brilliant glimmer of light danced across the man's chest as he moved.

"But the battle, it is that way." Looking back in the direction of the screams, Michaelis pointed toward other groundsmen who were being butchered.

"I know, but we do not have a prayer unless we can see Bebbel-uk's men before they are right on top of us and in the dark of night that is nearly impossible."

The seasoned warrior ran as fast as he could, getting as close to the illumination of the torches as possible, in order to prevent himself from being ambushed by the Malum, all the while staying out of it so as not to give himself away. Ducking behind one of the large tents, he tugged at Michaelis' arm.

"Get down, quick!" he rasped, glancing around the side of the tent, checking whether or not the enemy had seen them.

Michaelis bristled. "I mean no disrespect, sir but I am not a coward. I cannot sit by hiding, while the rest of our people are being slaughtered! If you have any courage left in your bones you will join me." And with that Michaelis jerked his arm away from the experienced soldier's grasp and sprinted back toward the battle. The older fighter looked on, wide-eyed as he witnessed what the boy selflessly dove into.

Crashing forward with all his might, Michaelis swung the blade in every direction his unskilled body would allow. The sword seemed to swing him as he struggled to contain its momentum. He aimlessly slashed through a mass of Malum standing unopposed over a mound of Lumen groundsmen.   Michaelis had something in his favor—surprise.

None of the Malum expected to see a member of the Lumen forces charging into their midst, especially at this point of the battle. By now, everyone who had not scattered was dead. Malum soldiers never chased after the men that ran, for they too knew the power of surprise. After the initial attack died down, they defended their position, staying close together as was their tactical method. Once certain they had driven the remaining men away permanently, the plundering commenced.

Michaelis' screaming charge from behind the tent caught them off-guard. Swinging his sword in an adrenaline induced rage he immediately leveled the two Malum closest to him. After that, any hope Michaelis had was dashed. The remaining Malum leaped instinctively toward his position. Strength quickly left his legs, the limbs weakening as youthful courage fled his body. Regret filled his mind. Fear of never seeing another sunrise clutched his heart. He felt himself falter, partly from the shock of the situation and partly from the thought of death, which ironically saved his life. When his body flopped to the ground, the Malum assumed they had killed him, like the other Lumenites, and returned to their nearby group. The last warrior to leave Michaelis reached down and picked up the groundsman's oversized weapon.

"Craftsmanship to match skill I suppose. Both quite lacking."

Michaelis was as still as the dead men around him. He was not only alive, but well aware of how his weakness saved his life. Lying in a most uncomfortable position, he stayed on the ground the exact way his body had fallen. He felt like a child hiding from friends, holding in every breath as long as possible, trying not to move, trying not to make the slightest sound. Every muscle twinge amplified in his brain. Every inhale, every exhale felt as if he were standing on a mountain shouting for his enemies to come catch him. The Malum had no idea he was still alive. Ultimately, they could not have cared less as they basked in their victory. Time seemed to drag on. Minutes were hours, hours were like days. Tension from being overly alert took a toll on Michaelis, eventually forcing his eyelids to close.

Chapter Two

The agony of sitting in a classroom waiting for the bell to ring was nearly over, for good. No more staring out windows at the springtime sun beating down on the dew-covered grass. No more pointless wishes of escaping from what was the equivalent of prison for most students. And absolutely no more trying to focus on the subject at hand simply for the purpose of trying to focus on the subject at hand.

History lectures were all but history, as were the head-nodding daytime snore fests that they brought on. Middle-aged monotone teachers two decades past remembering that they once were emotionally invested in relaying dusty details of days gone by were all but a lingering memory of a bygone era. Finals were nearly complete and with graduation only days away, Adam was more than ready.

A senior, he had been longing for graduation since the first day of high school. From the moment orientation ended Adam Malloy began counting the days. School was so easy for Adam that he rarely paid attention to the lessons discussed in the labs and lecture halls. Always anxious for tomorrow, he grew up fast, eager to get out of the confines of school and into the real world. To him, the emotional mini-world of adolescence was nothing more than a melodramatic stage for hysterical prom queens and testosterone fueled football stars.

Like most kids, Adam enjoyed the social aspects of school. The majority of his peers welcomed him. He was one of the select few able to transcend the established and protected clique boundaries. Adam got along with everyone. Although to him the extracurricular activities (sports, clubs, dances, even parties) were simply pastimes until he was able to chase his dreams.

Tired of the controlling atmosphere of school, Adam chose not to continue his education. College seemed like nothing more than a very expensive waste of time. Meeting with guidance counselors only solidified for Adam his view of higher education. He blamed their inability to direct him to a specific field of study, not realizing that most college students changed majors several times before figuring out what they wanted to do.

For years the boy felt that if ever given the chance, he could make a difference in the floundering world. According to Adam, his generation was missing the great causes romantically displayed in text books and docudramas. Movements that identified previous generations had become scarce. Considering himself intelligent enough to tackle such social issues, Adam deemed the stands of yesteryear vitally important for the health of a nation. The small-town boy wanted to fight for a cause, to right wrongs, and to help the less fortunate. After graduation he wanted to do something worthwhile, something worthy of being remembered.

"Dude, snap out of it. Bell's about to ring, you ready?"

"Ready for what?" he said, returning to the reality of his history class and the apparent conversation his friend Kevin was trying to have with him.

"The lake. Haven't you heard a word I said?"

Adam had been deaf to his friend's question. Bored, Adam's imagination floated off to the only thing he could concentrate on lately, getting out of town. He convinced himself that if he did not figure out a way to leave Lakeview immediately after being released from the clutches of high school, he would never escape.

Lakeview was a typical middle class, blue-collar town where the people dirtied their hands to earn a decent wage. A boomtown, the driving industry keeping the relatively isolated population alive was energy, specifically, natural gas. "The patch," as the residents referred to the gas fields, was the lifeblood of Lakeview. Abusive work that tortured the body, most graduates of Lakeview High strived to avoid a local career. Very few dreamt of long hours and back-breaking work in the patch. A majority aimed to leave town, to move to the city and make a name for themselves. Definitely not alone in this regard, Adam however took the threat of the patch a little more seriously than his peers. To Adam working in the patch was like a genetic disease that he needed to cure. He had seen firsthand what the oilfield did to aspiring youth. The patch claimed his dad as well as his two older brothers, overcoming them monetarily.

All that the youngest Malloy boy saw was people he loved trading hopes and dreams for the money the patch offered, their desires trumped by the gratification of making a big paycheck. Disgust for the industry ran deep through Adam's bones. The problem for Adam was that it was all he had ever known. He wanted to branch out and experience more than what Lakeview had to offer. The thought of staying in his hometown scared the teenager more than anything else. For Adam Malloy the patch symbolized giving up, settling.

"Sorry, I have to take care of some things at home. I'm not going to make it."

"C'mon, since when do you like spending time at your house?" Kevin stuffed a book into the canvas backpack on his desk.

"Normally I don't, but if I'm going to get out of town next week, I need to have my ducks in a row. Know what I mean?" Adam wrapped up his statement with a smile and a raise of his eyebrows just as the bell rang, dismissing class.

For nearly a year now all that Adam's dad talked about was how great it was going to be when his youngest son was in the patch. The subject made Adam extremely uncomfortable. So rather than upset his father by expressing his intent to leave town, he chose to avoid contact with his family as much as possible.

"Well if you get a chance, we'll be out there all night." Kevin patted Adam on the back as he passed him in the doorway.

Adam made his way out of the building among a crowd of his classmates. The cooped up energy of the students exploded onto the parking lot as hundreds of kids raced for their vehicles, each one hoping to get ahead of the unavoidable traffic jams.

Upon reaching his car Adam threw his backpack onto the passenger seat. The oxidized sedan was not much to look at but he was able to get around, and that was all that mattered. It was only a ten minute commute to school so Adam usually took a couple detours on the way home to make the trip last a little longer.

Today was different though. Today he needed the time to pack and tell his folks he was leaving town. Adam recognized that if he did not make his plans known now, then there was a good chance his family's reasoning and influence would persuade him to stay.

Turning onto his street, Adam felt his stomach knot up and his heart begin to pound. Sweat formed on the steering wheel under his fingers. Slowing down, he pulled the car up to the same spot he always did and parked.

The Malloy family had lived in this house for all but three years of Adam's life. This was home to them. Memories here were ones of love and happiness: many Christmases rushing down the stairs to open presents, birthday after birthday celebrated in the front room, and barbeques out back. The kitchen doorframe was a makeshift growth chart for all three boys, while the walls bore textured scars of roughhousing and horseplay. Adam knew he would miss his boyhood home the moment he left, but the pull was not enough to keep him from pursuing his dream.

The garage door was down, indicating his father was not home yet. While grabbing his backpack with one hand and opening the door with the other, Adam quickly climbed out of the car. Clammy and cold, his hands juggled a set of keys, searching for the one to open the front door as he made his way up the steps. An odd mixture of joy and sadness passed over Adam as he acknowledged the coming days.

Inside the house, he raced up the stairs to his bedroom. Dirty clothes were draped over the bed and covered the floor. His walls were haphazardly decorated with magazine pictures of million dollar cars and tattooed rock stars. Before he even set his book bag down the sound of the garage door opening hit his ears. Instantly his heart leapt into his throat as sweat formed on his brow. Adam dreaded the conversation he needed to have with his father, mostly because he knew it would not remain civil for long. The sensitive subject would escalate into an argument as soon as the words "leaving town" left his lips.

"Hey son, you upstairs?" Mr. Malloy's rough and raspy voice seemed especially high-spirited. Adam could picture exactly what his father was doing as he asked the question; coming through the door from the garage, placing the mail onto the kitchen counter next to where the newspaper was left that morning.

"Yeah, Pops." He could feel the stage fright begin creeping into his body. Whatever it took, he had to maintain his will to leave. Simply following through was all that needed to happen. He had already ran the pros and cons through his head, reminding himself that any advice his family offered would be biased toward him staying.

"Hey bud, I got good news." Footsteps thundered up the stairs. Adam's father was a large man who carried himself well despite his extra thick midsection. "I talked to my boss today and…" Entering his son's room, he saw Adam putting clothes into a suitcase. "What's this?"

"Dad," Adam kept his body fixed on packing the bag, trying desperately not to look at his father for more than a few seconds at a time, "I've decided to move to New York after graduation." The words cracked the concrete dam that had been holding back the mighty waters of his heart. All at once pressure ruptured the barrier, allowing the river to flow freely. Adam relaxed, worry streamed out of his body as relief quickly poured over him, washing away his anxiety.

"You what!"

Like flipping a switch, the tension in the room thickened instantly. Adam had verbally kicked his father in the stomach. Wounded, the parent was now about to retaliate. A shade of red replaced the color in the weather worn face of Mr. Malloy.

"Are you looking for a fight? Is that it? If you think you can just pack up and leave after this weekend you're-" Adam did not give his dad a chance to finish the sentence.

"It's not up to you Dad, it's my life and even though I know it's going to make you mad, I'm leaving!" Surprised that he was actually standing his ground, Adam waited for a response.

"Oh, so you're all grown up, huh? A big shot now? Just because you're graduating doesn't mean you can walk out on your family! This is your home son, this is where you belong!" A massive finger pointed at the floor as the loud statement echoed off the walls. "What gives you the right to disrupt everyone's life?" The older man moved farther into the room, causing Adam to take a few steps back, keeping a cushion of space between him and his intimidating father.

Reaching into the suitcase, Adam's father started throwing clothes all over the bed. "I talked to my boss today. You start as an Operator next Monday! That's one level higher than they normally hire new guys!" With that, he left the room.

"No, Dad. I'm not. On Monday I'll be on my way to New York City, on my way to a new life." Amazed by his words, Adam peered down the stairs at his dad. Turning around, the angered man looked back up at his child.

"If you think I'm going to help you pack your bags, if you think I'm going to support this nonsense, this attempt to slap me in the face, then you're mistaken." Adam could not believe his ears. His dad was speaking in a soft undertone, whispering so quietly that chills shot up Adam's neck. "Adam, I have fed you, clothed you, and put a roof over your head all your life. You have never gone without anything. Everything you've ever wanted I gave to you. I am not going to let you ruin your life, upsetting your mother and the rest of your family in the process. Now get into your room and put away your suitcase. This conversation is over."

For a second, Adam felt the impulse to do what his father said. After the initial desire to obey his parent's will passed, he remembered his ultimate goal. Adam wanted to change the world; he wanted to do something to fix it, to inspire others or to alter society's current path, which from his perspective was frighteningly depressing. His resolve hardened and the courage in his gut slowly built back up.

"Dad, it's not about you providing for me, it's not about all the things you've given me, it's about me following my dream, making the world a better place." The argument was now in full force.

"Dream? You call moving to the big city, to New York, a dream? No son, it's more like a nightmare! You're chasing a fairy tale. You're not going to get to Time Square and magically become some bigwig or rock star! It just doesn't work that way!"

"How would you know, Dad? You've never chased a dream. All you ever did was stay here in this crappy town! You don't know what it's like to want something more, to want to do great things, to climb high above the streets and shout your victory! You don't know because you settled for the patch." Adam knew he was treading on thin ice speaking to his father in such a way.

"Why don't you take a look at what you're trying to do? How many other people do you think have the same dream as you?" A long pause sliced through the argument. "If you have a problem with this town, with my job, let me tell you something kiddo, this 'crappy' place you hate so much has given us a life! If it weren't for the patch you'd probably be sleeping in a box somewhere. So before you go and knock my job, or my life for that matter, you better take a good look at what you have and how you got it!"

"Dad, I'm not trying to knock anything, I'm just saying, I need something more, that's all." Adam could tell he'd hit a nerve. He did not want to leave on bad terms, but he couldn't let his father's feelings get in the way.

"More, huh, always more with you kids. If only you knew what it took to give you what you have, maybe then you'd be happy with what you've got." Adam's father began descending the flight of stairs again. "Do what you want." At the base of the stairs he stopped and looked up at his boy. "Son, know that I won't be coming to visit you in New York, don't expect me to make that trip. Create for yourself a new world and live a new life, but know that it'll be without your family."

Hurt, Adam went back into his room. He had not meant to come across so ungrateful. Running the words back through his head he released a deep sigh of guilt. He was ashamed, knowing he could have conveyed his point more delicately. After all, he had expected his dad to react precisely the way that he did. Adam thought he had been prepared for the argument, his heartache proved otherwise. He mindlessly continued putting clothes into the suitcase, letting his father's last statement burrow deep inside his head. The Lakeview native did not have much to pack but if he did not do it soon, he might convince himself not to do it at all.

Mr. Malloy sat at the edge of the sofa, a broken man. He knew he could not stop his son from leaving. As a father, he wanted to give his child a chance to succeed in the world. He wanted Adam to have an opportunity to make the best of life. The patch had done him and his other two sons well. Never had he expected anything from his son in return for raising him, but that is exactly how he had come across. Guilt stricken, his head dropped down and his hands rose up until his face rested securely inside his palms. Tears formed that would never be known by his son.

Chapter Three

The voices of several Lumenite soldiers thundered through Michaelis' head like a herd of cattle stampeding across the prairie. It was nearly midday. The sunlight was warm and soothing, coercing the young soldier to remain asleep. His eyes squinted as the light of day shone into them.

"Well hello, my brave friend." The man kneeling beside him was the same cowardly warrior who had run from the Malum during the attack.

"I see justice did not serve you well." The sarcasm was dry and effortless. Michaelis slowly rolled onto his side, rubbing his eyes in an attempt to wake them.

"Aw, you are referring to my escape." The man chuckled. "You, my brave friend, are still quite young. You will learn that a dead man cannot help the fight any more than one who has a tendency to faint." A slight smirk crept across the corner of the soldier's mouth as he handed a small piece of bread to Michaelis.

"Fainted? The last thing I remember is trying to hold still." The bread muffled his words as he spoke.

"You fainted when the Malum attacked you. And that, brave groundsman, is what saved your neck. I am Baramatheus, Defender of the King, son of Nicholas, Servant of the Council." He extended his hand to Michaelis.

The title, Defender of the King, belonged to men who served as knights to the King of Lumen. They were specially trained royal soldiers who descended from the noblest Lumen bloodlines, elite Lumen warriors who were called upon to serve the king in a variety of ways.

"Forgive me sir, but if you are a descendant of the Council, why are you out here on the battlefield? Is it not your privilege to be excluded from all this?" It did not make sense to Michaelis. War torn fields of death were common for village groundsmen and the Royal Commanders (military officers of noble lineage), but not for kin to the Council. The boy did not know much about the inner workings of the kingdom, but he did understand that nobility was held to different standards.

"Good questions, my brave friend. First of all, we are no longer on the battlefield. We are now safe within the walls of the Lumen Kingdom. Besides, is it not everyone's duty to defend the kingdom from the evil trying to destroy it?"

Behind the kingdom's wall, Lumen was safe from the Malum. However, they still were in the wilderness, which was not quite as safe as Baramatheus made it seem. The open country of

Lumen was a perilous place, made up of forests, desert badlands, divided by rivers, creeks, and lakes, all spread out between mountain ranges and the valleys that separated them. Lumen villages, like the one that Michaelis was from, peppered these lands. It was the two types of dangers between these Lumenite communities that the knight seemed to be overlooking: man, of the undesirable sort, and beast.

The wild territory, which predatory animals, bandits, and conjurers called home was between the City of the Throne and the kingdom wall.

Michaelis could not see either of the two prominent Lumenite landmarks as he scanned the horizon in an effort to get his bearings.

The kingdom wall defined the outermost border of the land. Built out of massive logs and large stones, the barrier was incredibly strong. In key positions along the wall watchtowers jutted into the sky. The young villager, his knightly companion, and the party of soldiers they were traveling with were well within Lumen, for the formidable partition and its pylons were out of sight.

"We passed through the gate while you were asleep," supplied Baramatheus.

The gate was the only land entrance into the kingdom. It was supported by the wall along the eastern border of the country and made of solid lumenium. Green vines with randomly blossoming purple flowers climbed up its framework, creating the sense that what lay within the confines of the barricade was akin to a garden paradise. As the only land passage into the kingdom the potential for it to be exploited was high. Whether attacked merely as a distraction or as a genuine attempt to breach the barrier, the gate proved to be the primary target for the enemies of Lumen. For this reason the number of troops guarding it more than doubled any other outpost along the border. If the adversary ever seized the passage, he could send in an army at will, or choose to cut off the realm's trade and wait while the people starved.

The City of the Throne, or simply Throne City, sat on the western side of the kingdom nestled against the shoreline of the Tranquil Sea, a body of water revered for its mystery. Calm and clear, the water extended as far as the eye could see. Many voyagers had set out to explore its vast expanse and though some returned -always with wild stories of incredible encounters - most did not.

As the social, economic, political, and military hub of the kingdom, construction of the city was performed with painstaking precision. The city walls were designed to be the exact same length all around, a perfect square, while the tallest building within the city (the palace) extended up to a height equal to the length of each wall. Built to specific measurements, the dimensional cube symbolized the ingenuity, intelligence, and spirit of the Lumenite people.

To travelers approaching from the east, the City of the Throne was a marvel to behold. At dawn's first light, the city seemed to vanish. As the sun slowly rose, light bounced off the lumenium-inlayed designs that decorated the city's structures. Once the entire city was illuminated it became as clear as crystal, revealing an undisturbed view of the Tranquil Sea behind it until the sun was directly overhead. At dusk a different but equally compelling phenomenon occurred. The angle of the setting sun reflecting off the Tranquil Sea caused the artistry on the buildings to sparkle so brightly that the city appeared to be pure gold.

To the north and bending southeast directly in front of the city gate was the River Ax, so named for a great battle fought along its shores. The legend tells how the ancient Lumenites, being outnumbered and out-armed, retreated across the river to safety. The water split the two opposing armies like an ax. Separated by the river the Lumenite force had time to formulate a new strategy, turning the tide of the battle and eventually causing the enemy to surrender.

Mimicking the kingdom wall, Throne City also had only one entrance which, like everything in the capital, was visually stunning. The lumenium gate was adorned with an amazing ornamental work of art that depicted a victorious king standing in front of a multitude of people, sword in hand with the calf of a behemoth at his feet. A chalice and a bushel of wheat were above his head, tilted downward, as if the royal leader were being poured out of them. Standing nearly two hundred fifty feet high, the gate dwarfed the people who passed through it, sending an unmistakable message of the kingdom's power. Two enormous statues of behemoths stood in front of the gate, one on each side.

The large mammal, recognized throughout Lumenite history as the chief of all the world's creatures was incomparable in strength. The animal was capable of dominating anything and everything, yet chose to graze in the fields like cattle, solemnly feeding on the grassy hills while other wild animals played about. For this reason the giant brute was the Lumen Kingdom's prime symbol, embodying peaceful existence through means of might.

The sculptures of the behemoths stood steadfast in the waters of the River Ax with a cypress bridge resting between them. Those crossing the bridge could read an ancient promise engraved upon their bases: *As long as the Earth carries on, sowing and harvest, cold and heat, winter and summer, day and night will never end.* The stone creature to the right held an olive branch in its mouth, while the one to the left bore a series of six different colored gemstone rings, patterned after the rainbow. On top of each statue was a fire pit, burning continually day and night. The flames acted as beacons letting the people of the kingdom know exactly where their throne resided, and consequently, where their safe haven was.

At the city's center was the palace, the heart of the kingdom. The building's size was remarkable, a wonder of wonders. Having more rooms than could be easily counted, and a population exceeding that of the rest of the kingdom, it would be more accurate to think of the palace as a city unto itself. Markets, gardens, arenas, galleries, libraries, courtrooms, sanctuaries, taverns, indeed all aspects of city life existed within its walls. Everything in the palace was far more ornate than the rest of the Lumen Kingdom, making the stunning wilds of the land look drab in comparison. As the heart and soul of the land, the palace exemplified the potential of the Lumenites. Every day was a celebration. The residents carried out their duties with such joy and harmony that smiles and laughter were seen and heard each and every day. Witnessing the jubilant happenings of the palace emboldened trust in its chief occupant, the king.

Chapter Four

Baramatheus and Michaelis traveled by horseback along with a few other survivors of the ambush; the knight's mount was clearly distinguishable from the rest. Exclusively bred for the King's Defenders, it was sandy brown in color with an orange tail and mane. This breed had become their hallmark. Michaelis could not recall seeing the fire-haired creature in camp prior to the Malum attack, which he found odd since a horse like that would be almost impossible to miss. His curiosity nagged at him the entire afternoon as the group made their trip inward toward the City of the Throne until finally he sought to satisfy his curiosity.

"My Lord, your horse is quite brilliant. If I may ask, why do I not recall seeing it in camp prior to the Malum attack?"

"Has anyone ever told you that you have a sharp wit about you?" Baramatheus replied. "The reason is simple: I was not in the camp prior to the attack. I was traveling north, east of the encampment, when I spotted a garrison of Malum fighters preparing to advance on your position. I was barely able to alert the Royal Commanders of the forthcoming ambush before they were upon us.

"Sir, if I may ask another question, why are we heading toward the throne? Should we not be rallying with the other troops, preparing for our next defensive?"

"My brave friend, that is precisely what we are doing." Baramatheus looked surprised by the question.

"But sir, we are heading to—" One of the other riders sharply interrupted Michaelis.

"Petty groundsman, have you no humility? Do not question the actions of a Defender, especially one who is heir to a seat on the Council!" The man's indignant tone drove the words deep into Michaelis' head.

Baramatheus cringed at the comment. He had heard similar statements before. Despite the fact that he fought side-by-side with men from every village in the kingdom, he was never able to prove to the groundsmen that he too, regardless of his father's seat on the Council, had the duty and responsibility to carry a sword. The division he felt between the groundsmen and himself was not, however, reserved just for him. Animosity between royal soldiers and the groundsmen was a growing epidemic.

The knight listened to the man profess blind obedience. He accepted it with contempt, blaming it for the Malum's success. A firm believer in the sanctity of life, Baramatheus held that all men had an obligation to decide for themselves if they would die for a righteous cause, or even for a foolish one. Just as the soldier's chastising comment indicated, Baramatheus observed that men were no longer choosing how to die, but resentfully accepting that all they could do was die. The desire to serve their king joyously was now a past fantasy because the men did not view it as optional. Fighting for the sake of defeating the evil disease at the doorstep was an ideal held only by poets of late. Honor that came with protecting families from despair no longer mattered to the men marching out onto the bloodstained war plains. The war between Lumen and the Malum seemed endless. The loss of Lumen lives had been too great and seemingly without purpose. Through constant bombardment the enemy had managed to defeat the spirit of the Lumenites. The war was all but over now.

Growing numb to it all, Baramatheus started to give up hope. That is until he met Michaelis. In one selfless moment the young boy from an uneducated peasant family managed to reignite the flame of faith in the Defender's heart. Baramatheus smirked as he pondered how even in a simple unfinished question his new friend was able to unknowingly capture the essence of the underlying problem.

"Brave friend, I am aware of our heading." With a gentle smile Baramatheus eased, if only for a moment, Michaelis' questions. "Take comfort that we are acting in the best interest of our country."

Seeing genuine strength in his face, Michaelis' initial impression that Baramatheus was a coward dissolved. Although he did not understand why they were heading for the City of the Throne, he grasped that it was the right direction to be going.

"Sir, if I may ask, what will we do once we reach Throne City?" Michaelis could not stand being in the dark.

"My brave friend…" Baramatheus began to address Michaelis.

"Please sir, my name is Michaelis." The title of 'brave friend' sounded more formal the more the veteran soldier used it.

"Michaelis, my brave friend, have you ever heard of Oren the Ablaze?"

Michaelis recognized the title as belonging to one of the ancient Lumenites.

"No."

"Oren the Ablaze was a great warrior. He fought alongside the heroes of old and is said to have tutored King Apollas. A humble knight, he performed every task asked of him with great zeal for the kingdom. Oren is considered to be the father of the King's Defenders." Baramatheus looked over to Michaelis to see if he was paying attention. "This ancient knight is the only man to ever live through a fight with a livyatan."

"A livyatan?" Michaelis stared intently at Baramatheus, urging him to continue.

"Yes, my brave friend. No man has ever defeated a livyatan, though Oren came amazingly close. Numerous men have tried to repeat his venture, foolhardy knights. Many have fought against livyatans with sword, spear, dart, even javelin, but to no good fortune. Iron and steel are like straw and rotted wood to him.

"Livyatans do not flee from soaring arrows, nor flinch at the slinging of stones; to them they are mere dust and pebbles. Clubs are as splinters to the beasts. The proud men who dare to face one of them inevitably will bow before the monster, as if to their king. Livyatans have a strength which makes the mighty meek. Their skin is as thick as ten layers of armor; their teeth are like the tips of a hundred swords. The creature's back is impenetrable, armed with a row of natural shields so close together that not even air can permeate it. Their stomachs are not their weak link of armor either, for they might as well be made of a thousand sharp daggers. There are no other creatures like them. The livyatans even breathe fire, incinerating any foe attempting to conquer them." Baramatheus looked over at Michaelis only to find him entranced, hooked on every word the Defender spoke.

"The monster actually exists?" Michaelis had heard legends of the horrifyingly magnificent beasts, but never expected royalty to actually recount one as factual.

"Oh yes, they inhabit the seas and lakes of this country as if we were their servants. No man should risk stirring up a livyatan."

"I thought the livyatan stories were fairy tales." That someone such as Baramatheus was seriously conveying the ways and traits of such a fanciful creature dumbfounded Michaelis.

"My brave friend, do not be so quick to dismiss ancient tellings as trite myths of simple people. Most things throughout history that you might think are imaginative conceptions have a core rooted in fact. It is our generation which foolishly chooses to portray them as works of fiction, dismissing creatures and downplaying events. The animal most certainly breathes to this very day, as assuredly as do you and I." Baramatheus kept quiet for a while, guiding his courser along the prairie. He knew Michaelis was chewing on the account of the great livyatan, and he wanted to give him time to digest it.

Oren's Haven was their destination. The conversation had drifted off course as Baramatheus enlightened his friend as to the significance of the sanctuary. Soon enough, if all went well, the connection between Oren and Michaelis would become obvious to the young man.

Darkness was beginning to settle over the land. The sun that had so warmly awakened Michaelis was all but gone now. Only a residue of pink and orange remained in the sky. Behind the band of travelers a growing gray cloud approached. The agreeable weather was about to take a turn for the worse. Lightning cracked in the distance, spooking the horses. Concern encompassed the envoy as the storm raced toward them.

"I think, perhaps it is time to set up camp." Baramatheus did not want to get caught in the elements if he did not have to.

They had not had much time to gather supplies the night before. Bebbel-uk's army did a good job of looting most of the useful equipment. However, Baramatheus and the other survivors managed to salvage a few stable-blankets and rain-flies from what remained. The men used these to construct two makeshift tents. The accommodations were not ideal, but considering that the rain was falling in full force, they would do. Baramatheus took the first watch.

Michaelis volunteered to take the next.

Bandits had become a problem in the outer lands of the kingdom. Outcasts from Lumen villages and greedy outlaws from neighboring lands joined together and took advantage of the fact that the strongest men were off to war.

Near the end of the knight's shift sounds of clashing metal awoke Michaelis. As his body adjusted to consciousness he could hear the rain-muffled voices of men outside the tent. Not too far away the agonizing echoes of a brutal struggle rang out. Without thinking Michaelis dashed as quickly as he could toward the noise. He slipped almost instantly, splashing onto the mud covered ground. Wiping at his eyes he cleared away the pasty earth from his face. He had fallen at the foot of a conflict. The sight he saw was nothing short of spectacular.

There in front of him stood Baramatheus, a glimmering sword in hand, his cloak hanging heavy over his shoulders. The Defender's long hair draped across his face, clinging to his skin; his eyes peered out through the wet strands, focused intently on the robbers surrounding him. All of them were poorly armed, some grasping mallets while others gripped old, ill-treated blades. Baramatheus, from what Michaelis could see, looked calm and in a way welcoming of the situation.

The men tried rushing him, only to be deflected with such skill and fluidity that they retreated to a safe distance almost immediately. Baramatheus lunged forward, possessing more grace in combat than most portray on the stage. His extended sword pierced the chest plate of one of the motley men.

As soon as the marauder's flesh was punctured, the Lumenite sent his weapon in the opposite direction. It connected with an unshapely hammer, intended to strike the knight's skull. The instruments of death entangled before the first thief had even hit the soil and while Baramatheus was still in the air. Once back on the ground the nimble soldier stepped to one side without hesitation. Poised, he swooped the mallet from his opponent's hand, launching it through the rain filled sky. The Lumen warrior whipped his head around, locking onto two thieves racing toward him. He delivered his foot in turn to the faces of both men as he twisted his body around.

Michaelis' eyes widened as he watched the Defender easily repel his enemies. The men dropped to the ground unconscious. Baramatheus' cloak flapped like a flag in stiff wind as he spun through the air. Landing softly, he crouched down to rest his free hand on the ground, his senses alert. As if simply going through all-too-familiar motions, the knight twirled his sword, artfully stabbing his lumenium blade into the center of each man's chest in the process. Precision and accuracy guided the edge clean through their hearts.

Staring at the remaining men, the Defender jumped forward, slashing his sword upward toward the stars. The blade sliced the nearest outlaw's body from his thigh to his neck. Following through with the weapon, Baramatheus stepped onto the falling enemy's shoulder. Pushing off of it, he flipped backwards before dropping firmly onto the soggy earth. The mud splashing at his feet crashed like a tidal wave in Michaelis' face.

Only one man remained standing. His face expressed the unmistakable look of terror as he witnessed a single soldier destroy his comrades.

Baramatheus stared deep into his eyes as if to explore the man's soul. Was he at peace with how he had lived his life? Did he see himself as the wretched man he was or did he merely regret the decisions that led to his current predicament?

"Kill me or I will kill you," goaded the man uneasily.

Baramatheus slowly approached the intruder. The club in the man's hand was of no concern, an idle accessory at this point. The outlaw had watched the slaughter of his cohorts and knew it would be like a mouse chasing a cat if he were to attempt attacking the knight. Although he was no longer a threat, the Defender was obligated to uphold the duty he swore to the king. He was required to remove danger from within the walls of the kingdom. Though not harmful to the knight, Baramatheus determined that if spared, the bandit would once again threaten the citizens of Lumen.

"The evil of man's heart will be cleansed by the pouring out of blood." With each step closer to his opponent Baramatheus drew his arm back. Michaelis watched as his friend's sword moved forward through the raindrops, the scene seeming to slow down as the soldier sliced the raider in half. Lifeless, the body fell to the ground as if whole, splitting in two upon impact.

Overcome by sadness the calm look that had been on the Defender's face was gone now.

Michaelis picked himself up out of the mud as Baramatheus turned toward him.

"Are you all right?" The somber expression melted away as his focus shifted to Michaelis' wellbeing.

"That was amazing." The boy had never seen such beautiful fighting. "How did you learn to do that?"

"The death of men is not amazing, my brave friend. Taking another man's life is a horrible task, one that I do not enjoy. I would advise you to hold it in the same regard." Baramatheus moved toward the tent. He had had enough of the rain. Warmth and shelter would be his only consolation as he struggled the rest of the night to get the image of dying men out of his head. Even though he was aware that right was on his side, the reality of what he was forced to do by the bad choices of others weighed heavily on his conscience. Only time would ease the pain that stung his soul.

As it was about time for Michaelis to begin his watch, he let his friend rest in the tent alone. The rain showed no signs of relenting. The young groundsman walked to a tree near where the horses were covered, flipping his hood over his head in an effort to deflect the drops. The limp bodies of the slain men were much to close for comfort. He was not an experienced knight like his new companion and was not yet accustomed to the brutality of engaging the enemy. The first bloodshed he had ever witnessed was the slaughter of the night before. The call to war with the Malum had flung him headlong into manhood.

Mesmerized at the ease by which Baramatheus fought, his thoughts drifted back to his village as he stared blankly at the bloodied corpses by his feet. A week ago he knew nothing except how to tend to horses. Doing his duty after his father's death, Michaelis operated the village stables, receiving a few tips from the wealthier travelers. But times had grown difficult.   Rich men passing through his hamlet were rare.

Michaelis remembered a time, when as a young child his family traveled to the City of the Throne for the harvest festival. He watched for hours as royal men and women dressed in the finest clothing hurried about. Full of childish fantasies, he dreamed of one day being like them. As Michaelis grew older he realized that the world did not allow such opportunities to people of his stature. He served a position in life, however, and even though his vocation did not include the grandeur of others, he accepted it, fulfilling it to the best of his ability. Taking care of his family was all he required in order to be happy. As he matured, the fanciful ideas of his youth eventually faded.

The young soldier was unaware that his life was now on a different path. Unbeknownst to him he was currently heading to the City of the Throne with one of those royal men he watched at the festival as a boy.

The rest of the night was without excitement. Rain continued to pour while the occasional lightning crack and thunder boom kept Michaelis alert. He watched vigilantly for signs of trouble, all the while praying that none would show.

Chapter Five

It was a long trip to New York and Adam was relieved to have finally reached the city. With a well-worn duffel bag stuffed full of various odds and ends from his bedroom (an old alarm clock, a framed family photograph, little league trophies, etc.) and a scarcely used suitcase bloated with clothes in the backseat of his car he had made the trip from his parents' house in Lakeview. His small town was about an hour north of the interstate that brought him almost all the way into the city over the course of eighteen hours.

With each passing mile marker his emotions swung back and forth between his desire to follow his dream and the consequence of it: breaking his parents' hearts. But as he pulled his car to the side of the road and pushed the shifter into park, all that drifted away.

He had taken the first step. He left Lakeview and was in New York City. The small-town boy took a moment to relish his accomplishment. He had escaped the clutches of his birthplace. Adam had broken the Malloy family tradition and was feeling pretty alive because of it.

He was definitely not alone. It was not strange for people to flock to New York. The city was the epicenter for every possible kind of global activity. Stones thrown from the sky-piercing towers of the Big Apple caused many social, economic, and political ripples. In this great city, the men and women all spoke the same language, that of profits, progress, and dividends.

After the initial buzz of being in the midst of the hustle and bustle wore off, Adam set out to find a place to live. He stood at the foot of the fifth apartment building he had been to since he arrived. All the rent rates were far too expensive for him, especially considering he had not yet even found a job. Looking up at the tower he tried to convince himself that he could afford it. He walked through the door only to come out seconds later with a look of defeat on his face.

"How do they expect anyone to pay that much?" Culture shock was beginning to set in.

He slept in his car, which was not too bad; after all, he had spent many nights bunkered down in the backseat out at the lake.

The next morning Adam hit the apartment hunt with an excitement usually reserved for little children on Christmas morning. Determined to succeed, he was thrilled simply to be on the streets of New York. But by noon when he was still without a home, his expectations began dropping substantially. Reality was taking its toll. Accepting the fact that affordability was the most important issue, Adam began looking in the more undesirable parts of town. He noticed too, that as he looked at the cheaper places, friendliness and hospitality became increasingly scarce. The apartment managers acted as if they were doing him a favor by showing him the space.

Finally, at about nine o'clock in the evening, Adam settled on a place that he could afford, barely. It was in an older part of town, an area deserving of the label, "the slums." Adam saw what it looked like, the piles of garbage on the streets. He smelled the detestable odor lingering in the hallways, but he did not care. He wanted a place of his own, and more importantly, he wanted to start searching for a job.

Looking at his new home, he recalled the inspirational stories he read as a boy, classic tales of stars who struggled to make it to the top. They all seemed to have had very humble beginnings which had made them strive to be successful. He told himself that the shoddy conditions would someday make him a better person too. They would be his motivation. Adam smiled as he thought about how his dad would have considered the accommodations character-building. For now he was grateful to have a place to live and was intent on making the best of it.

The apartment was tiny. The kitchen and living room were practically on top of each other. His bathroom was the size of a portable outhouse. It was directly off of his bedroom, which was directly off of the living room. The paper-thin walls stained yellow with nicotine residue and cracked from water damage separated the young man from his neighbors. Both the small sink in the kitchen and the shower stall were almost entirely orange from the rust showing through the eroded enamel finish. There was only one small window. Despite its size it revealed the beautiful sea of red bricks of the adjacent building. Adam could literally reach his hand out the window and touch the building next door.

He had never seen such a ridiculous thing before. There was so much wide open space in the small town he was from that the big city seemed cramped. Apparently at one time the window had been a portal to the outside world, now it was simply a reminder that Adam was definitely not in Lakeview. He could not help but find the reversal of terms amusing.

That was not the only thing about his new world he found amusing. Two doors down lived an elderly woman who, regardless of the time of day, always wore a nightgown. In the afternoon she would open her door to let the air flow through her apartment. However, she had an ulterior motive. By opening her door she forced interaction with her neighbors and like clockwork, each time Adam passed by she would call out to him.

"Still huntin' young'n?"

"Yes ma'am. Not much out there these days." Adam was the only person on the floor who responded to the old lady's hollering with any kind of respect, so, he was the one with whom she preferred to converse.

"I s'pect not, if yer expectin' things to work out like they do in the movies. Mail clerk to CEO, right? Shake them fanciful thoughts, son, and look at whatcha got right in front of ya." Her voice had a grating pitch, touching nearly every octave of sound as she spoke.

"Yes ma'am, but then where would I be?"

"Perhaps yer right. I s'pose you could shake those fanciful thoughts and see if any foam rises ta the top."

The conversations were always the same. At first they seemed like any average neighborly discourse, but unquestionably at the end the woman would say something so strange that it would keep Adam laughing throughout the rest of the day.

"Chasin' that shiny brass ring eh, son?"

"Yes, ma'am."

"That's good. Someone needs ta try and reach them stars. The world would be a borin' place if ya didn't. Kinda like a car stuck in a rut, I reckon."

Usually it came as he continued down the hallway toward the stairs.

"Don't snatch them stars too quickly though, once ya've got 'em, yer breeches might not fit ya. Of course, I s'pose ya could always make a new pair." Adam concluded that the lady was a few grapes shy of a fruit salad, but worth a good chuckle nonetheless.

He finally found a job working at a fast food eatery as a cook and dish washer. Desperate, he took the job.

Six months passed.

He still had not found anything better. On numerous occasions his nutty neighbor suggested reasons for this.

"Young'n, don't ya know yer sights are set too high?"

"I don't think so, ma'am. This city is all about setting your sights high."

"Boy, that's not what this city is all 'bout. It's also 'bout humility and delis, lots of delis. Have you tried the one around the corner?"

"No ma'am."

"Blinded by pride, eh?"

"What? No. I just..." Adam stopped in midsentence wondering if they were talking about his failure to find a better job or delis.

"Don't be ashamed, son, just take the 'pompous goggles' off and see that there might be somethin' better out there."

"I'm sorry, what are we talking about?"

"Well, no wonder yer still flippin' burgers. Keep up. Yer makin' pennies doin' watcha doin' but yer not doin' nothin' 'bout it. Ya know meat and cheese go on a sandwich in a certain order, don't ya?"

"Yes ma'am.   What are we talking about exactly?"

"First ya dream, then you do. If all ya do is dream then ya find yerself in a routine where yer doin' nothin' but getting' bed sores. Though I s'pect with yer job ya'd still be doin' the world changin' work yer strivin' for, after all, ya'd be feedin' the hungry."

As he headed out of the building to work it was inevitable that he would pass his landlord, Mr. Santone. It seemed as if the guy was always trekking up or down the stairs. As many times as he made the trip, Adam wondered why the man did not just fix the elevator.

"Don't forget, rent's due next week, Smalltown."

Adam figured the nickname was just a grumpy old man's way of trying to belittle him. Santone had a name like that for everyone in the building.

Mr. Santone was a short man in his early fifties who bore a few tell-tale signs that he was not going to age very well. He combed what little hair he had left over his scalp to give the impression he had more than he really did. The nonstop consumption of coffee and cigarettes stained his teeth, the latter causing chronic hacking fits. Mr. Santone always appeared greasy, as if he had not showered in days. His wardrobe consisted of three basic articles, varying only slightly from one day to the next: wide strap suspenders, work slacks, and a sweat soaked t-shirt with food stains down the front of it. As if his hygiene were not bad enough, his enormous girth shortened his breath as well as his life expectancy.

Adam could tell by their brief encounters that Mr. Santone's life had been rough. As the landlord, he lived on the first floor of the apartment building, occupying a larger living space than the tenants, although not by much. Like many property owners in the city Mr. Santone was no better off than the people who lived in his building.

Santone's attitude resembled the building itself, unattractive and steadily degrading. It was already in shambles when he inherited it from his father and he had done nothing to improve it in the years since. "Don't worry, I know!" Adam did not miss a step. His momentum never slowed one bit. He had learned quickly not to make eye contact with the money-hungry rent-hound.

Upon reaching the main floor, Adam hurried by the homeless community that filled the entryway. Mr. Santone was continuously fighting to get rid of them. The losing battle added to his lifelong depression. On days that he felt especially motivated he would shoo them away, kicking them while throwing what few possessions they owned out into the street. Adam rushed past, nervously hoping to get out the door before one of them reached out for his legs, begging for money or food.

The young man hated confrontation with the street sleepers. It was not the people, but the frustration that he could not give them what they wanted that bothered him. He did not have any money to give. He himself was well below the poverty level. The uncomfortable feeling of being put on the spot day after day by these men and women worse off than he was should have been a warning, but Adam was too consumed by the rat race of survival that had become his life's routine. He was wandering in circles, merely existing.

Outside of the building was the three-ring circus of a city. No matter what time of day it was in the Big Apple, there were always people moving about. The metropolis was in a constant state of activity, millions of people from all walks of life going about their day-to-day routines. During Adam's short hike to work, a whole array of events unfolded.

Traffic-worn streets and trash-littered sidewalks greeted him at the door. The garbage, accompanied by stomach churning scents lingered in the air, each odor battling for prevalence. A construction operation was underway up the street, which added dust and debris to the already over-polluted neighborhood. One of the first things Adam noticed when he moved to New York was that someone was always fixing or cleaning something and yet nothing was ever fixed or clean. Half a block down, a group of kids danced under an open hydrant spraying out water like a geyser. At the end of the block was the same shameful scene as always. Three working girls territorially flaunting their product, each one outdoing the next as cars drove by. Right beside them, several toddlers innocently played in the gutter, the runoff apparently acting as an in-office daycare while mommy was working. A city bus stopping to pick up commuters broke up the scene at certain times of the day, as did the ringing of fire alarms and emergency sirens.

Upon arriving at the eatery, the day's excitement only increased. At work, Adam saw things that would have blown the minds of the slower paced, small-town folk in Lakeview. Things like the weekly screaming match between a married couple, complete with finger pointing, plate throwing, and the worst language he had ever heard. Add in a steady stream of drunken brawls, police arrests, purse snatchings, and even the occasional robbery and employment at the eatery was quite interesting.

Life in the city was not at all what Adam had envisioned. Things were hard where he lived. People struggled every hour of the day just to survive. Adam had not caught the kind of break he imagined he would. He was learning the realities of life the hard way. Somehow, he had managed to trap himself in an impoverished city lifestyle – one void of opportunities.

Chapter Six

By morning the rain finally stopped. Moisture covered the ground. Michaelis stayed awake and alert throughout his entire watch. The only danger he encountered was his overactive imagination, which startled him several times during the early hours of the morning.

The convoy began their journey to the royal city at dawn. They packed up what little they had with great speed. The dead bodies of the intruders helped motivate the men. Despite possessing the hardened attitude of soldiers none of them wanted to hang around the ghastly site and increasing stench of death any longer than was necessary. Baramatheus was inclined to bury the deceased, but time was of the essence, and so they abandoned the bodies to the elements.

Well-rested, they covered ground much faster. Following Baramatheus' lead the men pushed their horses to the limit, forcing the animals to move as quickly as possible. It was two more days before they reached the outside wall of the City of the Throne. Along the way Baramatheus had subtly been quizzing Michaelis, trying to uncover the young man's heart. It was paramount to Baramatheus that his friend have a good moral compass, for he took the life of a soldier very seriously and he saw great potential within Michaelis.

Upon reaching the city, the group parted ways. The soldiers headed home. Baramatheus and Michaelis made their way to Oren's Haven.

Like all the sanctuaries in the kingdom, the place of worship was monumental in size and elegant in style. It was typical of the Lumenite desire to cherish their heritage as it displayed fantastic artwork that paid tribute to the nation's noble history. Past kings, warriors, philosophers, monks, scholars, scientists, and poets were all honored by appropriately significant structures dedicated in their memory.

Oren's Haven was a sanctuary of particular importance to the Lumen knights. It was holy ground where all members of the King's Defenders were anointed and brought into the order. Not only did the Defender's quest of servitude to the king begin here, but so did that of the Royal Commanders who serve in the Lumen military.

The only real difference between Oren's Haven and other holy places was the unique artwork that covered the walls and the furniture within it. Along with the monasteries and abbeys, Martinian monks maintained all of the kingdom's sanctuaries and military memorials. They served not only as stewards of these sites, but also as spiritual council to all of Lumen.

"What is this place?" Michaelis asked as he stared upward at the marvelous stone walls adorned with beautiful engravings.

The pictures streamed together to tell a story. Grapevines crawling up the outside of the sanctuary added nature's sense of solitude.

"This, my brave friend, is Oren's Haven." Baramatheus saw the look on Michaelis' face and paused, allowing the young man to speak.

"Oren? Is this why you mentioned him?"

"Oren the Ablaze was a brave man. Like I said before, he is the only man to fight a livyatan and live to speak of it. The records say that he engaged the beast with the fire of Monk's Hell. When the time was right he struck a massive blow to one of its hind legs. It reared up, breathing down an inferno upon him."

Baramatheus led the way into the sanctuary, pointing at the narrative on the walls to help illustrate his story. "Oren knelt down with just enough time to raise up his shield. The flames blew all around him as the beast tried to char the great warrior. The fire was so hot that Oren's shield began to melt, scalding the arm with which he held it. Having no other option, he dropped the shield, stumbling backwards. Engulfed in the livyatan's breath, he dove into the lagoon that flowed into the cave. The livyatan continued to rain down fire on Oren, causing the water to boil."

Baramatheus pointed to a font of water at the front end of the haven's hall. "Oren was wise and knew that the water was the livyatan's habitat. If he wanted to survive, he would have to get back onto land.

"He crawled out of the bubbling caldron, and ran as fast as he could away from the flames. The beast moved quickly in his direction with a ferocious snarl. Oren clutched Chakkah, his sword, and leaped toward the giant lizard. The tip of his blade cut through one of its eyes. As the livyatan recoiled, Oren seized the opportunity and made his escape."

Baramatheus stood in front of a carving of Oren kneeling down behind a shield as a ball of fire rolled around him. "This sanctuary is where the men that are brave enough to go into battle, as Oren did, come to begin their role as knights of the Lumen Kingdom."

The story intrigued Michaelis. He looked intently at the artwork that surrounded him. Never did he expect to be standing in a place such as this. A sudden realization of why they were here struck him.

"Baramatheus, are you saying that I…"

"Yes, I am, my brave friend." The noble warrior moved past his younger counterpart toward a doorway at the edge of the hall. "Now, if you would be so kind as to tend to our horses, there is a stable attendant waiting out in the garden." Baramatheus gestured in the opposite direction and then disappeared into the doorway.

Michaelis did as asked. The attendant in the garden was an elderly monk. The Martinian greeted the young peasant with a relaxing smile and the two led the horses down to the stables. The groundsman was stunned. Just being in Throne City was awe-inspiring; knowing he was brought here for a reason made it more so.

* * *

Baramatheus walked through the doorway and down another hall into a small room adorned with books from ceiling to floor. In the middle of the room was an old and well-used desk. Sitting at the desk he found his father studying, which is exactly how Baramatheus expected to find him. His father was a researcher, his face buried in a book at every available moment. Nicholas was a very wise and humble man—most on the Council were. All twenty-four of the Servants took their responsibility with a weighty sense of importance. As part of the ruling authority in the kingdom giving support and advice to the king was their business and Nicholas took his duty with extreme sincerity and devoted attention.

"Father." Baramatheus bowed his head as he quietly tried to get Nicholas' attention. "It is of the utmost urgency that I address the Council."

Nicholas slowly put his book down as he turned to face his son. "Glad to see you have returned safely, my boy. Of what matter is this urgency?" Nicholas' speech lingered slightly, adding a sense of ease to the conversation.

"A young man by the name of Michaelis. I believe that he can aid us in our battle against the Malum." Baramatheus looked intently at his father in an effort to quicken his response.

"In what manner?"

"In the office of a Defender." The statement grasped the previously divided attention of the knight's father.

"A villager, I presume?" Nicholas spoke with unexpected confidence.

"Yes."

"Then I suggest he arm himself with the rest of the groundsmen."

"He is more than a groundsman, father. He is of royal caliber."

Nicholas' eyes widened at the statement. A whimsical expression crossed his face. "Son, that is quite the remark. Even among noble lineage very few can be found that are of royal caliber these days."

"That is why I seek the Council with such urgency. Michaelis is of a dying breed, his heart is holding fast to traditions of days past that he himself does not even understand. If we do not move to rectify the spirit of this kingdom, there will be no kingdom left to fight for." Baramatheus knew he did not have to preach to his father. Nicholas was playing the devil's advocate in an attempt to ensure Baramatheus had thought through every aspect thoroughly.

Nicholas knew his son was right. He understood better than most that the country was in crisis. However, he did not know if this was the proper way of handling the situation. "Bar, the Council will not be open to such a proposal. This land is a great and honorable kingdom. To blurt out that it will surely die if a peasant is not knighted, which by the way goes against the kingdom's customs, will infuriate many of my fellow Council members."

"Allow me the chance to present them my request, father. I will assuredly abide by the ruling of the land, but please call the Council so that I can at least be heard."

After a few moments the elderly man spoke, "I will call the Council."

Baramatheus bowed, "Thank you, father."

"Bar, know that I am also going to request the king's presence." Nicholas said before he left the room.

Chapter Seven

The Council gathered into the great hall along with the king and Baramatheus. It was attached to the sanctuary, where Michaelis had listened so intently to Baramatheus recounting the exploits of Oren the Ablaze. The hall was large and round in the center, with raised seating at the front. The king sat in an elaborately decorated throne in the middle, twelve men to each side. The beauty of the throne inspired reverence. So much so, that even in the king's absence one could not help but feel as if he was there presiding over the assembly. Directly opposite the Council, was the entrance to the meeting hall. Several benches lined the curved walls on both sides of the door. These were used only in special instances that allowed an audience.

Baramatheus stood at the center of the room. "I would like to thank the Council and my king for agreeing to hear me today."

Though King Josiah valued the Council and relied heavily on it for guidance, trusting in their wisdom more than his own, he did not always sit in on their meetings.

Josiah was a princely king, fairly young in appearance and relatively new to his office. His father, Charles, had passed away only three years ago, leaving the kingdom in the midst of war and in a growing state of division between the common Lumen people and the nobility. Josiah longed for a way to bring Lumen back from the brink of total annihilation. He was perfectly aware of the casualties suffered on the warfront and struggled to figure out how to inspire his military and mend the schism that was dividing the kingdom. When Nicholas requested his presence for a meeting on just such a topic he made it his priority.

"I come before you with the utmost urgency. As you are all well aware, we are losing the war against the Malum. They continue to slaughter our men on the field of battle, which in turn is defeating our men and women who remain at home in the villages as they deal with the painful and costly loss of their loved ones.

"The tactics they use to cut the throat of this land's morale are as effective as they are barbaric." Baramatheus began to move around the room as he spoke. "You also know that for some time now, I have been deeply concerned about the ongoing crisis affecting this country, our extended conflict with the enemy. That is why I have taken it upon myself to fight side-by-side with the groundsmen whom we have called up to defend our boundaries and our interests." Baramatheus' tone hardened.

"The attitude of our men is defeatist. They no longer have the desire to stand up for this kingdom or their king. Some, indeed, have gone so far as to abandon their duty, fleeing their homeland to live a life of shame rather than fight for what they deem a useless cause." Baramatheus looked directly at the king. "They see no hope in the future and no purpose in the present. For years now, I have watched as the men's pride has dissolved into a simple act of duty which contains absolutely no fire or desire!"

A Servant of the Council named Ethan interrupted Baramatheus. "Yes, yes. We are well aware of the lack of zeal that has infected our soldiers and that a sense of selfish disloyalty has spread throughout the villages. Are you going to carry on about your feelings all day or do you have an end point in mind?"

Ethan was notorious for his impatience and hasty judgment. He had little respect for Baramatheus' quest to put his life in danger and throw away the inheritance reserved for him, that of serving on the Council.

"Yes sir, I do have a point. It is this: I have come across a rarity amid the bloodstained lands between Lumen and the Malum Mountains. His name is Michaelis. Since I began fighting he is the only spark of light I have seen in these dark times and that is not at all an exaggeration. You speak of the depletion of zealousness among our soldiers as if it were an infection. Well, I am here to tell you there is a cure, and to plead for you to administer it."

Baramatheus could see on their faces that the Council members were confused as to where his spirited message was heading.

"I am before the king and the Servants of the Council today to plead for the anointing of Michaelis. I beg you to make him a member of the King's Defenders, that he may inspire the kingdom. I am asking that you fan the flame that is inside him and ignite this land with the valor of the common groundsman. Burn up the mindless, defeated souls and show the proud and strong people of Lumen who wish to fight the repulsive Malum that the sacrifice they make is not in vain. I implore you to do this that the enemy be driven all the way back to the caves they call home!" Baramatheus' clenched fists and flinty expression drove home his request to the king.

"Since you are imploring us to do this, I take it that Michaelis is not a descendant of nobility?" Ethan asked

The Council was slow to grant anyone the title of Defender. Allowing it to fall on a commoner was absurd. Lumenite society considered those of royal vocations chosen because of their family line, purposefully placed in their roles by a higher power. A convenient extension of this mindset refused to believe that a man could alter his societal role. Men did not have the right to make common countrymen more than what they were, just as royalty were not to do the menial tasks of the regular citizen. At one time Baramatheus adhered to this reasoning, but he had spent time among the so-called common countrymen, and had grown to realize that they were just as naturally endowed with talents as any noble; all they lacked was the education and lifestyle of the aristocracy.

"No, sir, not by the accepted standard. He is, however, Lumen to his core. This man would easily die for his land and his people at any time if asked to do so. I watched him charge a unit of Malum as if he were chasing a pheasant. He did so with no hesitation and with no regard for his own life."

"And this foolishness is what you call Lumen to the core? This is more aptly why we are losing the fight!" Ethan said.

"No, sir! The reason we are losing the fight is because the men we nobles so blindly ask to pick up a sword and march off to war are farmers and peasants who do not grasp why we ask them to do so. All they see is that they are protecting your comforts and luxuries. They see death claiming all of their kin and yet the king and his royal inner city dignitaries are still as safe as the day the Malum first attacked."

The Council was shocked. The king, however, seemed to be in agreement with what he was hearing.

"Servants of the Council, King Josiah, I do not intend to insult or to speak too harshly. I wish to awaken you to the events taking place in this country. Our society is teetering on the very edge of existence. I do not want to see our country fall to the evil foe. I wish only for the Kingdom of Lumen to thrive and to flourish, with happy people who love their home so much that they long for the opportunity to throw on the burden of armor and race off to conflict!"

Baramatheus dropped his head and then added, "Do you not understand that the age of nobility, as we know it, is over? Now is the time for the poor, the miserable, and the peasants to shed their skin and put on the overcoat of royalty, a task that carries with it the responsibility to do what must be done.

"The people of this land are numb to the plague that calls itself Malum; the disease has infected their bodies and rotted their very souls. You are right about that.

"I ask you to look honestly at the people you serve, and ask yourself if you truly are any better than they are or only better off?

"If it is conceivable for royalty, me, to fight side-by-side with lowly groundsmen, then why is it so hard for the groundsmen to stand side-by-side with royalty?" Baramatheus turned away from the Council in frustration. He knew what he was saying was not welcome and the odds of his changing their minds were nearly nonexistent.

The room was silent.

"Not only do I call Michaelis' decision to storm the enemy Lumen to the core," Baramatheus said, "I would go as far as to say he showed the bravery which Oren displayed the day he plucked sight from the livyatan. I implore you to consider that event in its entirety.

"Oren was a simple fisherman, not royal according to our society's standards, yet I believe we all would agree that he is evidence that nobility is to be found in the common man as well. Our focus on power, one's station in life, and the blood that flows through our veins has blinded us to the fact that true nobility is found in our villages just as easily as it is found among Throne City's privileged."

The Council members looked at one another in a brief moment of reflection before the chairman addressed the Lumen knight. "Baramatheus, Defender of the King, son of Nicholas, Servant of the Council, you speak bluntly and passionately about what you believe to be the situation this kingdom finds itself in. We, however, as members of the Council, have been discussing and studying the ramifications of the conflict since its beginning and find no weight in your presumption that if we anointed a village groundsmen, the tide of the war would shift. Therefore, know that we respect your insights into the daily struggles of our soldiers, since you have been with them in the valley of darkness, but we cannot take such extreme measures based on one man's opinion, however passionate."

The chairman of the Council spoke as if he already knew what the other Servants were thinking. He probably did. The members spent all day contemplating, studying, discussing, and thinking with one another on a vast array of subjects, with the war being the primary topic as of late. Any one of the Servants could rationally conclude what another member's view on a subject would be.

Baramatheus felt as if he had just been kicked in the stomach. He was positive that this had been the right move. The Council had to know that the war would end soon and in favor of the Malum unless they altered their current tactics.

His defeat was just beginning to set in when the king stood up.

"You may not be able to take the necessary actions based on what this loyal Lumen warrior has said, but I can, and I must." The Servants were startled at the king's words.

King Josiah, the highest of high royalty, was accepting the proposition to anoint a commoner? How could this be? The kingdom would certainly crumble if the king allowed anyone and everyone to cross the line and become royalty.

"With all due respect your Majesty-" the Chairman did not have a chance to finish his sentence.

"I have made my decision. Michaelis will be anointed. The men of this kingdom must understand that this land is as much theirs as it is mine." The king spread his hands outward in the general direction of the Council. "If I must choose between giving my throne over to the Lumenites or to the Malum, I choose the sons and daughters of this kingdom! Even if it means that there will never more be a king like myself."

The Council adjourned after the chair announced that the ceremony would be held at dusk. As they moved quickly to private quarters Ethan burst into a confused and frustrated tantrum, pausing only to ensure he was out of earshot of the king.

"How? How can the king go against our decision on this matter? Does he not see that if this happens, the entire kingdom will devour itself with anarchy?"

"Ethan, the king understands more than you, or the rest of the Council, give him credit for," Nicholas said as he gently laid his hand on Ethan's shoulder. "He recognizes that one way or another, the kingdom is going to change. He has chosen wisely. I, too, would rather continue to see Lumenites walking the streets of this city than those detestable Malum soldiers." Nicholas let the busy minds be, as he opened the door and headed down the hallway to where Baramatheus looked out into the garden.

"Son, the Council will follow the king's orders. They may not like it, but the king has taken the right course of action today. Michaelis should be thinking about his answers to the Council's questions. I have a feeling the Servants are not going to be easy on him."

"Michaelis' heart has the answers, and I know that they will please the Council," Baramatheus paused, "and the king."

Baramatheus approached Michaelis who was still near the stables. He had spent the time relishing the act of tending to such a fine courser. For a young man that had grown up caring for broken old workhorses and the occasional palfrey, this was quite a treat.

"Michaelis, I have brought you here for a reason. You are to be anointed as one of the King's Defenders."

"What? Me? But I am not nobility. I cannot be anointed. It is not allowed."

"You have shown what a true Lumenite's heart must be like if we are to be victorious in our present engagement. You, my brave friend, have the heart of a king. You are royalty here." Baramatheus lightly hit Michaelis in the chest with his fist, driving home the idea that it was the heart of a man that mattered, not the class of his birth. "The ceremony will begin at dusk. The Council will question you. Answer honestly, brave soldier, and you will be fine." Baramatheus turned and left, patting the long head of his trusted horse on his way by.

Michaelis stood motionless, trying to understand how he arrived in this situation. What had his friend said to the Council? The butterflies in his stomach began to flutter as he thought about being in front of the Council, and in front of the king.

Chapter Eight

Night fell on New York City. The sidewalks were just as lit up by all the glowing signs as they were in the afternoon sun. The nonstop commotion made it difficult for Adam to sleep. Each night he struggled to block out the sounds of the city. Each night the task became easier. He was acclimating to the culture of New York, learning to disregard most of the sounds: the screaming, the honking, the squealing of tires, the crying babies, the car alarms, the doors slamming in the hallway, and every other disruptive noise that festered in the neighborhood. At some point during the process of trying to fall asleep, it all just kind of washed away into the background.

Adam lay in bed thinking of what his life might have been like if he had stayed in Lakeview. He reassured himself that his decision to move to the city, leaving the quiet, dull life of his hometown was a good move. Before he knew it, he was dreaming.

Packages began falling from the sky, millions of them, raining down onto the streets. Adam watched as they hit the pavement, some crashing through the concrete surface with immense force, others landing as softly as a leaf on a patch of green grass.

People rushed to snatch them up, they were like children racing to the ground under an open piñata. As the crowd tore into the presents, a number of the boxes turned to ash, streaming through their fingers. Others ignited into massive pillars of fire, casting eerie shadows of unnatural figures on the asphalt. Yet some people pulled out beautiful musical instruments, each one varying in size. They played their instruments, many dancing as they did, making the most marvelous music with their newly acquired gifts.

Adam had never heard such wonderful sounds. The musicians did not seem to notice that the rest of the people were moaning in tears over what had happened to their gifts. Angry mobs began running all over the city, shrieking and violently waving their fists at the sky. For a moment, the profane language that spewed from their mouths drowned out the music. The sight was a dramatic contrast between those playing inspiring songs of harmony, and those hollering in chaotic dismay. Eventually, the music reclaimed dominance, completely muting everything else.

Adam's vantage point was from a small ledge on top of a building. Curiously, the building seemed to be infinitely tall. He could see the street below in the most minute detail. The gray color of the sidewalk sharply outlined the darkness of the pavement and the people on it, but somehow the building felt as if it continued on forever. Peering down to the street, the sudden rush of realizing how high up he was hit him with such power that he tumbled backwards, smacking his head against the pitch and tar of the rooftop. As he stood up, he swiped at the back of his sweatpants and t-shirt, dusting off the dirt and gravel from his clothes.

While the dirt was still rolling off his pants, Adam Malloy took notice of the floor beneath his feet. It was peculiar, not at all what one would expect on top of a building. Then, after looking around, he noticed that he was not on a building at all, but rather on the bridge of a huge ship.

Computer screens and radio equipment surrounded him. Every bell and buzzer was flashing with alarm. Gazing about the room, he realized that his hands were tightly gripping the controls of the vessel. How he ended up here was beyond him. Out in front of the ship, the only thing he could see was a body of blue water that was slowly melding into a dark red as the boat cut through the waves.

Farther past the bow, he could see what he knew to be the edge of the Earth. The image was reminiscent of a very creative painting depicting a flat Earth, a massive waterfall emptying into a cosmic abyss. His emotions surged as he frantically tried to turn the ship one way and then the other. The buoyant craft was already in motion and no matter what Adam did, he could not alter its course. Adam's stomach churned as he held onto the controls that were leading him over the world's dismal edge.

Out of nowhere, two fighter jets whooshed past the ship, heading in the same direction. He focused on the aircraft as the boat approached the watery cliff. The chemical trails extending from their tail-ends formed the vivid figure eight shape of the infinity symbol surrounded by a perfect circle. Time stood still as he stared hypnotically at the image in the sky.

Snapping out of the trancelike state, he recalled the current crisis on the ship just as the front of it began to tilt over the drop-off. Adam turned away from the controls, running as fast as he could toward the rear of the ship. All the while, more and more of the boat crossed the tipping point, falling over the edge. At the exact moment Adam reached the end of the ship, the entire thing plummeted downward. With every bit of effort he could muster, Adam leapt off the back of the huge vessel.

Suspended in midair for what seemed like hours, Adam floated aimlessly upward. Gravity had no effect on his body. He was able to glide through an expanse of nothingness for a while until finally, a dot of light caught his eye. It was barely even noticeable at first, a speck in the distance. Effortlessly, he began to move closer to it. The light became more brilliant as he neared, until eventually he passed through it as if through a tunnel, luminescent walls on all sides of him.

At the other end of the tunnel of light, Adam noticed a group of little children dancing under sheets of paper falling around them. There was writing on both sides, which Adam could not quite make out. The pieces of paper were absorbed into each other while drifting through the air.

Adam thought of the bed in which he had gone to sleep, each blanket covering his body like the layers of paper falling onto the children. The safety and comfort of the bed eased Adam's bewildered emotions while he intently watched the paper drape over some of the kids, conforming to the shape of their bodies until the children disappeared. Those remaining made a game out of the situation, laughing splendidly as they ducked and dodged. Adam could not help thinking of a simpler time in his life, a time when he was carefree.

A few moments passed before a mysterious gust of wind swept down to the ground where the kids were playing. Quickly, the unusual breeze headed upward with a train of paper and children following, eventually disappearing into a golden sky.

To his right, Adam could see a mountain range that reeked of violence. The mountaintops were crashing into one another, fighting like bulls trying to establish dominance. The Earth quaked and stones crumbled as each peak smacked into the other; however, the sound was not that of earthen structures colliding. It resonated with that of metal clashing against metal.

On his left, Adam watched a new tree rapidly grow out of the ground. White flowers, each with five petals started to blossom. A hint of pink doused the tips briefly as the flower expanded. Palm-sized red and green fruit fell from the branches almost immediately. Every stage of the growth cycle took place in a matter of seconds.

He looked around in an effort to take in all that was happening when he spotted an older man walking toward him. The man was humming a tune. It was at the same time very beautiful and yet a little disheartening. Adam's first impression of the man was distrust; he was an intruder invading this peaceful place within Adam's dream. The distrust was replaced with a feeling of great union with the stranger, like they were linked somehow.

The stranger wore a white t-shirt, a pair of khaki pants, and no shoes. Adam got the sense that the man had traveled a great distance. His feet were dirty, although as Adam looked at the man's feet they did not seem to be moving. The stranger was not actually walking, but rather gliding along the ground. His clothes were slightly tattered, giving the impression that he had been wearing them for a long time. Adam inherently knew that the man had been wandering all over the Earth, traveling back and forth, looking for something. As the traveler moved, a bright light followed him, calming Adam's apprehension. Uncertain of how to react, Adam tried to hide behind the tree that had sprung up before him.

"I see you."

The words rang out sweetly as the man looked directly at Adam, placing one hand on his knee and bending over as if to get a better look, much like a child playing hide and seek. He then began to sing the words of the melody he had been humming.

> "The place to hide, I can find
> The one with the power.
> But I, in stride, may assist the mind
> Of him in this hour."

The way he sang the words made them stick sharply in Adam's head. Adam did not understand what the lyrics meant, but they were in his mind, loud and clear, as if written there.

Adam turned away from the shoeless stranger, sitting down with his back against the trunk of the tree. To his surprise, there was a stunning woman standing in front of him. She looked down at him, her expression full of curiosity. The stranger's song rang out again. The woman looked up, turning from Adam to the direction of the captivating tune. Adam, too, turned back toward the traveler. He was still singing his short melodic words.

In his hand was a round fruit from the tree next to him. He tossed it up into the air playfully, watching it fall back into his hand. The motion was spellbinding. Adam and the woman followed the fruit's path. Upon catching it, the traveler examined it closely. Satisfied with it, he then turned away from Adam and the woman as the words of his melody streamed from his lips.

While the man slid away, he continued to toss the fruit up into the air. Just before he was too far away to be heard, he threw the fruit straight back. It whizzed past Adam.

The woman caught it with remarkable reflex. Adam looked up at her again. She was now eyeing the fruit, inspecting its every detail, rolling it around in her palm, as if she were in the supermarket picking out produce. The longer she viewed it, the more the look on her face changed; finally, she focused her gaze once more upon the traveler. A smirk crept across her lips as she watched the strange man walk away.

She took a deep bite of the fruit and then vanished. The fruit dropped into Adam's lap. A sweet smell floated up to his nose, begging him to eat. The aroma was so enticing that Adam lifted it to his lips and bit into it. Instantly, a pain sliced through his body.

Doubling over, he wrapped his arms around his waist. Never in his life had he experienced such agony. Tears flowed from his eyes. His intestines were on fire. His gut wrenched violently in reaction to ingesting the fruit. Within seconds Adam was vomiting, his throat and stomach working in unison to rid his body of the foreign substance. He looked at the fruit. Nothing was wrong with it. What was happening? Why did he feel like he was dying?

All of this took place at the foot of the tree that Adam had been hiding behind. The close connection he had shared with the stranger was now gone. His attempt to move away from the tree was unsuccessful. As he slid his hand along the ground behind him it bumped up against a brick wall. A wall that quite obviously had not been there before, for it stood exactly where the woman had disappeared only moments before.

"Where did that come from?" Adam did not understand how the wall got there.

He beat his hands against it in an effort to get away. All the while, the mysterious tune of the traveler was getting louder and louder, tormenting him. Although the tune was in his head he could not help but look over his shoulder, checking to make sure the traveler was truly gone. In a shocking moment of discovery, Adam realized that the words were getting louder because he had begun singing them. Uneasiness filled his heart upon this revelation.

The fear resonating within his body pushed him to hit the wall with all his might. The bricks exploded into dust. Adam felt a wetness under his hands as he crawled forward. The damp ground was getting thicker and deeper; it became easier to swim rather than crawl. He did not have to swim far before reaching solid land again.

Panicking, he pulled himself up and out of the thick crimson river. He tried to move quickly, but the weight of his wet clothes bogged him down. He struggled for each step as he stomped his way forward. A sense of urgency befell him as he realized that despite how hard he was trying, he could not move any faster than his current slow pace. He shed his clothes, leaving them lying on the bank of the river.

He saw his bed from his parents' house back in Lakeview. Without a second thought, he turned toward it and began running frantically for the one thing he recognized, a memorable image of comfort and security. The time it took to run the distance was all wrong. The bed had not appeared very far off and yet it took forever to reach it. Once there, exhausted and out of breath, he fell to the floor and climbed his way up and onto his old bed, tears streaming from his face.

It felt great to be lying there. Youthful feelings of warmth and innocence encompassed his heart and mind as he reached down and pulled the sheets over his naked body.

A sudden knock at the door of Adam's apartment startled him. It seemed like he had just closed his eyes. Rubbing the side of his head, he dropped his feet to the floor, not yet fully awake.

"Hold on. I'm coming, I'm coming." Adam stepped into his sweatpants and pulled his t-shirt over his head, the melody of a familiar tune meandering through his mind.

Chapter Nine

Anointing a knight into the order of the King's Defenders was a significant event. Only a select few soldiers ever received such an honor. Never in the history of the kingdom had a village groundsman been given the privilege. The qualifications for the title were nearly unobtainable. After the validation of a soldier's royal ancestry, the leaders of the Defenders and the Council scrutinized his conduct to ensure his valor as well as his ability to follow the Defenders' code of ethics. This vocation within the Kingdom of Lumen was highly sought by royal men, not to mention that it garnered respect from all in the land.

Michaelis stood in the center of the room, exactly where Baramatheus had stood hours earlier. The young man was petrified. He had no clue what to say or how to act.

He looked up toward the Servants of the Council with such a natural humility that even the king questioned if he was truly the right man. The Servants looked very distinguished to the lowly stable boy. Each of them possessed a demeanor permeated by greatness. Most of them wore long, thick beards which concealed their aged facial features. The confidence in their eyes expressed a wisdom greater than that of twenty men. Baramatheus sat in the back next to the door along with the chief strategists of the King's Defenders.

"Michaelis, citizen of the Kingdom of Lumen," the chairman of the Council spoke, his stern voice echoing throughout the room. "The bravery you have shown in the face of danger has been recorded and conveyed to the Council by Baramatheus, a respected and loyal Defender of the King. Your king has found it in his heart to grant you nobility in exchange for your undying service to this country."

Already nervous, Michaelis felt tiny as he listened closely to the words of the Council.

"In tradition, after the manner of Oren the Ablaze, this Council anoints you as a member of the King's Defenders, an honor of the greatest magnitude. As Oren fought the livyatan, you too have proven yourself in combat. It has been said, 'Remember the battle, for you shall not wage it again.' Like Oren, the actions that brought you the honor being bestowed here today will never again be obtained, no matter how many more victories you may have in the name of your king."

Generally, the highest ranked member of the Defenders received the pleasure of anointing the newest member. Not this time. Without warning, the king stepped down from his throne and walked over to the font placed in the room. Taking the cup and dipping it into the ointment, King Josiah moved in front of Michaelis. A look of shock appeared on the faces of everyone as the king began to speak.

"Young man, brave soldier of the Lumen Kingdom, you have shown great courage in the face of death. You have displayed enormous love for your fellow man and for your country. In doing so, you have shown great loyalty to your king. Please kneel." Michaelis knelt without hesitation. "Do you accept responsibility for your courageous and virtuous deeds, which were performed out of the purest of motivations?" The king stopped to give Michaelis the opportunity to respond.

"I do, and I will to the best of my ability for the rest of my life." Michaelis was surprised when his voice did not shake. Despite living life as a peasant, he found that he was remarkably calm in the presence of the king and his Council.

"Then, by my title, King of the Lumen Throne, and in the fashion of Oren the Ablaze, I anoint you with the Flame of the Livyatan as a member of the family united by the order of the King's Defenders." The king dripped the oil over Michaelis' head. After the cup was empty, he placed it on the table from which he had picked it up.

He then moved to another table covered with pieces of armor. "As a soldier of Lumen I implore you to bear your armor well."

Standing reverently at the head of the table was the abbot of the sanctuary. The Martinian picked up a belt and placed it in the hands of the king. In turn, King Josiah then lowered it in front of Michaelis.

"This belt will help support your weapon, therefore wear it with pride as a reminder to be honest and truthful to your brothers in arms who in turn will support you in battle."

Michaelis reached up and took the belt from the king. He had never seen such fine clothing.

The king turned back to the monk, who lifted from the table a breastplate made of the finest lumenium. The metal was rare and highly valued for its strength and reflective properties. It shone brightly in even low light making it a symbol of the kingdom as well as the ideal metal for a knight's armor.

"This breastplate is meant to protect your most valuable asset, your heart. For with your heart you can stand for what is good when others cower from what is evil. Wear this piece of armor with integrity, taking care to be righteous in all your actions, on and off the battlefield."

The breastplate shone brilliantly as it reflected the light in the room. In the center of the armor was the king's symbol, a behemoth. The beast appeared to be standing guard over the knight's heart. Michaelis thought of the first time he had seen Baramatheus and how his armor had shimmered in the moonlight.

King Josiah took the next piece of royal armor from the abbot.

"With this you will be able to stand firm in the midst of conflict, trusting that you will walk off the soil that flows with the blood of men. Take up this shield. Grasp it in good faith, as Oren did, knowing that as long as you can hold it, the flame of your foe will not overtake you."

Michaelis grasped the shield's handle.

"Just as you wear the breastplate to protect your heart, use this shield to protect your senses. It will allow you to keep your wit despite the abounding chaos."

Next, the king placed a helmet over Michaelis' head. "Keep your mind clear and focused in times of trouble and you will be delivered from death."

The armor felt awkward to the young Lumenite. When he was called up to be a groundsman, all he had was his father's old sword and an overused satchel to throw over his shoulder. Now, here he was fully dressed in the garb of a knight, kneeling before his king.

The king wrapped his fingers around the sword, removing it from the outstretched palms of the monk. It was the last tool needed to equip Michaelis for his new station in life. King Josiah placed his hand on Michaelis' shoulder. "Young friend, your strength will most certainly inspire those around you, calling them to take action to defend what is theirs. I beseech you to speak words of motivation and empowerment, launch their spirits to the realm of offensive action against the Malum and any other threat we may face in days to come."

The king raised the sword slightly above his head and said, "Michaelis, son of the Lumen Kingdom, may the courageous spirit that possesses you be shown to all through this royal blade!"

He then lowered it back down and placed it directly in front of Michaelis.

"Take the hilt of this mighty weapon, the sword of your king, and rise to your feet, for I declare you a royal servant of the Kingdom of Lumen under the command of my Defenders."

Grasping the sword, Michaelis wasted no time rising to his feet, standing face-to-face with the king.

Baramatheus, followed by all the others in attendance, applauded in celebration. History had just been written. A new era had begun in Lumen.

Chapter Ten

The pounding at Adam's door grew louder and faster as he put on his shirt.

"You know what day it is, Smalltown! You know! Open up this door!" Mr. Santone was early. He always made the rounds on the first of the month, but today, it seemed, he was attempting to set some kind of world record. Usually he had the decency to wait until eight o'clock before beginning to disrupt the lives of the tenants.

"I know you're home, Smalltown. You work the late shift so you gotta be!" Mr. Santone hated getting stiffed on the rent.

"I have it, don't worry."

Adam unlatched the four locking mechanisms that secured his apartment so that he could open the door. His movements were slow and groggy. All he cared about was rubbing the sleep from his eyes. Last night's vivid dream had caused him to toss and turn all night. His bloodshot eyes were heavy and burned with every blink.

Mr. Santone was standing at his towering 5'7" right in front of Adam, abnormally close to the door frame. In fact, it was obvious that the money-monger had been trying to peak through the crack of the door before it was pulled open.

"You know, Smalltown, if you were a good tenant you would have me my money prior to its due date. That way I wouldn't have to come around and wake your lazy butt up."

"Here you go, sir. Sorry it's not wrapped in a pretty pink bow. I'll try to do that for you next month." The sarcasm in Adam's voice fell on deaf ears. Santone was not in the mood for smart-aleck remarks. He just wanted his money.

"Well, maybe if you would get a real job..."

Half way through the sentence Adam began to tune the slum-lord out. It was always the same thing with Mr. Santone. All Adam could think about was how badly he wanted the sleazy old man to leave, or better yet, for him to zip his mouth shut. And with that last thought, Adam's life changed forever. As Adam visualized his barking landlord's mouth being zipped up, it actually happened. In mid-sentence, Mr. Santone's lips began to come together with tiny, interlocking metal teeth as a zipper tab moved smoothly across his mouth. The terrified look on the slumlord's face caused Adam to step back in fear.

Mr. Santone panicked. Was Adam still dreaming? He distinctly remembered awakening to the abrupt sound of Mr. Santone pounding on his door.

The man became frantic. He could not open his mouth and yet he still was trying to talk. In fact, he was desperately trying to yell. He mumbled horrifically for Adam to help him.

In a panic, Adam quickly slammed his door. As soon as it shut he fell against it, letting his body slide downward until he was sitting on the ground, his back against the door. He cocked his head back until he was looking straight up. In an effort to grasp the reality of what happened he sat there thinking, his eyes wide open, intense and perplexed.

Sounds of his mumbling landlord still echoed in the hall.

"All I did was think it." Adam sat there for hours, never moving from the door.

Absentmindedly, he began to hum and then sing:

> "The place to hide, I can find
> The one with the power.
> But I, in stride, may assist the mind
> Of him in this hour."

Repeating the second line several times, he felt that there was something special about the song. The strange man in his dream had sung it to him. At the time, it did not mean anything, but now it was beginning to make sense.

Adam Malloy observed, "I must be the one with the power."

He sat in that same position all day long. Entranced with the short little verse, he tried to figure out what was happening. He eventually forgot that Mr. Santone must be frightened to death. All he could think of was himself.

How his landlord was doing was of little concern to him.

An entire night passed and eventually the sun came up again. Adam still sat, stunned. He fell asleep a couple times but awoke shortly after because of the thoughts rolling through his mind. Like a child before the first day of school, he was restless, excited about what he had done. Adam was also terrified and nervous. The emotional mixture blended into an unusual baffled jitteriness. What now? Would all his thoughts become reality?

Tempted to test his newfound power, Adam dragged himself off of the floor and walked over to his makeshift night stand (two cinder blocks stacked on top of each other). On it rested an alarm clock. Just about everything Adam owned he had brought with him from his parents' house. The alarm clock was a hideous relic from his childhood. The white front of the clock was in the shape of a clown's face. At the center, where the hour and minute hands met, was a red circle that looked like the nose of the clown. The rest of the clown's body held the clock up in a cartoonish way. Adam had owned the timepiece for as long as he could remember. It was ugly, but he could never bear to part with it.

Deciding to use the clock as a trial run of his new found ability, he would try to repeat what he had done to Mr. Santone. The first incident was an accident.

The second would be intentional.

He concentrated on his thoughts, saying to himself, "If the clock was slightly taller, it would be better." Adam watched as the clown grew taller. The look of joy that crossed Adam's face was priceless. He was thrilled.

"The nose should be a little brighter." The nose of the clock became the exact shade of red Adam had pictured in his mind.

"Wider." And it was wider.

"How about a digital alarm clock?" It instantly began changing into a regular alarm clock, complete with green backlit numbers and a snooze button on top.

"A candle." The buttons on top of the time piece began to drip down the front of it.

Adam could not believe what was happening. Somehow, he had received an amazing gift. People would kill for such an ability. Playing around with the clock grew old quickly. Glancing across to his window he remembered how silly he thought it was that the building next door was close enough for him to reach out and touch the bricks. He walked over to the window, gazing downward toward the ground.

Thoughts began to roll through his head, "An empty lot for the neighborhood kids to play baseball."

Nothing happened at first. But as Adam closed his eyes in concentration, he felt a cool breeze brush against his face. Opening his eyes he found that the building was gone. In its place was a grassy lot. He could see the path where the kids ran the base line. The red bricks of the building had disappeared. No more staring out into the expanse of stone and mortar. Now he could watch and listen to children playing games down below in the field he created. It never occurred to him that people were more than likely in the building he had just annihilated.

Adam sat down on his bed rather proud, realizing that this was what he had always wanted. He could change the world with a mere thought. He could right all the wrong things that went on every single day. A smile crossed his face as he reveled in what he had done. He was responsible for giving the little children, kids that usually played in the gutter, a much better and certainly much safer place to live out their childhood.

"What else?" Adam was itching to try out his gift again. Looking all over the room for something else he could fix, he settled on the room itself.

"I need enough space for a king size bed." Gradually the walls separated until the room was quite large.

"And now, the king-sized mattress and frame." His bed puffed up like it was about to explode and then gently eased down to its new size.

"Fantastic! This is unbelievable. What else?"

Changing of household products was fun, but the excitement was already wearing off. He wanted to get to work, to do something that mattered. As he thought of ways to help the dying world, he looked down at his feet. Among the rest of the trash that had collected in the living room was an old newspaper. Adam found his opportunity on the front page. The headline would give him the chance to test his ability on a much grander scale. It was time to see what he could really do.

Chapter Eleven

The headline of the newspaper read: "14 Killed in Tunnel Collapse." Adam figured this would be a great place to start helping those that could not help themselves. All he had to do was think that the tunnel had never collapsed and the headline would rewrite itself. Or at least that was how Adam hoped it would work. So far, every change he made was relatively petty, with the exception of Mr. Santone, of course.

Adam read the article carefully to find the cause of the tunnel collapse. The culprit was faulty concrete. According to the story, the cement company had apparently mixed the chemical additives improperly. Deciding that this was the primary cause, he knew he could fix it if he thought hard enough. While sitting on his bed and looking down at the paper, he began thinking of how the concrete used was not defective but rather a perfectly normal batch. Adam spoke the words, clearly defining the alteration. Within seconds the newspaper's headline began to change. The letters bled into a black pool, until finally the ink reconfigured on the paper. Now the title read "Foreign Diplomat to Visit New York." Accompanying the caption was a photograph of a dignitary descending a flight of stairs attached to an airplane, an entourage of officials all around him.

Filled with excitement, he sprung off his bed and quickly changed clothes, putting on a slightly dirty long-sleeved t-shirt and a pair of old jeans. He put his shoes on as he hopped through the door. Reaching out and closing it with a sharp slam, he raced down the hallway. The elderly neighbor lady that lived a few units down from Adam was standing at her door when she saw him come barreling out of his apartment.

"In a bit of a hurry eh, son?" The woman always looked forward to talking with Adam.

"Yes, ma'am! I've reached the stars!" He jogged right past her.

"I see. Yer breeches do look a tad smaller," the woman whispered to herself.

Adam would not have heard her anyway, for he was already in the stairwell. On the street, he could not help noticing something different. Immediately, he heard an amazing noise coming from the lot next to his building. Kids were laughing and yelling with great sounds of joy. He could not believe what he was hearing. Adam Malloy looked across the street where he expected to see several little children trying to float makeshift boats down the gutter. They were not there. The largest grin Adam ever smiled popped onto his face as he sprinted toward the lot. Today the shop keeper's runoff from hosing down the sidewalk was going to waste and Adam was ecstatic about it. Stopping at the corner of his building, the small-town boy leaned up against the cold concrete to simply watch for a few minutes. Children were doing exactly what Adam had pictured when he thought of the lot.

A group of boys and a few girls split into two teams to play baseball. A speedy little kid with freckles all over his face was rounding second base as a girl clobbered the ball as hard as she could. Adam sat there awe-struck watching as a game of pickle ensued. The freckle-faced kid dashed back and forth clumsily, trying not to get touched. An immense sense of accomplishment began to swell up inside Adam.

With a speed walker's pace, he headed down the street away from the baseball field. He was making his way to the eatery, although he was not sure why. Despite the fact that Adam was not particularly good friends with anyone there, in this moment of celebration, he felt like being around other people. He dearly wanted to tell someone about his newfound ability, but at the same time he knew he probably should not. He figured that by being out in public he could at least satisfy his urge to talk to someone.

The restaurant was packed when he arrived. Every booth was crammed full, patrons constantly rotating in and out. It was the normal daytime crowd taking advantage of the eatery's quick service and convenient location. One thing was certain: the quality of food was not the reason for the volume of customers.

At both ends of the dining area were two televisions, each mounted in the corner so that everyone eating could see the screens. During Adam's shift the TV was usually on a channel that showed nonstop reruns of classic programs: black and white renditions of a false world, a world where people got along and everyone laughed on cue. Today, however, the customers were watching a network news channel. Adam noticed a group of people were crowded around the television set in an effort to hear the breaking news. A cloud of silence hovered over the food counter as a woman began to speak from the news desk.

"This is just coming across the wire as we take you live to our reporter on the scene. Bill, can you hear me?" The news anchor was a fairly attractive middle-aged woman. She stared intently at the camera as she tried desperately to hear what her man in the field was saying.

"Yes, Pam, I hear you. The activity here is quite crazy and, well, noisy. I'll do my best and hopefully you're getting this back at the studio." Everyone at the eatery inched closer to the TVs in anticipation of what was going to be said. "Approximately fifteen minutes ago, an apartment building, which also had several major retail stores here on the street level, collapsed, literally crumbling to pieces. Now it is still unconfirmed, but we are getting accounts from eye witnesses that the wreckage extends for blocks. We have not been able to verify that due to blockades restricting mobility in that direction. As you can imagine, there is an unbelievable amount of activity down here. I can say this, casualties are more than likely very high."

Another break in his report left people with their own thoughts of the horror.

"On a side note, Pam, one of the witnesses mentioned that she saw a 'parade of limousines' passing by just prior to the collapse. Since we are only blocks from the UN it is certainly possible that she did in fact see a diplomatic convoy en route. There is concern that it may have been the foreign diplomat from Kahrlzbekistan that arrived just this morning. We'll keep you updated as soon as we get any more information. Back to you, Pam."

Adam could not believe his ears. He had just read about the diplomat's arrival, it was the headline that replaced the one he prevented. He took a seat at the counter as the news anchor was adding her comments to the unfolding story, confusion covering every inch of his face. Adam saved fourteen people from the tunnel collapse, but at what cost? He stared down at the menu, trying to figure out what to do next.

"Hey, cutie. You're not supposed to be here until later," a waitress about Adam's age said. She always had some flirtatious way of talking to him when they bumped into each other. For as long as he had worked at the eatery, she had been interested in him.

"Yeah, I'm just here for a burger." Adam said, barely noticing her. "A double with bacon, if you don't mind."

She placed his order and then walked back into the kitchen saying, "Sure thing, sweetie. It'll be ready in a jiffy."

Sitting on the bar stool, Adam watched as the man next to him struggled to get ketchup out of the glass bottle. He empathized with the frustration that came with the effort.

"All the technology in the world and restaurants still insist on making us earn our condiments."

Adam thought intently about the red paste falling freely out of the bottle. A second later the ketchup began to slide out, almost too fast. He smiled as the man let out a sigh of relief followed by a subtle "finally."

It was not long before the double bacon cheeseburger Adam ordered was in front of him. While he was enjoying his meal, a news update about the building collapse came on the television. Casually directing his attention toward the screen, he listened while he ate.

"Folks, we have breaking news concerning our main story. Bill, what can you tell us?"

"Well, a lot of new information has unfolded in the last fifteen minutes. First, Pam, we have been able to verify that the foreign emissary we mentioned before was indeed en route to the United Nations building when the high-rise gave way. We have made several phone calls in an effort to get an answer of his whereabouts, but at this moment have not been able to get any sort of definitive confirmation from the Kahrlzbekistan embassy. Also, we are being told that the cause behind the collapse is believed to be, well, basically, what equates to bad cement being used in the foundation of the building. Authorities report that there is going to be a news conference soon and more information on that aspect of the story will be made available at that time. I must add, Pam, that rescue teams are in full force down here. According to earliest estimates, casualties may be in the thousands."

"Thanks, Bill. The station has indeed received information regarding the possibility of faulty building materials being the primary cause of the catastrophe. We will keep you updated as soon as we find out any more information on this devastating event."

The news hit Adam like a punch to the stomach. The word "cement" stuck in his mind like a sharp knife. That was what caused the tunnel incident. He quickly stood up. Dropping his food, he started for the door when the waitress called out to him.

"Hey, sweetie! You forgot to pay." The girl was leaning over the counter as the bell above the doorway rang from Adam's exiting.

Adam thought about the exact amount of money to pay for the meal plus a generous tip, resting on the counter. A moment later, there it was.

"Oh, never mind." The waitress was looking down to grab his plate when she saw the money lying there.

Racing up to his apartment, Adam grabbed the newspaper, which was still lying on the floor where he dropped it. Scanning the article, he was dumbfounded that the headline he changed turned into this substantially worse incident involving the man on the altered page. It was not supposed to be happening like this. He had saved people, but now more were dead. Nervous about the events unfolding, Adam thought about a TV along with satellite so that he could watch the news. Just like every other time, his thought produced material results.

For the next few hours, he sat in the light of the massive television screen, careful not to think anything that he might regret later. The connection between the tunnel cave-in and the collapsing building was obvious. He desperately wanted to know why something bad still occurred.

Chapter Twelve

Michaelis pondered his life as a knight of the King's Defenders. After the anointing ceremony, Baramatheus brought him to a monastery where the untrained peasant honed his skills among the monks of the Martinian order. The seasoned warrior mentored him, instructing him in various fighting techniques, teaching him everything from the fundamentals to the more complex methods of defensive and offensive combat. He spent time illustrating good and proper practices when traveling long distances, emphasizing preparedness and detailing ways in which to remain unnoticed.

At the same time, the monks, who were the kingdom's only scribes, taught Michaelis about his country. The Martinian monks were entrusted with protecting and maintaining the truth of the kingdom. Founded on ancient knowledge handed down from before the dawn of the

Lumen age, it was their duty to guard the past from distortion and misinterpretation. They took their obligation seriously and educated all the royal members of the nation with the accurate account of historical events and Lumen legends. Various brotherhoods existed, all of them Martinians. Each monastery perpetuated the stories of the ancient times by copying the accounts in countless volumes. These universal accounts, central to the history of the Lumenites, were at every abbey. In addition, each brotherhood took special interest in detailing the happenings of certain significant people and the events involving them. It was in this manner that they guaranteed the existence of the kingdom's history. The records were captivating to read. The way in which the monks wrote was more like picking up a heroic tale or epic legend than it was like reading a chronicled history. The adventures were riveting, and marvelously detailed. It was only the solemn nature of the Martinians that kept people from mistaking their writings for grossly exaggerated episodes of lore.

Michaelis enjoyed all of his training. He grew closer to Baramatheus as the experienced soldier guided him through the trials of learning. Eventually he came to view him as more of a father, rather than a mentor. Michaelis was a new man, much more mature in mind and heart. He stood with a sense of dignity, although he had vowed to himself shortly after his anointing that he would never forget from where he had come.

The whole time he was training, the fight with the Malum grew more costly. Men were dying daily as they braved the wilderness in an attempt to defend themselves. The Malum army was making advances toward the Lumen gate. Michaelis grew impatient; he longed to help his fellow countrymen fend off the evil curse.

"It is time," Michaelis grunted as he raised his sword to meet Baramatheus'.

"Time for what?"

"For what? To put this practice to work!" Michaelis swung around, sweeping his blade across his body, slicing through the air toward his instructor.

"So, you believe you are ready to charge off into battle?"

"Of course I am ready. I could not be any more ready!"

Their blades met, spraying sparks with every clash. All the while, the two men debated whether the timing was right to engage in life-or-death battle. Baramatheus knew Michaelis was ready, but saw the opportunity too great to pass up. The days of light-hearted fun were about to end and he wanted to delight in them for just a little longer.

The younger knight was not yet aware, but he and his mentor were about to part ways. The two great soldiers entangled their swords. The moves of both men were graceful and executed with remarkable skill. After several moments, the more experienced man brought down the student with a quick and unexpected move.

"Yes, my brave friend, I believe you are indeed ready." Baramatheus stood back, extended a hand, and helped up his pupil. A subtle smirk rested on the corner of his lips. "Only, remember that there is always more to learn. You can only go so far within these walls. Your lessons will continue beyond them."

Turning his back to Michaelis he wiped off his sword, removing all the metal shavings and mud from the surface of the blade. "I am saddened to say, we more than likely will have to take different paths to the frontlines."

"What are you talking about, Bar?" A ring of shock resonated in Michaelis' voice. He did not want to hear anything about separating from Baramatheus.

"You are a good soldier. You will do well on the battlefield."

"Yes, right next to you as we lead the men of Lumen to victory." Michaelis' voice was unsure.

"We must lead separately. I will continue to do my part. Now you must do yours. You have what it takes to lead. It would be a waste of resources for both of us to be in the same camp. The training you have received will serve you well. I have prepared your way. Now you must proceed down the path which is yours." Baramatheus placed his hand on Michaelis' shoulder. "Do not worry, my brave friend. I will see you on the safe side of this conflict where we will feast in celebration."

Michaelis shrugged his shoulder away and took a few steps back. He looked out into the distance.

"You have taught me well. Thank you, Bar, for all you have given me." A deep sigh escaped the young man's chest. "I will do you and this kingdom proud." Michaelis looked right into Baramatheus' eyes as he spoke.

"That I know." The two men gave each other a look of encouragement and then Baramatheus turned and headed for his quarters.

With the training over, there was no time to lose. They had spent long enough away from the battle. Both men were anxious to do their part. They would meet with the other members of the King's Defenders to lay out their strategy. The time was nearing for either the claiming of victory or the acceptance of defeat.

At the Defenders' keep there were many rooms, most of which were for training, planning, and discussion. Near the end of the entrance hall was a large gathering room. In it were three men who were leaning over a huge table covered by a map, a variety of food, drinks, and a collection of burnt down candles. The men were planning the defensive strategy against the Malum.

The King's Defenders were in charge of the country's major fighting force. The army received its direct orders from them through a series of ranked royal soldiers. The king would give orders to the

Defenders and they, in turn, would figure out the most effective way to carry out the order.

The men jumped with surprise as Baramatheus and Michaelis walked into the room, for they had been ensconced in retreat for days with only the servants entering to resupply them with food and candles.

"Pardon the interruption, gentlemen, but your servants, Baramatheus and Michaelis, are at your disposal." Baramatheus, followed by Michaelis, bowed to the men.

"Ah, the mighty monks have decided to join the ranks of warriors."

Gidaen, along with the two other men in the room, were the chief leaders of the Defenders. The three of them acted as a system of balance for the order. This system prevented the Lumen knights from being manipulated to serve one man's purpose.

"Michaelis is trained and ready to put his sword to work for his king." Baramatheus looked down at the map. "And it seems just in time." A dire and perplexed expression spread across his face. "Is this really how things stand?"

The map showed five camps set up outside the gate of the kingdom, all of them about six thousand men strong, some more, some less. One camp was trying to hold off the Malum to the northeast near Devastation Valley, which was particularly odd because even the Malum were hesitant to travel through it. Another was directly north, almost near the coast. As for the other three, they were clustered together in the south. All together there were roughly 32,000 Lumen soldiers. Gidaen leaned over the map, pointing to the far north encampment.

"Our men have been fighting a group of Malum soldiers that were apparently trying to sneak in along the shore. All reports state that the Malum troops are moving ships through the region. We believe they intend to surprise us by coming in from the Tranquil Sea and up through the harbor. The camp at Devastation Valley is currently hunkered down. The latest message from them reports a force of at least twenty thousand Malum fighters moving down the valley in their direction."

"That is amazing. Not even the Malum like traveling through that valley, let alone in such a cumbersome mass."

"Well, apparently they do not mind so much anymore. Safety in numbers, I presume. The three camps to the south, though they have suffered severe casualties, are pretty well fortified for the time being. A rider is en route, ordering them to merge their camps," Gidaen said as he looked at his two colleagues, both of whom bore a look of defeat.

Baramatheus stood looking at the map, pondering troop movement and the probable outcomes. He eyed the table as if he were playing a game of chess, the markers on the map the game pieces.

Michaelis was standing at the far end of the table, peering down from the perspective of the Malum Mountains. "What is your plan, if I might ask?"

"That is what we have been trying to figure out for the last several days, young monk." A slight sense of sarcasm punctured Michaelis' ears. The fact that he, a battle-ready soldier, had been training in a peace-filled monastery was rather amusing to some of the seasoned knights. Most Defenders trained at the keep. The cause of Michaelis' unusual circumstance was that he was in as much need of learning the history of the land as he was in learning the art of war, given his humble roots. "It seems we have come to a turning point in the struggle against the Malum. We cannot seem to figure out a way to survive this predicament. There are no reinforcements to send except what is already out in the field. It seems we are being forced either to sacrifice one pathway into the kingdom for another or to stand fast, attempt to hold our positions, and inevitably die."

The men looked exhausted. It was obvious that they had run scenario after scenario through their minds in an effort to maneuver free from what looked like the endgame for the Lumen nation.

Michaelis looked over at Baramatheus, making eye contact. Both of them knew the table was essentially up for grabs if they could come up with a feasible plan. As if on cue, they both looked down and studied the layout. Baramatheus shuffled over, bumping the three strategists out of his way. Michaelis stayed where he was, tilting his head in thought. The look in his eye was of pure determination. He was not about to lose this kingdom to the hands of the evil foe. Looking at the table through the eyes of the enemy obviously helped. After only a few minutes passed, an idea came to Michaelis.

"Sirs," his voice interrupted the silence, "I know a way to win this war."

"With all due respect, Defender of the Records," the title a condescending reference to Michaelis' training, "we have been looking at this map for days. I doubt you have the answer to all the questions in mere minutes." The man was gruff in appearance. He looked battle-worn and tired.

"Perhaps not all the answers, but I think maybe you needed to look at the map as if you were in Acerbus, from the Malum's perspective, from Bebble-uk's angle." Michaelis gestured to where he was standing.

"Well, we are waiting. Speak up!"

"It seems to me that the only option is to pull the men from the north and move them south to help the forces at Devastation Valley," Michaelis started.

"Young man, you obviously do not understand what you are saying. If the Malum get to the Tranquil Sea they will come at us from the west, through the harbor," Gidaen bluntly interrupted.

"Yes, I understand that. I also understand that the city has a very highly trained army whose sole purpose is to protect the City of the Throne. There is nothing between the docks and the city; therefore, if we leave the city's forces to do what they are trained to do, we can move our men to aid the others."

The three Defenders were astonished that Michaelis had come up with such an idea. It was brilliant, it was simple, and it was obvious. A tinge of embarrassment rolled over Gidaen and his cohorts. Baramatheus moved over to Michaelis' side of the room and placed his hand on the shoulder of his friend as he often did.

"Well done, my brave friend." Baramatheus was just as astonished as the others.

"That is a good start, but who is to say that the two combined camps will have any better luck fighting off the twenty thousand Malum?" Gidaen was ready to listen to Michaelis now.

"I am, and Baramatheus, of course. And it will not be two camps. It will be five. That will put us at one force, thirty-two thousand strong." Michaelis knew without a doubt this would work. "I will ride south and lead the men north to Devastation Valley. Bar will ride north and lead those men south to the valley. When Bebbel-uk sees what we are doing, we will have forced him to adjust his plans in reaction. With all the camps together, we will outnumber the Malum force moving through the valley. With those kinds of numbers Bebbel-uk will see the potential threat and will not want to risk losing that many men.

"I suspect the Malum will shift their men in the south to assist the valley troops. That will put the numbers back in Bebbel-uk's favor. The Malum forces heading for the sea will be cut off as they will continue with their plans. The only concern then is being outnumbered." As he spoke, Michaelis noticed that Gidaen was looking intently across the map at him and Baramatheus.

"I do not like it much either, sir. However, I think it will be an excellent catalyst for our men. We are setting the stage for one final battle between Lumen and Malum. Our men need to know this is the struggle to end all struggles. If they can be shown that it is life or death, I know the Lumen spirit will prevail." Baramatheus placed his hand on the hilt of his sword.

A chill passed through the room as they all stared at the dawning future before them.

The plan was in place. Michaelis loaded up the supplies he would need for his journey south. Baramatheus did the same for his flight north. Time was certainly not on their side, and the voyage was long. Michaelis had a nonstop flutter in his stomach. He felt capable of doing that which had to be done, although worried that the men would not see the situation for what it was. He knew the groundsmen were tired and downtrodden; they would surely see him as just another leader spouting empty words. Baramatheus finished stuffing a satchel of food into his saddlebag as Michaelis mounted his horse.

"Ride quickly, and remember to trust your horse. The breed is truly noble, more intelligent than some men. If you lose your way, trust the courser." Baramatheus had depended on his red-haired steed many times throughout the years and as a result he knew exactly what the beasts were capable of.

On one occasion he had been hurt so badly that he passed out while traveling away from a Malum attack. The weather began to shift and snow started to fall. Baramatheus regained consciousness a couple times, but not long enough to do any kind of directing of his horse. The steed took him to the shelter of a secluded cave, lowered him off its back, and lay down next to Baramatheus to keep him warm.

"Will do, Bar. Protect yourself out there." Michaelis hated to part ways with Baramatheus.

Once Baramatheus was ready to ride, he looked over at Michaelis as he turned his horse in the direction he was headed.

"I will see you at Devastation Valley." Baramatheus whipped the reins and let out a holler.

Michaelis followed suit. The two warriors rode off in opposite directions, leaving a path of dust behind them. The three chief Defenders watched from a perch high above in the tower of the keep.

"Pray that wisdom lies within this plan, brothers," one of the rugged strategists spoke, a cloud of doubt looming over his heart.

"The fate of many rests upon the courage and wisdom of two," Gidaen added.

He did not know whether the plan would work, but it was all they had. All they could do now was hope.

Chapter Thirteen

"It is apparent that the cause of the building collapse in downtown New York City was, in fact, the result of a miscalculation that occurred while construction of the building was still at the foundation stage. Geotechnical engineers are telling us that the materials used in the foundation were not sufficient to support the weight load of the building. Investigations are already underway to learn more about this deadly error. As far as casualties, sadly the number has reached seventy-four as of this morning. Among the deceased are the Ambassador of Kahrlzbekistan and his aides. The motorcade was traveling on the adjacent street when the building fell. For more on that side of the story, we turn now to our correspondent in the region of Kahrlzbekistan, Samuel Burk. Sam, what have you learned so far?"

"Well, Pam, not too much. The representatives of the Kahrlzbekistan government are not giving us any information. But, I can tell you this. The ambassador was in the US on a relations-mending mission hosted by the UN. The two countries have not been on good terms for nearly three decades, not since, as some of our older viewers might remember, the fall of the Engelsian presidency. America cut ties with the regime that had conducted the coup which ousted President Engels when their methods became violent. Kahrlzbekistan is a small country with a limited number of exportable goods. It is our understanding that the ambassador was in New York to meet with the secretary of foreign affairs tomorrow with hopes of working toward establishing a trade agreement and possibly to request aid to help ease the nation's economic hardships. Since the building collapse, we have been hearing a lot of talk on the streets here, mostly scared voices spreading a rumor that the leaders of our nation somehow planned the incident to cover up an assassination plot on the ambassador. I know it sounds crazy, but the people here honestly believe that it was an elaborate conspiracy. Back to you, Pam."

"Thanks for the report, Sam, and keep up the good work. There you have it. The situation grows more intense as now it seems we might have an international conflict brewing."

Adam went over to his fridge and grabbed a soda out of the door.

"What have I done?"

All he wanted to do was save the people in the tunnel accident, and now he might have inadvertently started some sort of political skirmish.

Thoughts raced through his brain as he desperately tried to come up with a way to fix this problem he created. All kinds of questions bounced about in his mind. Why did people still end up dead? How did it become a worse accident than before? Why did the Kahrlzbekistan people think it was on purpose? What would correct the incident without causing another one? Given that both events involved concrete and structures collapsing, he even wondered if maybe the same fourteen people that were in the tunnel accident, were also among the new casualties, as if their deaths were the result of some sort of fate. Nothing was too far-fetched. After all, he had the power to reform reality by simply thinking.

It was while these ponderings were afloat in his head that he started humming the tune he had first heard in his dream. Minutes went by without Adam even noticing that he was repeating the melody, and then all of a sudden, he was aware of the song. He immediately connected it with the solution to his questions.

> "The place to hide, I can find
> The one with the power.
> But I, in stride, may assist the mind
> Of him in this hour."

"That's it!" Adam was convinced that the little poetic verse contained the answer he was looking for, a way to fix the problem he created. Although he did not know how or why, deep down he believed that it must be the key.

He began to think about the details of the problem. First, Adam thought about the factory where the bad cement originated. He not only stopped the construction company from using the mixture, but also made the employees at the factory aware of the error. The geotechnical engineers responsible for providing the information necessary to build a safe and solid building, did just that. There were no miscalculations. A new version of the incident replayed in the gifted young man's brain. The cement company discovered the faulty mix and junked the entire batch while the foundation was designed and developed flawlessly. After he crossed all the T's and dotted all the I's he turned the television back on, intently watching for clues of a rewritten story.

In midsentence, the news anchor switched the story she was reporting. Now it was not about the rescue operations at the scene of the fallen building, but rather about how several New York Yankee infielders were donating a portion of their salary to renovate a downtown historical high-rise building.

Adam sought to be proactive. He never wanted to cause war or political turmoil, negatively affecting thousands if not millions of lives. The idea of Kahrlzbekistan and America engaging in an armed conflict because of his thought terrified him.

One thing was certain: Adam wanted to help people, not hurt them. This whole incident taught him that when he was confronted with the uneasiness of ruining lives, when his conscience was stricken, he could remove that burden by changing the details of the situation. He was convinced that if the results of his alterations were not to his expectations he could always adjust it to be something better. Longing to provide safety and peace in the world, he hurried to remove the textbook evils from across the globe.

Naïve and well-intentioned, his first monumental adjustment was to rid the world of all the evil "isms" that plagued mankind with conflicting ideologies and extreme actions. Communism was the first to go, as it was the classic foe of the American history classroom, Adam's primary reference for political and social differences in the world. With one thought the ripple effect began.

The consequences of his thought ran much deeper than he could have ever imagined. The moment communism in its primitive state disappeared, so did every similar form of governance and socio-economic structure. More importantly, however, was that the opposing systems ceased to exist as well. In short, the removal of communism, even in a very infantile form, resulted in the end of capitalistic free democracy. The contemporary capitalistic paradigm shifted so drastically due to the lack of communistic influence, that the entire system came undone. Every contemporary governing body across the globe was revamped.

The consequences were staggering and yet to Adam, everything continued to operate very similarly. He reached his desired result. There would never again be strife between the capitalistic free world of the west and the communistic states of the east. Unfortunately, it was at the cost of so much more.

Adam tackled major issues as he thought of them. He had no idea what he was doing. He just kept thinking, changing and correcting, erasing and recreating. Alone in his apartment, he obliterated the world as he knew it, without a hint to the ramifications of his thoughts.

Taking a break from changing the world, he sat down on his new recliner to watch the news in order to see how things were developing. He had no doubt that he had improved life on Earth. Feeling fairly confident in what the TV would tell him, he did what any young bachelor would do if he was about to sit down and relax in front of the tube: he ordered a pizza and breadsticks. Like a worker at the end of a hard day, he just sat there, mesmerized by the reports and eating his dinner.

All seemed well in Adam's adjusted world. People everywhere appeared to be working together. Not once did he hear anything about war, or mention of world crisis. Everything was going smoothly in his eyes. He did not notice the stock market ticker streaming across the bottom of the screen, which would have been the first clue that things were not as perfect as he had thought.

The numbers were low. All sorts of market issues changed. American technology firms were competing with foreign markets that had more employees and cheaper resources. The domestic energy industry slowed to an almost complete standstill as imports became extremely cheap. The price of oil plummeted due to a real open market. American dependence on oil from countries hostile to her was no longer an issue. This, in turn, had an impact on the drive to come up with alternative energy sources. Innovation at nearly all levels, across all industries, came to a stop. Corporations who, yesterday, were making items used by militaries in all countries across the world were no longer making such items for their largest customers.

An entire industry was all but annihilated. Soldiers who had manned the armed branches of the various global powers were now standing in line for jobs. This did not take into account all the men and women who were trying to compete with their foreign counterparts, not able to survive on the bargain basement wages of the people in other lands. Domestically, and in many places across the planet, the workforce was flooded with able-bodied help, a situation that had never been experienced in history at this magnitude.

The thought never dawned on Adam that good could come from the bad things of the world. Of course, war was not a good thing. But the cost of operating armies was very good for economies, if in no other way than that they employed soldiers, feeding them and paying their wages. The number of families supported by a service man or woman in First World countries was almost unimaginable. After Adam's thought, most military jobs were nonexistent. Gone were governments' excessively funded military researchers, analysts, strategists, office personnel, covert agencies, and of course, soldiers. Most of the support roles filled by the military no longer existed. Countless political committees and think tanks were of no use, because war was not a primary concern. By no means would anyone suggest that war was good, but the threat of war did have its positive social and economic aspects, that obviously Adam did not understand or fully comprehend.

For days he walked around his apartment full of pride. In his heart he knew he had done a good thing, and indeed his intention was good. Adam took time to think of some things that would make his life easier as well: a new car, top-of-the-line computer, videogame consoles, kitchen appliances, furniture, clothes, and fine foods. He even took the time to send his parents several nice gifts, instantly, of course. Basking in the knowledge that he had, from his limited perspective, rid the world of war, Adam Malloy reveled in the realization that his dream to be somebody that would make a difference came true. From his perspective, millions of people were sleeping easier at night because of his thoughts.

An abrupt knock at the door caught Adam off-guard. He had not seen anyone in nearly a week. Skipping, he hurried to the door. Opening it, he found a visitor he normally would not have been too pleased to see. There, in the hallway, stood the waitress from the eatery he used to work at. Her name was Evalynn and she looked a lot different from how he was used to seeing her.

"Hey, cutie." The young woman was wearing a worn out khaki dress and a pink blouse that looked slightly too big on her. She had fixed her hair and made an attempt to put on some makeup. "Haven't seen you at work in a few days. You inherit some sort of fortune or something?" She intended the question to be sarcastic but as she caught a glimpse of Adam's apartment, she realized that maybe she was not too far off. "What in the world? How do you afford all these things?" She was amazed at the array of stuff he had.

"I don't think I'll be working at the eatery anymore. I kind of found a new job." Adam knew he was stretching the truth a bit, but he was not prepared to explain how he had acquired all his new possessions so quickly.

"Apparently, one with much better pay." Evalynn was still amazed at all the things Adam owned. She stood in place turning in circles, looking at everything, for what seemed to be hours. "Why have you been working at the eatery if you can afford all of this?" She stretched her arm out and picked up a controller for the latest videogame console.

"Like I said, I found a new job." Adam quickly pulled the gadget out of Evalynn's hand, putting it down on the coffee table. In the same motion he picked up some dirty dishes that had accumulated over the past few days and headed into the kitchen. "All this is sort of a new-hire bonus."

"Wow, some bonus. Who are you working for, a drug dealer?" Evalynn snickered under her breath.

"No, of course not. I'm working for…" Adam stuttered slightly. "I'm working for a social firm; it's amazing what I'm doing. It's actually a global company." He knew it sounded unbelievable, but in his mind it was close to the truth. After all, he was changing things all over the world and he was acting, in his way, for the social good of man, or so he told himself.

"Okay, whatever, if you don't want to tell me how you got this stuff, fine. I came over to check on you because you kind of just disappeared the last couple of days. I see you're alright, so I'll leave you alone, sweetie." Evalynn opened the door to leave.

"Wait!" Adam could not let her leave.

If people in the neighborhood knew about the stuff he had, everyone would begin to wonder how he was getting all of it, and he did not want a bunch of nosey neighbors poking into his business. Concern for privacy pushed him to do something he otherwise would not have done.

"Stay for a while." He could not believe he had just said that.

On a normal day, he would do anything to avoid talking to Evalynn. All she ever did was flirt, hoping to develop a relationship. Now, here he was asking her to come into his apartment and stay. Admittedly, she looked much better in regular clothes than in her work uniform. There was something about her that was appealing. Although she obviously was not very skilled at prettying herself up, she had a subtle natural beauty that made up for any lack of makeup and accessories.

As Adam looked at her, she closed the door and came back inside. He decided to tell her the truth. He was dying to share his ability with someone, why not her? He did not know her all that well but he was fairly confident she would not go running off and blabbing to everyone about his secret. Besides, no one would believe her anyway.

"Evalynn, I'll tell you where I've been getting all this stuff and why I'm not working at the eatery anymore."

Adam was getting nervous. The memory of what it felt like when he mustered up the nerve to tell his dad he was leaving Lakeview popped into his head. That same fluttering feeling in his stomach was back. A bead of sweat dripped from his scalp. He remembered the fight with his father, which caused all sorts of emotions and memories to flood his mind. He still was not talking to his dad and although his mom had promised to visit, she had not yet made the trip to New York.

Evalynn sat down on the couch, still scanning the room, checking out all of the new and expensive things.

"Would you like something to drink, Evalynn?" Adam asked as he walked toward the refrigerator.

"Sure, what do you have?"

"Anything you want. Name it." Adam opened the fridge door and waited for Evalynn to name her drink of choice.

"Iced tea, please."

Adam's expression showed a hint of disappointment. With a quick thought he turned a can of cola into a nice tall glass of iced tea, complete with a slice of lemon. He closed the refrigerator and went back into the living room.

"Here you go, one glass of iced tea." Adam sat down next to Evalynn on the couch. "Okay, you want to know where I've gotten all of this stuff?" Adam paused for a second, taking a big breath. "I thought it all up." He stopped, waiting for Evalynn's reaction. He could not believe he just came right out with it. He thought it would have been much harder to let the cat out of the bag. The response he received was not what he expected.

"Whatever." Evalynn firmly placed her glass down on the coffee table in front of her. Standing up, she brushed her hand through her hair. "If you don't want to tell me, fine, but don't treat me like some kind of idiot." Evalynn was making her way back to the door.

"No, really! All I had to do to get these things was change the stuff I already had to what I wanted it to be in my mind!" Adam was frantically trying to impress upon the girl that he was telling the truth. "Evalynn, why would I make up a story like that?"

"I don't know Adam, but do you really expect me to believe all you have to do is think and you get what you want? I might not be the brightest person on the block, but I'm not that gullible." Evalynn turned again in an effort to leave.

Adam was desperate. In reality it was not too important that she knew he was telling her the truth, but for some reason he felt like it was a matter of life or death that she believe him. He was tired of keeping his ability to himself. To Adam, the waitress' trust became of the utmost importance.

"Look at your shirt, Evalynn."

Adam thought about her shirt fitting correctly and how it would look better in red. On cue it changed to a tighter red blouse.

"Oh, my goodness!" Evalynn was pulling at the bottom of the shirt, stretching it out away from her body so that she could see it better. "You're telling the truth! How can you…?"

"Evalynn, I have the ability to alter things. All I have to do is think about what I want them to be and they just change. It's amazing!" Adam sat back down onto the couch.

"So, you've just been creating all these great things for yourself all week."

"No, I've changed some of my things, but I've also been fixing some major problems in the world. I've eliminated war. I've saved innocent people from dying in accidents. All kinds of important stuff." Adam moved over to his favorite spot in the apartment, the window overlooking the empty lot that was now much bigger than it had originally been, while he waited for Evalynn to say something.

"War? There's no war." Evalynn looked confused.

"Not anymore. I changed the way things work," Adam spoke with pride.

"No, there hasn't been a real war for a long time. I mean even I know that it's been decades since anything more than a small conflict has occurred." Evalynn looked at Adam in distrust. "I believe you can change things, like my shirt. I don't know how, but I seen it with my own eyes." She pulled at its seam again. "But don't try and tell me you're responsible for world peace when we've essentially been war-free for ages. That's absurd." Evalynn stood up and went over to his entertainment center.

Adam was now terribly confused. He had just changed the social and political systems of the world a couple days ago. How could Evalynn think the world had not had a major war in centuries? A week ago, there was war and conflict in every corner of the world. The entire planet seemed to be coming undone.

"Evalynn, two days ago all kinds of countries were threatening war with each other. In fact, extremists have been causing wars across the globe for years." Adam was in total shock.

"Cutie, the only thing people fight over anymore is the job at the end of the unemployment line downstairs. Stop playing silly games and show me what else you can do." Evalynn was more interested in Adam making her a new dress, than she was with the governmental climate he claimed to have created.

The young man stayed in front of the window for quite a while, pondering how Evalynn could think the world had been the way he made it for years, when it had only been that way for days. He was confused because Evalynn clearly knew he changed her shirt. It was not as if she always thought her shirt was red. No, she saw it change and therefore knew

Adam changed it. Why were the bigger things different? No one noticed when he altered the tunnel accident. The story changed just as if it never happened, all the people reading the paper did not realize the article shifted to something else even if they were in midsentence when it changed. No one was aware that things were changing right before their eyes, unless it was literally right before their eyes.

"That's it!" Adam was on the right path. Evalynn and Mr. Santone were the only two people that noticed a physical change as it occurred. They were aware because they had seen it happen. With all the other events it was as if things had been that way all along. Adam rubbed his forehead in an attempt to understand what was happening. Evalynn was still fingering through all of his new things.

She was becoming obsessed with the thought of having whatever she wanted.

"Adam, do you think you could think of a new dress for me?" The waitress was dying to see the alteration happen again.

"Sure." Adam was busy questioning the workings of his talent. Quickly he thought of a new dress for Evalynn and continued trying to figure out the mental dot-to-dot in his mind.

Evalynn's dress transformed just as her shirt had. Her eyes lit up, sparkling with the realization of the power that the man she had a crush on possessed. Exciting possibilities began to soar through her imagination as she thought about all the things she could have. While creative ideas were bouncing around in her head, she eyed Adam, who was oblivious to her staring at him. She returned to the thought of how much power he possessed over and over again as the two of them sat silently in the living room. Adam was trying to wrap his brain around the mind-boggling ways of his alterations, while Evalynn obsessed over what she could gain from her sweetheart.

As they sat there, her desire for him shifted from mere puppy love of a co-worker to lustful adoration of a god. She no longer saw a man struggling to get by as she was, working in a dead-end job living paycheck-to-paycheck, but now she stood in the presence of a powerful man who, if he wanted to, could give her the world. She was certainly attracted to Adam physically, but her passion for him was rapidly transforming into an idolatrous worship of his gift.

Chapter Fourteen

The weather was by no means kind to Michaelis as he traveled south toward the encampment. He made it midway across the open country of Lumen when the sky opened up and it started to rain. The water had been pelting his face nearly half the day. The wind was blowing so hard that the rain appeared to be falling horizontally. Disoriented, the knight questioned whether he was traveling in the right direction. Visibility was horrible. Every time he attempted to look forward, the sharp bite of the wind-driven water stung his cheeks.

Michaelis marveled at his horse's sense of direction; that the mount knew which way to travel was remarkable. Several times the weather forced him to stop so that he and his animal could take shelter. During one of these breaks he ran into the first test of his training, the first physical threat on his journey to help save the kingdom.

The terrain was desolate. The ground was thick, lined with cracks that ran every which way across the crust of the barren earth. Even with the rain, which was starting to turn into sleet, the earth was still as hard as bone. Michaelis stood against an earthen wall under a slight overhang, taking advantage of the natural roof. Given the conditions, the ability to make a fire was out of the question. In an effort to stay warm, he pressed his body as close to his horse as possible.

It was while in this position that he allowed himself to be ambushed. Not by raiders or thieves, but by a wild creature. Without warning a massive mountain lion dropped down beside him. The beast landed so naturally it seemed to fall from the sky as if just another raindrop. Michaelis had encountered mountain lions before, but never one of this size. From time to time, back in his village, mountain lions would come in from the wilderness and prey on the cattle and chickens. It was at least twice the size of an average mountain lion.

The giant feline let out a nasty snarl as it landed. Michaelis jumped, startling his horse. Huge incisors protruded from the ferocious animal's mouth. A raspy purr resonated from the lion's body. Stepping sideways it hissed, its lips rolling back, revealing menacing fangs. Tension was evident in the animal's legs as it prepared to pounce.

Michaelis reached down, gripping his sword. Moving ever so slowly, he began to pull it out of its scabbard. The movement, however slow and steady, spooked the enormous feline. The cat leapt at Michaelis. He was barely able to draw his sword before the beast slammed into him, forcing him to the ground.

Both of the cat's paws gripped his shoulders, its razor sharp claws digging into Michaelis' upper back. Excruciating pain ran all throughout his body. The animal was extremely heavy. As the two hit the ground, the echoes of the lion's roar washed out Michaelis' agonizing yell.

An ordinary horse would have run away as soon as the predator made its presence known, but not this breed. The royal steed learned to stand steady in the midst of danger, a massive horse bred to assist its rider. In this particular instance the horse stayed close but was doing nothing to aid his master.

The cat turned away from the now bloodied man and attacked his steed, a much more rewarding kill. The horse kicked wildly in an effort to defend itself. Michaelis, injured and in tremendous agony, knew that he could not let the lion make a meal of his horse. Without it, there would be no timely way of getting to the camp, and consequently, no way of convincing the men to follow him to Devastation Valley. At that particular moment, the horse meant everything to him.

With the imminent importance of his task before him, Michaelis rose to his feet, disregarding all the pain in his body. The lion was making a valiant attempt at breaching the horse's defensive maneuvers, moving in slightly closer with its every kick. The courser had so far been very fortunate, as it connected with several bucking thrusts, sending the lion flinging backwards into the dirt walls of the ditch. Shaking off the blows, the lion moved in again, looking for an opportunity to demobilize its prey.

Michaelis jumped toward the cat. Letting out a great yell that was a combination of both pain and adrenaline, he flew through the air, his sword extended. When the feline heard his battle cry it snapped its head around to catch a glimpse of what was happening. Without hesitation, the animal began to move away from the threat. The Lumen knight's blade connected with its side as it tried to escape from danger. In response, the lion lashed out at Michaelis, knocking him down to the ground, the sword buried in the cat's flesh.

Michaelis was picking himself up when the beast began limping toward him. He was not fully upright when the monstrous predator growled forward, biting at his face. The Defender's reflexes proved amazingly fast as he dropped back to the ground, away from the clamp of the lion's jaws, which were now directly above his torso.

In a desperate move to save himself, Michaelis kicked upward with his right foot. The motion connected with the lion's throat. The monstrous creature jerked back but quickly heaved forward again, pinning Michaelis between its teeth and the earth wall behind him. With both hands shakily holding the lion's mouth away from his body, the warrior grabbed hold firmly so as to swing his weight up and around, landing on the cat's back.

With blood pouring out of both opponents, the thrashed Lumenite warrior began bluntly pounding the skull of the lion with all his might, clenching tightly with one hand to the lion's fur. The animal was staggering around, manically trying everything it could to get Michaelis off its back. Finally, it drove him into the crusted soil of the ditch's thick wall. Despite all the Defender's efforts to hold onto the ferocious beast, he slid off the back of the creature, snagging hold of his sword in an attempt to stay on his nearly-defeated adversary.

Michaelis found traction on the ground as he withdrew his lumenium blade from within the mountain lion. In a sense of relief the lion circled around twice before realizing the protrusion had been removed. With a sudden awareness that it could now move more freely, the four-legged creature went in for the final blow. Michaelis could see in its eyes the pure animalistic desire to kill. Nature's fierce hunter was fed up with the little man before it. Positioning himself in a decent defensive stance that compensated for his injuries and protected his vulnerabilities, Michaelis was as ready as he would ever be for the lion's attack.

Chapter Fifteen

Evalynn was stunning. Entranced by Adam's power she begged him to think up a few improvements to accentuate her best features. He did as she asked, altering nearly everything about her. She had new hair, was taller, thinner, her teeth were straightened, and her complexion was slightly softer. An increasingly immense sense of pleasure filled her with every enhancement. Adam too, was enjoying himself as he let adolescent thoughts of airbrushed coeds take root in his mind. The sinful thoughts flourished as he surrendered to his desires, ultimately making a physically perfect woman. Both the artist and the artwork were elated, addicted to the experience.

Adam's very first alteration had been a physical change, zipping Mr. Santone's mouth shut. It was a combination of reality and cartoon-humor, a hauntingly hideous image. Evalynn's makeover, however, was much more pleasing to the eye. She was drop-dead gorgeous now and consequently, more attracted to Adam than ever before. The lust in her heart reached the boiling point. She could not contain herself. Consumed by her goddess-like features she longed to utilize her attributes. With every stroke of his mind her inhibitions lessened.

Fueled by the creative power of his ability, Adam did not shy away from her either. He was excited by the fact that she was the result of his carnal imagination. Throughout the hedonistic flesh sculpting, Adam thought of several corrections for himself as well. He became the epitome of Greek perfection, his statuesque form putting Michelangelo's work to shame.

The pair was the embodiment of a generation overcome with shallow values, encouraged by attainability, and propagated by instant gratification.

Satisfied with her new body, Evalynn realized she too possessed a very powerful talent. While she stood before Adam, she noticed the covetous look in his eyes and sensed opportunity. She smiled seductively, "Adam, take me to dinner."

Evalynn was caught up in the superficial luxuries in life, especially now that she gained access to them. Adam, on the other hand, was thirsting for another chance to use his gift. Addicted to the ability, he longed for any excuse to exercise the power within his head. Like an athlete that loses the capacity to compete, Adam felt empty without something to alter. He craved the opportunity to fix the things around him that he deemed wrong.

Adam produced a limousine for transportation to dinner. Before they arrived at the restaurant, he mentally added their names to the reservation list. For Evalynn, exiting the limo was exhilarating. Paparazzi were everywhere, hoping to cash in on a photograph of controversial stars. Camera shutters snapped and flashes popped, flooding the night sky as the former waitress gracefully climbed out of the car. Beautiful people were all around her. Adam interlocked arms with her, escorting her to the entrance of the dining room, where the maître d' greeted them. It was as if they had been born among the elite. No one would have been able to guess that they were social imposters.

Time seemed to slow down as Evalynn walked toward their table, her breathtaking beauty causing everything in the room to momentarily stop. Adam's presence was not overlooked either. Strength radiated from him as he moved with unmistakable confidence.

Along with all the other men in the room, Adam could not stop staring at Evalynn as he ate his meal. She was a magnificent sight. But while the other men were struggling to keep their hormones in check, he was more interested in the intricacies of his skill. He analyzed her like a plastic surgeon looking at his craftsmanship after a patient completely healed.

"Adam, wouldn't it be great if life were always like this?" Evalynn spoke like she was on a vacation that would inevitably end.

"It can be, Evalynn," Adam responded flatly as he glanced around the room to see if anyone famous was in the restaurant.

"No, I mean you and me together in this fancy place, living this fairytale lifestyle. I just wish there was a way it could last forever."

"Evalynn, it can and will. Remember, all I have to do is think it and it will happen." A thought occurred to Adam as Evalynn spoke. He could easily make himself wealthy and powerful, he could make his name known throughout the world, he could even make himself live forever.

"What are you saying, handsome? Are we really going to have this life forever? You and me among the rich and the spoiled?" Evalynn smiled, a slight tone of resentment fluttering throughout her words.

The idea of making himself immortal had not crossed his mind until he heard her words. Why not? All it would take would be a single thought. If things got bad or he did not want to remain how he was at that point in time, he could just think about something else and change it again.

Adam gazed upon the brilliance of the woman across the table, briefly debating within whether or not to eternally extend his life. Evalynn nibbled on her desert, a delicious apple cobbler, ever so enticingly. Drunk with images of godlike immortality, he happily thought about spending the rest of a very long life with Evalynn.

A series of chemical reactions in Adam's mind was all that was needed to cheat death. Initially, he thought about being wealthy and influential, admired and significant. Then without any further delay he thought, "As long as there is earth to stand on, Evalynn and I will live forever." He included Evalynn in the process, giving her among other things, what he considered to be the greatest gift of all, a long life with him. As he thought he stared over at her as she pulled her fork out from between her lips, the small piece of warm fruit filling her mouth with its delicious flavor, everything about her stunning face captivating his attention and causing him, almost instinctively, to add "her beauty never ever fading."

"Yep. You and I will forever be among the elite." He proudly grinned.

Thrilled, she could barely contain her emotions. Adam was her very own Prince Charming, rescuing her from the overworked, underpaid, poverty-stricken lifestyle she otherwise would have had to endure.

Upon finishing their meal, they were treated even better than when they had arrived. Walking to the doorway and out to the limousine, crowds flocked to see them, flowering the gorgeous couple with adoration, cooing as they passed by. It was all they could do to make it into the vehicle. Even as the modern chariot pulled away from the restaurant, the sea of people stayed with them. The attention was intoxicating.

Their destination was no longer Mr. Santone's rundown apartment building. Adam's new home was a building bearing his name. The Malloy building was the epicenter of New York City, a new tower in a restructured city that revolved around Adam Malloy.

"This isn't right," Evalynn noted as she looked out into the night. "Where are we headed?"

"You didn't think I was really going to keep living in that crummy old apartment, did you?" Adam was smiling from ear to ear.

During the ride home he made all the preparations for their new lives, giving them everything he could think of. He added every material possession possible to his list of belongings, creating a life of royal proportions for the two of them.

Like a child blinded by excitement, the young man was still ignorant of the ramifications of his talent, unaware of the reality that all choices have consequences. His power soaked mind and lust-drenched heart refused to see the masses of homeless people on the street as his glimmering car paraded by them. Narcotics were nothing compared to the addiction of Adam's gift. He was out of control, hopped up on his ability. His accomplishments were destroying the world, while he itched for another fix. Evalynn, too, forgot how life was merely hours ago. The couple was given the world. There was nothing they could not have. There was nothing they could not do.

For Evalynn, the ride to the new building took forever. All she could think about was Adam and what an amazing life he was sharing with her. She peered over at him, consumed by his bodily perfection while the knowledge of his talent burned inside her. Lustfully, she yearned to thank him for every one of his thoughts. Without hesitation she leaned in and kissed him. Stunned, a piece of the small town boy peeked through his new image as he pulled away, separating their lips.

"What was that for?"

"To say thank you, sweetie." Evalynn licked her lips and then leaned in again for another kiss. The level of intimacy continued to rise until they arrived in front of the Malloy building.

"We are here, sir," the limo driver rang out over the intercom.

The door opened, revealing the lights glistening off the windows of the building. They rushed out of the car. A doorman welcomed them home as they dashed into the lobby. Neither of them had ever experienced such extravagance. In the middle of an elaborate marble floor Adam noticed he was standing on top of a massive 'M.' He gazed upward at an inconceivably ornate chandelier hanging directly over his head.

"Wow!"

"Wow is right! You thought of this?" Astonishment filled Evalynn's voice.

"I guess so. Things are a lot simpler in my head when I think about them." Adam finally snapped out of his shock, making his way to the elevator.

Everything in the building was made of the finest materials: rare woods and marble, fine gold and precious stones covered every surface, sparkling magnificently. The ascent to the suite was long; the Malloy building was the tallest in New York City. Despite this architectural fact, the reason time dragged on was that Evalynn and Adam could not restrain their desires. The wild couple gave into their flesh with flagrant recklessness. They desperately wanted to be in the seclusion of their new home so as to continue their shameful deed.

With an abrupt ding they reached the top floor, the elevator letting them out directly into the living space of the suite. The furnishings in their home were even more impressive than the rest of the building. Evalynn touched everything, entranced by the life of luxury that was now hers. Adam, too, forgot the intended throes of passion and headed for the balcony. He had dreamt of this ever since he decided to come to New York. When he finally became successful, he would stand at the top of the highest building in the city and stare out into the jungle he fought through, letting out the loudest yell he could muster. It was a grand and romantic thought. Unfortunately, he did not have to struggle much to achieve it. There was no effort involved in his climb to the top. Yes, he lived in poverty for some time, but his triumph landed in his lap without any work on his part.

The view was remarkable, the lights of the city shone brighter than the stars. It was not like Mr. Santone's apartment, where he could hear the sounds from the street below even when he was inside. No, up here standing out on the balcony, he could only faintly hear the sounds of traffic below. New York City looked stunning from this vantage point, a paradise made of jewels, each building reflecting off one another, lights dancing off the windows of the structure next to it.

Adam was speechless: the site was breathtaking and the feeling that grew in his body was indescribable. He had made it, and in good company too. Every possible wish he made came true. For the time being he and his new friend were going to enjoy it together. Nothing could have erased the smug smile on Adam's face as he stood reveling in his accomplishment.

Chapter Sixteen

The time it took for the mountain lion to decide how to move in on Michaelis seemed to take hours. With every breath the Defender took, hope of another filled his mind. It was an iconic scene: a wounded knight planted steadfast, waiting for his foe to make a move toward him. His heart pounded like a tribal drum while his chest rose dramatically with every breath. The animal finally raced toward Michaelis. Dropping to one knee, the warrior extended his sword upward. Piercing the lion under its head, the sword sliced from the creature's throat all the way to its heart. The weight of the mountain lion knocked Michaelis over as its limp body gave in to the forces of gravity. The battle of champions was finished.

At a glance, it was uncertain which one of them defeated the other. The Lumenite gladiator lay on the ground, his body weak and in pain. Michaelis did not remove the sword from the animal's carcass. He simply lay there, sword in hand, until he passed out. Adrenaline escaped his body until he could not gather enough strength to do anything more. After a few moments, his horse came and lay next to him, almost as if he were standing guard. It was the courser's turn to protect his master.

The rain continued to pour the entire time Michaelis slept. His body was in desperate need of healing, as was his spirit. His first trip out into the world as a member of the King's Defenders and a hungry animal nearly devoured him. These were the days that would test the fiber of his resolve. He learned a lesson the hard way in the ditch, a lesson engraved in the soldier's mind forever, for by letting his guard down, he nearly lost his life.

He slept for days. Suffering from chills and severe fever, the inexperienced knight was in shock. It was quite fortunate that he was not among civilization, for if he had been, the people tending him could have easily arrived at the conclusion that he was dead. The lion had mangled the Defender. His breath shallow, his pulse faint, and he was lying in the cold of night with sleet slapping the ground around him.

When he finally awoke, his initial movement triggered horrendous pain in his shoulders. Gritting his teeth, he rolled up onto his knees. The dead beast still lay beside him. To his other side his horse sat, staring him square in the face, as if awaiting an expression of gratitude.

"Thanks, boy."

The sleet had stopped and the sun shone, highlighting the blood-covered ground. An urgency to get moving came over the Defender. Enough time had been lost due to the lifeless creature next to him. With an agonizing pull, Michaelis unseated his weapon from within the lion's body. His muscles were sore and his injuries restricted the movement of his arms. After cleaning the sword, Michaelis placed it into its sheath and moved over to his horse that had lowered himself down to aid the rider's mount. Michaelis slid his leg over the animal, straddling the saddle.

"Ready, boy?" A slight slap on the horse's side sent horrible twinges into Michaelis' shoulders. "We need to get to the camp." Michaelis forced himself to pat the side of the orange-haired courser again.

The horse stood up, raising Michaelis off the ground. The two of them made it out of the ravine, and were back on their way. It was late in the day and although it was not wise, Michaelis decided to continue traveling throughout the night. He had to make up time. If he did not reach the Lumenite troops and convince them to follow him to meet Baramatheus, the plan would fall apart. Both Defenders needed to be successful if they were going to have a chance at victory. The Malum were a fierce enemy and heavily outnumbered the Lumen forces. Heart was going to be the key factor in winning this conflict.

The terrain was rough, especially for a wounded rider. With the horse's every step, pain spread through Michaelis' body. In a bizarre way, he welcomed it. He used it to stay focused; the agony acted as both motivation and reminder. The manner in which the wild cat had attacked brought the Malum to Michaelis' mind. Both used the elements to their advantage. It was after this thought that the Defender made himself a promise: he would never again let his guard down. Next time he would be the one using the environment to gain the upper hand.

The daylight disappeared quickly and soon the journey continued in the thickness of night. Michaelis used the stars to navigate through the desert land, a technique the Martinians taught him. Not yet even at the border of the kingdom and already he was battered and broken. He spent the night chiding himself for his carelessness, the thought of the hungry feline ruining everything infuriated the young Lumenite.

Just before dawn, Michaelis spotted a flickering light bouncing about the horizon to the north. Was it a torch? He continued on his path, being ever so careful not to lose track of it. The glow of the sun coming up in front of him was at the same time comforting and slightly disturbing. As the sky brightened, the light was beginning to disappear, fading into the backdrop of the blue-gray sky. Michaelis carried on toward the encampment, his senses attuned to everything around him, telling him to be vigilant.

He covered a lot of ground before needing to stop for water and tend his wounds. Cleaning his injuries was quite the task. Both arms were nearly immobile from the shoulder down. As he strained in excruciating discomfort to wash one side, he had the pleasure of looking forward to disturbing it again when he switched arms to clean the other.

Michaelis draped his cloak over a large stone next to his sword. The spot where he chose to stop was a small water hole in a patch of waist-high bushes. It was not ideal for protection but it was the best he could find given his time frame. He barely began to pour the water over the bloodied claw marks when he heard the scuffing of pebbles a few feet away. Michaelis' pain vanished in an adrenaline-filled flurry, allowing him to take up his sword with great speed. The bright lumenium of his blade shone in the morning sun.

He ducked down as low as possible, creeping toward the noise. A figure dashed around among the bushes quickly. The glare of the sun made getting a good look at what it was impossible. As Michaelis played a game of cat and mouse with the silhouette, he contemplated how his mentor would handle the situation. Whatever it was, it was fairly large. Not as big as a grown man but it was definitely not a mere rodent. At this point Michaelis would have welcomed the invasion of a badger or a groundhog, but he could tell from the way it moved through the brush that it was more than that.

As Michaelis chased the thing around, trying earnestly to catch a good glimpse of it, he began to make out certain attributes. Most noticeably, that it was wearing clothes. Was it a man? It could not be Malum, for Michaelis was still in the Lumen Kingdom. Perhaps it was a raider, or possibly a conjurer, but either of them would have been more aggressive, at least until they knew whom they were dealing with. The dance was getting tiresome; Michaelis looked for an opportunity to corner the being and then sprang out from the brush, landing on top of it. They tumbled to the ground, flailing and fighting against one another.

"Don't hurt me!"

Michaelis jumped up, startled. Laying on the ground before him was a frightened boy of no more than twelve.

Michaelis stood above the child, his sword aimed down at the boy's chest, his free hand holding the child's neck to the ground. The child's eyes were wide open, bulging with fear as he looked up the gleaming blood groove of the Defender's weapon.

"Please, no!" The boy was cowering into the earth as much as he could, his teeth gnashed together in expectation of the cold sting of the sword penetrating his heart.

"A boy?" Michaelis stood up, releasing the out-of-place youth. "What are you doing out here?"

"I was following you, sir." The young Lumenite sat up, dusting his clothes off as he put more space between himself and the weapon that nearly ran him through.

"Why? Was that your torch I saw?" The Defender spoke sharply at the child.

In a different time and place the scene would have looked amusing, like an older brother scolding his younger sibling. Unfortunately an unnatural maturity was one of many consequences of the war, a side effect that both Michaelis and the boy suffered from.

The stealthy child wore tattered clothing, covered with twigs and leaves. It looked as if he had been playing in the woods all day. A shabby piece of rope held up his pants. Judging by the way his shirt hung off his small frame, it must have belonged to his father.

"Well, it is just that I saw you and was curious as to where you were going. I was hoping you were a scout."

"You know, if you are going to sneak up on someone at night, you should not use a torch." Michaelis was squatting above the pool of water, splashing it onto his back.

"You saw it, huh?"

"Yes I did; you are fortunate that I did not mistake you for a raider. What is your name?"

"Pura." He answered quickly and with a surge of confidence.

"Well, Pura, I suggest you turn back toward your village and head home."

"Can I not come with you?" The boy stepped closer, no longer afraid.

"No, I am in somewhat of a hurry. Now get back home. Your mother is probably looking for you." Michaelis finished redressing his wounds and had managed, painfully, to put his shirt back on. With a grunt he threw his leg up and over his steed.

"No, sir, she is not." The boy's eyes looked down and his shoulders dropped.

Michaelis knew that there was only one reason why the child's mother would not be looking for him. Sympathy filled his heart.

"What about your father?"

"Sir, my father fought the Malum." The expression on the boy's face was a mixture of pride and regret. "He was a groundsman and did his best." Pura did not need to say anything more. It was apparent that his parents were no longer with him. The child was an orphan, left to fend for himself, to get by however he could.

All of a sudden Michaelis faced a difficult decision. He hated to leave the boy in the wilderness, not knowing what would become of him. On the other hand, if he brought Pura with him he would be putting his life at risk.

"Pura, you will earn your keep as my arming squire. You are a bit young, which is actually quite fitting, considering that I too do not hold the traditional requirements for my title. And you will have to do as I say."

"Yes, sir!" Pura's face lit up. He was thrilled to simply be traveling with someone, to have companionship.

The wilderness was a hostile place for a lone traveler, especially a boy as young as Pura. In fact, Michaelis was amazed the child had not been caught by conjurers, which were known for taking grave risks to push their beliefs upon the young and the wavering, people that did not quite have a firm hold on their lives. Pura, all alone in the open country, would have been a welcome target.

The child rode on the back of Michaelis' horse in silence for the rest of the day. The knight was not about to stimulate conversation for he still struggled with his decision; he was certainly not in need of a page. On the other hand, Pura was much safer with him than without. But for how long would that safety last? Once they made it to the camp, the boy would be in harm's way again. Making decisions that affected the wellbeing of others was difficult. Michaelis wondered how it was that Baramatheus made it look so easy.

Chapter Seventeen

Night came quickly. The Defender and the boy rode all night and all day to get close to being back on schedule before they stopped to rest. Although he was satisfied with the amount of ground he covered, it did not change the fact that the run-in with the giant feline cost Michaelis a great amount of time.

"Pura, you told me you were hoping I was a scout." The boy tossed a twig into the fire. "Why are you looking for the Lumen troops?" Michaelis looked up from the fire pit, eyeing Pura's mannerisms as he responded.

"Sir, my mother died when I was born and since my father's death I have no one. I left home in search of Lumen soldiers, hoping to help fend off the Malum threat. I had set out not knowing which direction to travel and had been wandering about for weeks."

"Well, you managed to survive."

"I picked up some skills that helped."

"I see that." Michaelis looked at Pura's feet.

"Yes sir, I found that I was able to move a lot quieter by tearing the edges off my cloak and tying the pieces around my feet. Whenever I spotted someone, I would track them, like I did you, in hopes that they were groundsmen en route to the conflict. I want to fight the Malum, sir."

"I can understand that." Michaelis could imagine how the boy felt. He too had lost his father to the Malum forces, the difference being that Michaelis still had his mother after his father's death. Pura had no one.

"Pura, do you know what I am?"

"I know you are a soldier." Having never before seen a member of the King's Defenders, Pura was clueless as to the kind of soldier Michaelis was.

"I am one of a special group of soldiers. Knights. The King's Defenders. Have you heard of us?" Michaelis felt kind of uncomfortable talking about his new vocation. In his heart he still felt very much like the child in front of him. He did not feel like royalty, and he especially did not feel like a knight.

"Are you a groundsman?" It made sense that he would only know the lowest class of soldier. After all, that was the position of every peasant who went to war.

"No, the Defenders are different from groundsmen. We usually travel alone, but we aid the groundsmen and other soldiers when they need assistance. We also perform many other unusual tasks."

"Like what?"

"Our primary purpose is to defend the king in whatever fashion we can. And that might require any array of duties."

"So, you are servants to the king."

"Exactly, we serve the king, even unto death. In any case, Pura, you should know that we are headed to an encampment of Lumen fighters."

During their conversation, Pura had been casually gathering firewood. Upon hearing Michaelis' words he immediately dropped the wood in front of the pit. His face beamed with the news.

"So I will get a chance to serve the king too? I will get to fight the Malum?"

"Do not worry. You will get your chance to serve the king," the Lumen knight said as he placed a log onto the fire.

"And fight the Malum?"

Michaelis did not want to tell Pura what the boy obviously wanted to hear, partly because the cold reality was that if the child fought, he quite assuredly would meet his death.

"Trust me, you will face the enemy. I cannot promise you that it will be in the way you desire, but you will serve your king."

Michaelis knew that the boy would more than likely see battle. But he did not want him to cling to the hope of it, for he recognized the child's motivation. Michaelis did not doubt that Pura wanted to serve his country wholeheartedly. He did not want Pura to become obsessed with fighting the

Malum in revenge for his father's death, a passion which could easily consume a son. The objective was to put a final end to the war between the Malum and Lumen, bringing peace to the land. Unfortunately, the task took the form of fighting Bebbel-uk's Malum warriors.

Pura had no response for Michaelis. His burst of enthusiasm softened to an adventurous smile. The orphan returned to the business of collecting fuel for the fire. Michaelis was confident that eventually Pura would understand why he did not want him wielding the sword against a foe who could easily devour complete brigades of grown men, let alone a small boy. The Defender was only trying to protect his new friend.

The night was calm as the two travelers slept. Michaelis kept his senses sharp as he closed his eyes. A falling leaf could have awakened the nervous dreamer. He tossed and turned as the images of dying Lumenites filled his head. He was not naïve. Many of his fellow countrymen would die in the coming days. Droves of them were already dead. Even he might not make it to the other side of this arduous task. During the day he did not bog himself down with thoughts of this type, but at night when his imagination took over, his mind played out all the suppressed images he tried to bury with such difficulty. Michaelis slept in short spurts, a half an hour at a time at best, tightly gripping the sword on his chest.

* * *

On the other side of the kingdom, Baramatheus was just reaching the nation's wall. He had ridden hard the entire distance. Currently, he was on track to be at the northern camp by sunrise. He pushed his horse to the point of exhaustion, stopping only long enough for the animal to get a drink and catch a quick breath. Several times he had spotted raiders in the distance, but thought little of it, for he was moving so fast that not even a hawk, its wings full of wind, could keep up with him. The battle was nearing and the men would need all the time they could get to prepare. Baramatheus was somewhat skeptical of the reaction of the groundsmen. He knew that what he was going to propose to them would seem more like a death sentence than the kingdom's saving hope. He prayed that compassion for their fellow man would encourage and move them to follow him to Devastation Valley.

Lumen's history was brimming with tales of men performing unbelievable acts in the face of great resistance; he hoped the men would see the current task as a chance to defy the odds in a similar fashion. Ever since the "Battle of the River Ax," Lumenite soldiers braved the plains of war with thoughts of victory seeding the soil of their heart, but that will to win was waning. Baramatheus knew far too well that the core of a man, his very worth, was tested by facing the fiercest of opposition. The hideous acts of the Malum were eating away at what it meant for a man to firmly stand in his beliefs, to defend his kingdom, culture, and brother with courage and faith. Their barbarous warfare caused an entire generation to forfeit their responsibility. The threat holding the kingdom hostage blurred the understanding of what it meant to be a Lumenite man. He trusted that this grand and final maneuver would drive the truth down into the weakened spirit of his Lumenite brethren and embolden them.

Two Lumen guards peered out into the moonlit night, steadily watching for any signs of danger. From the watchtower they spotted Baramatheus approaching. A cloud of dust billowed out from under the hooves of the lone rider's horse. As he grew closer they became more attentive to his actions. Since he was on the Lumen side of the wall, he posed very little threat. Raiders were too full of cowardice to come near the tower, conjurers rarely tempted their fate, and the scavengers preferred to stay away from the edges of the kingdom to avoid run-ins with the military.

"Look, the horse's mane, it is orange!" The guard recognized the horse as belonging to a Defender. Moonlight illuminated the hair in such a way that the strands looked like flames.

Baramatheus was coming upon the wall in full gallop. Since there was no gate, only the tower, the guards questioned the haste of the rider. Assuming that he was a messenger, they followed protocol and summoned a soldier to prepare to meet him. And because it was obvious by the mount that the rider was of royal blood, the post's commander had the unpleasant surprise of being the one to be awakened.

To get to the top of the guard tower, the soldiers had to climb a steeply-angled open staircase protruding out of the wall. There was no railing or awning. As Baramatheus approached the wall he altered his course slightly, heading for the side of the tower while maintaining his pace.

"Sir, he is not slowing down!" the guard hollered down from the tower to his commanding officer on the ground who was waiting anxiously for the messenger to arrive.

Baramatheus was moments away. With a tug of the reins he slowed his horse down considerably, although still moving much too fast for someone preparing to stop. The guards watched with curiosity as he guided his courser in the direction of the stairway. Everyone that was awake watched as the knight climbed straight up the staircase leading to the tower. The men on duty stepped back, stumbling to get their crossbows locked into firing position. With an amazing show of skill, Baramatheus directed his horse in an almost full gallop up the stairs, pulling back on the reins at just the right moment at the top of the wall, causing the horse to leap gracefully, succumbing to the forces of gravity. Along with Baramatheus, the animal braced for the firm landing. The knight held on tight as his mount landed at the foot of the wall just outside the boundary of the kingdom.

The commander had raced up the stairs after Baramatheus and was now standing at the top, next to the two watchmen, peering down at the stranger.

"Sorry for the disturbance friends, but time is of the essence." Baramatheus trotted the horse in a circle allowing it time to regain composure. Smiling up at the soldiers he gave the steed a kick, and raced away.

The Lumen guards stood in total disbelief, watching as the dust cloud billowed out from behind the flame-like tail of the royal knight's steed.

Chapter Eighteen

Living at the top of the world was more than a figure of speech for Adam and Evalynn. As days turned into weeks and weeks into months the couple experienced everything they could possibly think of until one night as Adam lay in his bed staring up at the ceiling, restless and eager for morning to come, snow began to fall. It was a peculiar occurrence this early in the year. The golden leaves of autumn had barely started dropping from the trees and the air was gently beginning to cool down. On an average day a person could get away with a light jacket and jeans, but not today. The snowfall continued well into the morning. Adam stood in front of the balcony door, staring out into the curtain of white. It was so thick he could hardly make out the basic form of the nearest building.

"You know, spring is nice. I like the spring. It's perfect, never too hot or too cold." Adam did not even know if Evalynn was listening, but he continued to talk as if she were. "The winter slows things down, traffic gets congested, businesses shut down, ice storms cause power outages, and negative-degree temperatures make vehicles stall out. In fact, I've read of people dying from exposure because they were stranded in a snowstorm. Not to mention air travel is harder and some folks can't afford to heat their homes." He paused, thinking. "I would go so far as to say that winter is nature's roadblock to progress. It's like Old Man Winter is sitting in a chair looking in on this snow globe we call Earth and sees that things are getting along pretty well. So what does he do? He shakes up the globe and everything bogs down again." Adam looked outside shaking his head in disgust, sipping a cup of coffee as he waxed philosophic about the intricacies of nature. "He does this to us every year. Ev, how do you like spring?"

Evalynn was soaking in the massive hot tub two rooms down the hall.

"Spring? Springtime is nice." She had no idea why he was babbling on about the season.

She laid her head back, her hair draping over the edge of the bathtub. The glow of many candles illuminated the room with a warm and soothing ambiance. The last thing on her mind was the inconvenience of weather patterns. Life was perfect as far as she was concerned. Once Adam interrupted her solace she could not help but think about all the good things of spring.

"Yeah," a curious glimmer filled Adam's eye, "spring time is nice."

Adam began humming the tune from his dream as he thought about how much nicer everything would be if it was always spring in New York. He figured other places in the country would appreciate it if they were never plagued by winter as well. Resolute, he began to segregate the seasons.

He thought of the four seasons confined to specific quadrants of the world. He was charting unknown waters, unsure of the ramifications. Unaware of how he received his skill, he never quite grasped the particulars of how the thought provoked alterations worked. Nevertheless, with the control of a sun-deprived teenager playing a video game, the young man placed winter in the northeast quadrant, spring in the northwest, summer in the southwest and autumn in the southeast.

It was absurd, but as he thought about it, the snow stopped, resulting in a smile. Amending the weather made things unusual to say the least. From that moment on, if a vacationer wanted to enjoy a nice warm beach on a hot summer day they would need to travel to South America; or to go skiing, one would have to go to Asia. Just like that, Adam fixed what he surmised to be another one of life's hindrances.

The world changed drastically upon this thought. In order for this adjustment to occur, to sustain life, the laws of nature were amended according to the new parameters. Earth's tilt recalculated from the relatively stable 23.5 degrees prior to Adam's thought, to a much greater axis angle that continually shifted in order to keep the northeast quadrant of the planet from directly facing the sun, consequently directing the southwest quadrant precisely in line with the bright star.

Constant bombardment of the sun's ultra violet rays rapidly thinned the ozone layer over the southwest quadrant helping to keep the air warm all the time. This created low air pressure in the southwest, air from the northeast rushed toward the southwest by way of currents traveling across the southeast and northwest quadrants. These new wind patterns assisted in the axis tilt change by providing constant wind pressure that pushed on the oceans. The time it took for the planet's range of motion to go from west to east dramatically sped up in order for the seasons to stay confined in their designated areas.

For the Earth's axis to change angles the liquid core at the center of the planet, which spun independently from the rest of the world, accelerated, revolving much quicker than before. This increase in revolutions created massive tidal waves of magma splashing about within the globe. Bigger currents in the center of Earth altered the magnetic field and relocated the planet's poles.

Understanding of the known world and even the universe changed instantly. As before, the people were none the wiser because everyone was aware of this new thought as if it were the way things had always been. Landmasses changed, seas and oceans were no longer the size and shape they had been before. The distance from the Earth to the moon totally reconfigured so that the ruler of the night could continue its role in maintaining life on Earth. Animal habitats repositioned with respect to climates, weather patterns, and temperature ranges. The entire ecosystem reconfigured in an unrecognizable fashion. Environmentally, the world looked tremendously different than it had. Other celestial bodies were completely reorganized so as to protect the Earth from being annihilated by the marvels of space. Each planet and moon moved about like thumbtacks on a map.

Adam only wanted nicer weather, but in getting that, he erased the canvas of the world and started a whole new painting. Things were vastly different and yet he could not tell anything had changed. New York City was still exactly as it had been, at least from Adam's perspective. The only change he detected came in the form of fresh spring air.

Pleased with his actions, Adam turned from the balcony and went to the couch. He flipped on the TV to witness people enjoying the new climate. There was not a word. Of course not; as far as the people were concerned the weather had always been just as it was.

The news network was reporting on the record-breaking unemployment rate. Video footage showed horrible images of people struggling to get by. A correspondent was in the middle of an interview with a man that had been out of work for quite some time. He was describing the conditions in which his family lived and how they daily wondered if there would be food on the table.

His family sat behind him. They looked happy, but it was obvious they were trying to downplay their impoverished conditions. The man's wife came across very dignified and proud, despite her lifestyle. The kids appeared bored, the camera crew nothing more than a bother to them. On national television they tugged at one another's clothes, bickering back and forth like siblings.

The picture the man painted was awful. Adam was nearly in tears as he watched the interview, knowing he had caused the pain and grief the man contended with every single day. He changed the channel to another news network. More of the same. He flipped again and again, finding an unsettling theme on all the channels: poverty. It was everywhere!

It was evident to Adam that by thinking away one problem, he had created another. All those people starving, and without hope. Adam had become the primary cause of pain in the world. A hard-hitting question erupted in his mind. How many people would die because of his thoughts? Pacing back and forth, Adam tried to think of a solution. Several minutes later the answer dropped into the room in Newtonian fashion.

"More time!"

Adam conceived a way to employ the countless masses that were out of work. Longer days would create more time to work; to compensate, companies would have to hire more employees. Contemplating the idea, Adam began thinking the words to put his brainstorm into action.

He added enough time in the day for an entire shift. Recalling how hard his dad worked when his company was busy, the blue-collared boy foresaw that the additional hours in the day might cause the already employed to have to work longer hours. To nip that potential problem in the bud he instituted a law limiting the number of hours in a shift to eight. The thought was an admirable one; however, blinded by his insatiable need to fix what he broke, Adam unknowingly took the first step back toward the type of government he had already dismantled. Thirty-two hours was the length of the new day, adding in time for a fourth eight-hour shift.

The same radical alterations that occurred in the cosmos to allow for the seasonal division occurred in order for the day to be lengthened. It was odd that Adam conceived this idea given that his limited work experience left him completely ignorant of managerial issues. The only reference he had for this thought was the memory of his childhood. Whether he realized it or not, the recollection of his father never having enough time to spend with the family weighed on his action. Mr. Malloy would come home from work tired and depleted of all energy. Household duties were awaiting his attention, things like fixing the garbage disposal, or clearing out the rain gutters. Adam would stand at his father's side begging to play. The only response he would get was, "If only there was more time in the day." Well, now there was.

Adam watched as the unemployment rates dropped before his very eyes on the TV.

"What are you doing, cutie?" With a white towel wrapped around her body, Evalynn leaned up against the arm of the couch.

"A lot. I fixed the unemployment problem. Oh, and I stopped the snow." Adam pointed over his shoulder to the balcony door.

"What are you talking about? It never snows around here." Evalynn moved over to look outside.

Adam sighed loudly as he coped with the fact that Evalynn was not aware of his most impressive accomplishments. Breathing in again, he acknowledged that he was all alone. Only he could remember how things had been before his improvements. It was a depressing side effect to his amazing gift.

All of a sudden a light bulb lit up in Adam's head. Adam smiled: all he had to do was think it and everyone would know about his power and what he had done. Adam mulled over the idea for the rest of the afternoon as he watched to see if his longer day would have any kind of adverse effect on people.

More people were working, which was a good thing. Several reports detailed how the average worker was making less money than ever before due to the strict mandate on the number of hours a person could work. Many folks needed overtime pay to make ends meet and now they were not getting it. Adam put an end to that quandary real quick. He was determined to make things better.

Innovation and invention was the answer to the lower wages. Adam's theory was that if people were creative and used their imagination to bring new products to the market, then that would act as a catalyst, thus igniting a chain reaction. This would create demand for more people to be employed in order to operate the equipment producing the material needed for the guy working the assembly line putting the parts together that the packaging guy could ship to the trucks which would take the product to the retail stores who in turn would sell it to the consumers, generating money for the company to be able to come up with more products, resulting in businesses being forced to hire more employees.

In theory, it sounded as good an idea as any. Once the concept was put into motion the only problem was that there was no way of dictating what the scientists and researchers would develop. Adam never considered that man might invent himself right out of a job by coming up with ways to make work easier and quicker, eliminating the need for employees at all.

Evalynn was clueless as to the extent of Adam's power, a fact that bothered him tremendously. He felt like Aesop's lion, a thorn of pride sticking in his paw, stinging with every miraculous thought. Fortunately for Adam, he did not need the assistance of any Androcles. Focused on getting his due credit, he thought about Evalynn being aware of every alteration he made to the world. Thinking about Evalynn's awareness, he made sure to include every last adjustment. He badly craved the glory for all his actions. Oddly enough, the once-reserved boy, who wanted nothing to do with the girl that so noticeably ached for a relationship with him was now opening up to her, confiding in her because the frustration of containing the truth was driving him mad.

Evalynn burst into tears, furious with Adam.

"How could you? You're a monster!" She was flailing her fists against Adam's chest. "You ruined my life! Live forever? I'm your slave! You've bound me by your decision to live on this mutation of a world you've created!" Her knowledge of how Adam connected their lives to the existence of Earth, coupled with how he had distorted so many of the things that made life bearable infuriated her.

"You asked for it." Adam was confused. "It was your idea! Don't you remember? You were the one fantasizing about how wonderful it would be to live a life full of wealth and possessions forever!" Adam's tone was frightening her. He pushed her away. "Me? What about you? You loved the idea before I enlightened you to the when and how of it happening. Just two hours ago you were soaking in the hot tub talking about how splendid spring was! Don't get mad at me! I did exactly what you would have done if you had my gift."

"No Adam, I would not have done the things you've done. Don't you realize what a mess you've made? You've destroyed everything I've ever known, everything you've ever known. You're only a man. What gives you the right to play God with the world? Maybe you didn't like the way things were. Guess what? Others did. Compared to what you've thought up, the old world was paradise. What gives you the right to do what you've done?" Evalynn hid her face in her hands, tears dripping from her eyes as she sobbed.

Enraged, she accepted responsibility for planting the seed in Adam's head that blossomed into such a monstrous nightmare. Even though at the time she did not know what the man could do, she was not innocent. Adam tried to tell her about stopping wars. He made the attempt, but she was too caught up in the despair of her own thoughts. The desire to be attractive and rich had consumed her. She had fed at the trough of lust and envy, nourishing her hedonistic inclinations on the realization that men and women fixed their passions on her flesh, and if not on her admirable features, then on the ornaments that adorned them. She was as guilty as Adam. Whether she liked it or not she gave Adam the idea and in so doing, initiated his quest to rewrite the way the world operated.

"Evalynn, you and I will live forever! Don't you understand? We have dipped our fingers into the fountain of youth. With my gift nothing can stop us from experiencing whatever splendor comes to mind. Olympia is our home, the Earth is our playground! We have an opportunity most would kill for." Adam spoke as if he were trying to sell her a used car. "Evalynn, I was given the wondrous gift to make everything the way I see fit. We are no longer restrained to the confines of the old order of the world. Whatever your heart desires, I can give it to you. It's yours, just tell me and I will think it."

Adam hated to see her hurting.

Evalynn picked her head up out of her hands. Streaks of makeup ran down her cheeks, the whites of her eyes already bloodshot.

"You know, I understand what that old saying 'ignorance is bliss' is all about. I want things to be the way they were. I want to go back to not knowing. I want to be able to live the way I was intended to. Can you think that for me?"

"Why would you want that? You can have whatever you want, and you want to go back?" Adam was walking over to the window just as he used to do in his old apartment. Only now it was not red bricks blocking his view. It was a mountain range of concrete, steel and glass. There were no children playing baseball, no empty lot, just the expanse of manmade structures.

Interestingly enough, Adam did not realize the similarity between where he was today and where he had been when he started testing his skill. Once a building blocked his view, so he removed it, creating a safe place for neighborhood children to play. Now all he could see were buildings. Where was the joy of watching boys and girls frolic and laugh? Somewhere along the line he began abusing his special talent, bending it to his will, becoming completely self-absorbed. What brought him the greatest satisfaction drove all of his motivations. Adam was coming to a bitter and brutal realization. Emotions rained down over him. Anxiety, anger, shame, guilt: the list of feelings dripping off his soul grew dark.

Leaving the apartment, he stepped into the elevator and descended to the lobby. At ground level he walked outside where he then crawled into the limo that was always waiting for him. He gave the driver the address of his old apartment, his mannerisms cold and weak. The trip to where he lived only a short time ago seemed to take forever.

Adam was grappling with what he had done, how every time he thought a selfish thought to make his life better, he disrupted someone else's. The various consequences of his thoughts hit him like a freight train, running over his heart like a penny on the track.

Oblivious to the happenings around him, the good within Adam seemed to turn off: his eyes glazed over and his face froze solid in an effort to not look out his window at the atrocity he had made of the world. Terrified by the knowledge of his deeds, he tried hard not to even think, afraid of changing even one more thing. The area he was heading to was still a bad part of town and the expression on the driver's face showed the concern as they entered the questionable neighborhood.

"Sir, are you sure you want to come down here?" The driver squirmed a little in his seat as the view darkened.

"Yeah, just take me where I told you." Adam said.

As soon as the car pulled over, Adam opened the door, not waiting for the driver to get out and come around. Moving straight forward and into the building which looked exactly as it had before Adam started his meddling. The driver stood curbside, terribly confused as to what his boss was up to. Heading up the stairs and down the hall toward the apartment, Adam passed the old lady that loved talking to him. Looking up at the sound of footsteps, she was mumbling to herself as Adam came closer to his old home. As he walked past, he could hear her voice, but could not make out a word she was saying.

Just as he grabbed for the doorknob, he heard with perfect clarity the woman say, "How's them breeches fittin' these days?" She was as crackly as ever.

Shocked, Adam stopped, staring in her direction, bewildered. Jerking himself out of the stunned state he quickly moved inside the apartment. Nothing had changed, it was just as he and Evalynn left it. Even the glass from her iced tea was still on the coffee table. Immediately, he went to his window to look at the lot below. It was precisely as he made it. No children were playing on it at the moment, but the field was still as it had been.

Looking at the door, he pondered what the old woman said. He recalled Mr. Santone and how he discovered his gift. Adam put his hands in his pockets and walked over to the door, leaning his back against it. He slid down until he was sitting, just as he had done before, now in the exact position he was in when he realized his power. Evalynn's words ran through his head while he sat there on the floor.

What gave him the right? He did not know the answer. He began questioning himself.

"Why was I given this gift?" Adam wondered.

It was a valid question, one he had never really taken the time to ask. After all, he was not highly educated; a high school diploma from a small town in the middle of nowhere hardly qualified him for the tasks he performed. He possessed no experience in any of the fields he so easily ruined. Adam scratched his head as he laughed to himself in a tearful depressing manner. Assuredly, he had messed things up. For some reason he had been given a chance to live a great life with an amazing, supernatural gift. He had taken that gift and wrapped it in evil. Ignorance prevented him from understanding the complete implications of his dealings. He thought as a child despite having the responsibility of a man. Dropping his head even lower, he sulked for a while until he came to a conclusion. He would just put everything back the way it was.

Hopping to his feet with a sudden burst of energy, Adam knew what he had to do: he would undo all the things that he previously altered, starting with the very first. Without hesitation, Adam verbally recited his thoughts, wanting verification he actually was rectifying his malpractice.

"Return Mr. Santone's lips to normal."

The burden on his shoulders lightened. Atlas was once again confident in his ability to bear the weight of the world. Pacing around the apartment for a minute Adam recalled the events, taking note of the order of his changes. He dashed into his bedroom frantically, looking for the melted candle that was once his boyhood alarm clock. Holding it in his hand he examined it, the clock was a sad symbol of his negligence. The two bells on the top had melted down the face of the clock. Adam began to think precisely with succinct mental words that he wanted the clock to change back into the clown.

He waited patiently, expecting the clock to transform at any moment. That moment never came. The clock stayed exactly as it was, causing extreme confusion to subdue him. "Why is it not changing?" Adam's voice echoed off the empty walls of the apartment.

Had his talent finally faded? Desperate to see any result, he looked at his wall while thinking about a different color of paint. Sure enough as soon as the words went through his mind, the wall changed colors. He looked back down at the clock. Again he thought about it returning to its original state. Nothing happened. With an outburst of anger, Adam chucked the clock against the wall.

He ran his hands through his hair as he turned around looking for something else he had manipulated. The newspaper that contained the tunnel collapse story was lying on the floor. Immediately he tried with all his might to return the headline back to its original verbiage. Panic stricken, he thought of each word slowly and with a determined focus. Nothing. Frustration flushed through Adam's veins as his heart began to race. Apparently the blessing had its limitations. Without explanation as to why, or for what purpose, he concluded that anything he altered could never return to its original form. Horror set in.

Evalynn was right: he had destroyed the world.

A tear formed at the corner of Adam's eye, rolling down his face, eventually dropping to the floor with a silent splash. The puppet master stood motionless, his brain wrestling with the scope of the situation. A dark cloud of anger hovered over him. His eyes hardened as the goodness in him extinguished like candles on a cake. If it is true, as people say, that the eyes are the window to the soul, Adam boarded his up in preparation for a storm. A soft low hum began to resonate in the room, a tune that slowly became louder and louder in harmony with Adam's temper. All of a sudden the confused man started to repeat the one verse to the song tattooed upon his mind.

> "The place to hide, I can find
> The one with the power.
> But I, in stride, may assist the mind
> Of him in this hour."

Chapter Nineteen

Michaelis and Pura made excellent time.

"How are we supposed to get over that?" Pura was patiently waiting for Michaelis to answer him, as they both gazed up at the kingdom's border wall, a stupefied expression on their faces.

"Well, my friend, that is a good question. I suppose we are going to have to climb over it."

"What about the horse?"

"How about you get us some food? I will figure something out."

Pura dug around in the saddlebag until he came to a few pieces of Lumen traveling bread. It was actually more like jerky than bread, containing the basic sustenance a person on a long journey needed to survive.

Michaelis stood planted in one position looking up at the wall. He was as still as a tree, his eyes indicating his confusion. He had not thought about the wall, or the obvious problem it posed. The wall was a notable beacon to his inexperience; Michaelis' strategy lacked some foresight. He was puzzled. Curiosity of how Baramatheus handled the obstacle controlled his thoughts. The two men left Throne City, one heading south, the other north. The one gate into the kingdom was east of the city. The only explanation Michaelis could fathom was that Baramatheus must have known of another way around the obstruction due to his past experiences. Experiences. Michaelis smiled as he remembered what his mentor had said at the monastery, "Only, remember that there is always more to learn. You can only go so far within these walls. Your lessons will continue beyond them."

"We will walk." Michaelis gave into the fact that there was no quick way of getting his horse over the barrier.

"What about Red, here?" Pura rubbed his hand on the side of the courser. "We can not just leave him."

"I would not worry about him. He knows his way around this kingdom better than you and I." Michaelis grabbed a pack from the horse's back.

He had two packs with him. One was a leather bag containing his armor; on the outside he attached his shield, cinching down a flap that hid most of the metal. Although the lumenium armor was light, when carried on foot, all the pieces together in a cumbersome bag weighed enough to slow any man down. The other pack contained rations and field supplies, food, a blanket, and some cookware. Everything he carried was well-thought-out. Redundancy was a staple in the Defender's preparatory planning. He used rope to bind the two bags together and then had draped them over the hindquarters of the horse like a saddlebag. This same rope easily wrapped around his shoulders and waist to support the pack on his back. Using the same item for multiple purposes enabled the knight to travel quickly and with more flexibility. The practice was a valuable asset since Defenders mostly traveled alone.

Michaelis rigged up the supply pack for Pura to carry and then prepped the other one for himself. Once the two were ready to head up and over the wall, Michaelis patted the side of his horse as he told him to head back to the City of the Throne. The animal galloped off, leaving the knight and the orphan standing at the foot of the massive stone barrier.

"Watch your footing and stay close," Michaelis told Pura as they started up the wall.

The Defender went up first, with Pura following directly behind him. The face of the wall was difficult to maneuver. After all, it would defeat the purpose of a defensive barrier to be easily ascendable. Michaelis meticulously chose his handholds while carefully working his way upward. The boy, on the other hand, scampered up with ease. In fact, the only thing keeping him from climbing the wall faster was his older companion directly ahead of him.

Relatively speaking, up was not the hard part. At the top was where Michaelis wished they would have found another way around the obstruction. He turned and began a steady and careful descent into the wild territory between him and the thousands of Lumen soldiers at the camp. Pura moved down with as much ease as he had climbed up. His movements resembled a squirrel hopping from one tree branch to another. Reaching the bottom, the Defender looked back up with a sense of accomplishment and relief.

"Not bad, Shorty." Michaelis patted Pura on the shoulder, much like his mentor did to him when he was impressed.

The two started their much slower journey across the meadow, heading for the camp. Michaelis figured they would still make decent time. If he recalled the map correctly, the territory between their current position and where the soldiers were was relatively flat meadowlands.

Along the way the two talked about numerous things. Pura was a very friendly child. He had all kinds of questions for his older friend, mostly about Throne City and the King's Defenders. He asked about the Malum and why they wanted to conquer the Lumenites. Michaelis did his best to answer the boy. He did not want to keep him in the dark, mainly due to the fact that his young friend would see soon enough, firsthand, what they were like. Michaelis relayed what he learned from the Martinians concerning the Malum and their ruthless leader, Bebbel-uk. Several times he included too much detail and noticed Pura's eyes glaze in boredom. Michaelis explained the plan he devised and how everything depended on the efforts of the groundsmen. He pressed upon the orphaned boy why it was important that the men follow him north to meet Baramatheus and the rest of the troops.

Michaelis told Pura all about his mentor and how he had taken him in and convinced the Council to trust in the heart of a lowly stable boy. The stories cut into Pura's soul. The tales mesmerized him as if they were some sort of ancient legend. The two travelers confided in each other, sharing their entire life stories by the time they arrived at the southern encampment.

Pura explained how his father hated the fact that he was called upon to serve the king. He told Michaelis that his dad served willingly, but with an animosity that filled his heart with anger. No one in Pura's village understood why so many men had to die. They all watched as their loved ones marched away, never to return. The community tried to take care of the orphaned child but he was not interested in being a burden on them. His father had always emphasized how important it was for a man to stand on his own two feet, to earn his own way. Michaelis recalled that his family and his village felt the same way in regard to the war effort. By the end of the journey, the pair knew all there was to know about each other.

When they stopped, Pura gathered wood and unpacked the food while Michaelis started the fire. Generally, after they ate the younger would fall asleep while the knight stayed awake, ensuring their safety through the night. Several times along the way Pura convinced his new friend to teach him some techniques with the sword. Initially, Michaelis resisted but eventually he came to the conclusion that it would do more good than harm to show the young boy how to protect himself. The Defender's sword was quite heavy for the child despite being lumenium. Pura did his best to hold it in the fashion Michaelis taught him.

As the boy handled the blade, Michaelis explained how important it was not to live by the sword. He talked to him about how exceedingly better it was to study the writings of the ancient teachers and how that would benefit the boy much more than a metal blade. Of course in perfect student form, Pura wanted none of the advice. His only interest was to follow in the footsteps of his tutor. He wanted to be a brave knight and defend the land from evil. Michaelis knew his words fell on deaf ears but spoke them anyway, hoping someday the orphan might recall them and put them to use. A father-son relationship developed. Pura grew closer to the knight, connecting him with his fallen father, a soldier in service. Michaelis began to understand how Baramatheus felt about their relationship: a sense of responsibility, of sympathy, and hope for the less-fortunate person by his side.

"Do you think Baramatheus has reached the northern camp yet?"

"I suspect he probably has. Although I am not sure how he dealt with the wall. That could have hindered his pace as it did ours." Michaelis was certain that his teacher had prepared his journey to include a way around the most obvious of obstacles.

Although Michaelis was about to lead an army of men into battle, he was still very much a student. He learned how to defend himself and how to attack. He studied the history and culture of his homeland and was even taught how to heal others, a tool that would certainly come in handy in the midst of battle. But it was all knowledge gained in the confines of the monastery, behind the secluded and protective walls of the monks. Now he was "putting the steel to the flesh" as it was said and learning how to use the logic, reasoning, and application skills that played as much a part in the role of being a knight as the ability to handle the Defender's sword. Michaelis would be a fine warrior and was confident Baramatheus had taught him well. He only wished that he already possessed the knowledge that comes with experience, experience he obviously did not yet possess.

"Baramatheus is a much finer Defender than I. He undoubtedly prepared for all the occurrences of his journey."

"The sun will be setting soon. Are we going to stop near those big rocks over there?" Pura asked.

There was a cluster of massive stones on the horizon. It was obvious that their arrangement was not a natural phenomenon, but manmade. The formation was in disarray now, but it was apparent that at one time the stones formed a circular shape. One section of the henge was still intact, providing insight into the original architecture of the site. The megaliths measured about twenty feet high from their grassy base to their skyward top. Several of them were capped with a lintel, creating the simple shape of a doorway. It was clear that the stones were not native to the region. Between each doorway was a series of much smaller blue rocks which sparkled with a greenish tint in certain angles of light. All in all the location was the perfect place to make camp, but Michaelis was anxious to get to the men. A superstitious discomfort swelled inside him as well. He did not know anything about the place, but the way the formation was disturbed made the soldier wary to use it as a shelter.

"No, Pura. We will keep moving tonight. We are nearing the end of our trek and can make it to the camp by sunrise if we keep walking," Michaelis answered, knowing it was a lot to ask of the boy. He had no option if he wanted to give the men plenty of time to prepare to travel to Devastation Valley.

"What do you think this is?" inquired the boy.

"I am not certain. The monks speak of a struggle that took place centuries ago. I cannot be sure, but perhaps this is where it took place. Whatever it was, it has long been destroyed."

"It is eerie feeling, that is for sure."

"Yes, the legend tells of a conjurer who was so powerful that he was able to move mountains with his mind. He transported stones from foreign lands to build a temple, an altar to summon a certain spirit."

"Do you think this is that temple?"

"From the looks of it, perhaps. The story goes that when the spirit came forth it brought an entire army with it. The very spirit the conjurer so badly wanted to harness, consumed him and the evil army spread across the land, destroying everything in its path."

"Did the king stop them?"

"This was long before the Lumenites were a people. In some twisted and perverse way the conjurers revere the event. They all marvel at the power of the spirit realm and long to complete the task their forefather failed."

The two of them turned about as they walked, gazing up and down, looking at every inch of the ruin. Their imaginations raced in every direction, while the dark tale of the conjurer ran through their heads.

As they made their way past the destroyed rock formation, the boy glanced back. He dropped his head in silence, the thought of rest disappearing as the stones shrank in the distance. He was not looking forward to hiking all night, especially now that he had an image of evil covering the land. The dark posed a much more frightening scenario for the youngster than it did for Michaelis, for he was still very much at the mercy of his imagination.

The Defender however, welcomed traveling at night. The darkness provided a natural cover for them. After the initial adjustment of the eyes it was easy to become used to the lack of light. Once his senses shifted he could make his way past objects quite easily. In addition to this, the darkness created an early warning system for him. The torches of any unwelcome traveler would be detectable well before they crossed paths.

The night passed quickly and before they knew it, they could see the Lumenite camp in the distance. The sun was rising, illuminating the fortified gathering on the horizon. Michaelis applied his training, taking note of the layout. It was the typical Lumen arrangement, established many years ago. A well-conceived design for its day that proved to be effective up until the unexpected paradigm shift of the enemy's tactics, which had made the model vulnerable. No longer was the enemy of similar thought. Now the opposing force moved sporadically, without any known organization.

The Lumen strategists were unable to comprehend the logic behind the enemy's war plan; all they knew was that it was effective. Bebbel-uk's army was barbaric, refusing to follow the unspoken guidelines of civilized warfare.

The Lumen soldiers spotted Michaelis and Pura while they were still far off, but then again the two weary travelers were not trying to conceal their approach, but were simply walking directly toward the camp through the open field, under the ever-brightening morning sun. At first glance, Michaelis and his sidekick seemed to be leisurely approaching the encampment as if they had all the time in the world. In reality, the two were extremely exhausted from their nonstop hike throughout the night.

An entourage of men greeted Michaelis, including several groundsmen along with a scout, and one of the camp's commanding officers.

"This is a Lumen outpost under the authority of King Josiah. State your business." The officer was firm and to the point. The last thing he needed was the disruption of a wandering traveler.

"My business is Lumen business." Michaelis tossed his cloak over his shoulder: the pink glow of the sun danced across his belt, a symbol of his title.

"Oh, my apologies, sir."

The Lumen officer was in charge of the groundsmen, but a member of the King's Defenders outranked every officer on the battlefield. Only the king himself or an elder Defender was higher in the chain of command.

"Not a problem, sir. You were merely doing your duty, sir. Will you please show me to the officers' tent? And show my aide to somewhere that he can get some rest."

Michaelis purposely addressed the officer with the dignity of "sir." Addressing a lower-ranked soldier with a title was not expected, but since the military man had more experience and was much more knowledgeable as to the interworking of battle respect was warranted.

Michaelis looked down to Pura and tapped him on the back, signaling that everything would be okay. The two parted ways: Michaelis followed the officer to meet with the other Royal Commanders, while the boy tailed a groundsman to a servant's tent.

The accommodations were more than Pura anticipated. Inside the tent was a table full of food, a bed covered in the finest linen, and a stack of sleeping gowns. To the side of the entrance was what the boy imagined to be a royal throne. It was actually only a common chair for taking off boots and undressing, but such beautiful Lumen carvings adorned it that the unlearned child had no idea it was scanty in comparison to the actual Lumen throne.

Michaelis entered the tent to find an argument underway. A man was standing over a table, his finger stabbed down onto it, a map pinned between the wood and his fingertip. He was expressing his views on a subject pertaining to the point on the map. Four other men, all of whom were irate, surrounded the map in disagreement. They were all officers with the exception of one, who was a Defender.

Michaelis hesitated as he entered. He was not used to being in the company of the elite. These men were all well-educated, seasoned soldiers, and he was an inexperienced groundsman turned Defender. The task before them was difficult. They were in control of thousands of lives. None of them took their position lightly, and consequently all of them thought they knew the right way to go about protecting their men and, ultimately, protecting Lumen. The objective was clear to them, but the means were not. They had become callused from years of watching their troops die in the grapple of combat. They were just as tired of the situation as the angry villagers and their actions indicated as much.

Chapter Twenty

A hateful gloom pumped through Adam's veins. He had no one to blame but himself, a truth that just would not do. He quickly found a scapegoat, placing the blame solely on the back of the gift giver. The only problem being that Adam still did not know who that was. Although the thoughts were vague in substance, the basic aim of his blame was a bizarre combination of the civil-social framework of the world, the universe, the demiurgic deity of materialistic ideals, and the expanse of time. The accusations fell on anything and everything he could think of. He was, however, far from the truth of who had given him his very unique gift. Filled with disgust, an internal fuse lit; it was only a matter of time before Adam would explode. Frustration brewed in the young man's gut like an ulcer, his heart sizzling with anger.

Why was he cursed with the power to manipulate the planet according to his will? Why had he been burdened with such a cruel ability? He questioned everything, wanting so badly for it to all to go away. Water gushed from his eyes. If only he could start over, push the reset button and reboot the system. The fact was, he could not. There was no disc to eject, no "game over, please try again" message. The lesson he was learning was a hard one. Choices have consequences, good and bad.

Self-abhorrence fermented in his mind, slowly growing more and more potent until eventually he erupted, tumbling around his bedroom, thrashing and swinging his body through the air. A temper tantrum of nuclear proportions sent shockwaves across the globe. Ground zero: the apartment where it all began.

Adam began cursing loudly, denouncing his power, denying its existence and the choices he had made. His nails dug into the sheetrock of the walls as he clawed his way across the room. Fine white powder filled the room from beneath his fingers. He had no particular destination, his body flailing in every possible direction in violent spasms. He kicked, threw punches, and convulsed, and all the while verbal abominations echoed from his throat. The horrifying scene carried on for quite some time.

The neighbors looked worried as they all, one by one, opened their doors and peeked out towards Adam's apartment.

"I 'spect he's tryin' to take his breeches off," the elderly woman said. "They're too small ya know." She nodded in assurance as the tenant across from her shook his head, dismissing her ridiculous conclusion.

An emotional inferno engulfed Adam, driving him down to his knees. The sound of sobbing was the only noise remaining.

"Why? I just want to know, why?" He could taste the bitter flavor of tears as they rushed past his lips. "You promised to help me with that stupid little song. I know it means something, I know it means something!" Adam was yelling at the top of his lungs in an attempt to call out to the author of the lyrics that were branded on his soul.

What hope remained, vanished in a single instant. There was no long contemplation to weigh out the consequences, no analysis of the outcome. Adam simply gave in.

Like a conductor in front of an orchestra, he raised his hands and began to let thoughts roll through his head, apocalyptic visions. His thoughts and his movements coincided perfectly as Adam molded a world that trembled in death pangs. With a powerful upward motion he raised his palms. The Earth began to shake and the valleys opened up, spraying lava from the molten core. Volcanic eruptions covered the world. Thinking of massive uplifts, pillars of solid stone shot like rockets to the sky. Water splashed violently against each gigantic landmass as the oceans shifted, draining into the steamy furnace of the Earth. With a quick jolt outward, stretching his arms away from his body, Adam blew the sides off the building he was standing in, revealing his existence to the vastness of the black, ash-filled sky above him. While lowering one arm to his side, he slowly extended the other outward across his head, as if he was making a huge swipe with a paintbrush. At that very moment his malicious thoughts released the stars. Galactic missiles aimed directly at the Earth began to scream across the matte black backdrop of the heavens. Adam sent thousands of meteors crashing into the planet. The young man imagined every natural disaster his mind could conceive: tornadoes and hurricanes, earthquakes and ice storms, tsunamis and floods. Then with the posture of a stage magician he unleashed them all on the world, like birds out of a cage. The look on Adam's face was pure evil.

Guilt for what he had done sent him over the edge.

The disdain he felt for himself turned suicidal. Rage blinded him from the pain his thoughts were inflicting on the people of the world. Longing to be free from the truth of his actions, his only desire was to make the end of the world a reality. With every destructive anomaly the world cried out in terror. Millions of lives were slaughtered at the whim of the distraught man.

Despite his best effort, what he was trying so desperately to do was pointless. In an exhausting show of merciless fury, Adam summoned every ounce of his creative mind to try and kill the world. Yet Earth continued to spin. With all his power,

Adam could not destroy the world, only its inhabitants. At present only a remnant survived Adam's fit. The planet continued to make life possible. He did not understand how life could go on, but it did. The ramifications were worse than anything he had done before.

Adam's limp hands dropped to his side with a bounce. His chest deflated as he exhaled a breath of defeat. The tirade was finished. He had taken his heartache out on the people of the world. He could do no more to his home. He realized in his misery that despite all his power, he could not create the utopia he so desperately desired.

What happened next could be perceived as the lunacy of a madman, but it was not. Adam was many things; insane was not one of them. He began holding a conversation, a conversation that would have looked extremely peculiar if someone had had the chance to be a fly on his wall. He was talking to the traveler from his dream, only the traveler's presence was not detectable to anyone but Adam.

Mistakenly, he addressed the man as if he were the gift giver himself. "You promised me. You told me you would help me. Where have you been?"

"I have been assisting you." The stranger's calmness escalated Adam's anger.

"How? You haven't lifted a finger to help me!"

"By guiding you to make the choices you've made."

"But I've made a mess of everything. I've made bad decisions. I've destroyed the world and I can't get it back." Adam's pitch was soft, void of life.

"Oh, no. You have made the choices I knew you would make." After a brief pause the mysterious being spoke again, "Adam, do you not feel better knowing you are living in your world? A world you conceived? You are no longer captive to the parameters established before your creation. You've chosen to live your life the way you want to, in the truest of possible senses." The old man looked upon Adam with a consoling expression. He was hard to read. He seemed to care for Adam by the soft, steady way he spoke to him, but there was something about him that made Adam squeamish.

"But my world is horrible. People are in pain, they are starving, they are forced to work harder while they receive less, they struggle to merely live." Adam's tone was a sad confession, as if his words would urge the man to fix everything.

"Oh," the traveler chuckled, "they are much worse off than that now. With the exception of a few, everyone is dead. And I would say you did an excellent job at that. Not only did you kill them all, you managed to rid them of faith along the way. But now you know what it is like to be in control. Does that not comfort you?"

"Comfort me? The death of countless people is on my shoulders. I'm responsible for all the agony in the world! All of it! I wrecked the world. I'm nothing but a selfish, foolish murderer!" Adam punched at the air, losing what little resolve he had as he tried to pummel the man before him.

"Yes, that is a cold and agonizing truth, but you can change that too. You still have your gift." The man smiled. "Let me help you, Adam. After all, I have only been trying to aid you, to free you." The stranger took a step toward the edge of the floor which overlooked the ruins of the city. With perfect demeanor he stood, dignified and in control. His posture was solid, that of a statesman. "Were you really meant to live life the way it was? It can be so much better." He paused for a moment. "I can help you, if you will let me."

Adam finally realized what was happening. In a word: manipulation. From the very beginning the gift bestowed on him, his mental prowess, his thought-dominion over the world, was being controlled by this being. The entire time this deceiver had been encouraging Adam with his melodic persuasion. The man from his dream was after the gift. Adam was a pawn, a vessel to wreak havoc on the planet.

"You've helped me enough. I turned to find comfort in the tune you sang. I thought it was the answer, some mystical key to show me the path. But it wasn't. It was only a ploy, a ruse to gain access to my ability. I tried to find help where there was none. Lies and empty promises, that's all you gave me. Don't offer me help! No!"

"Puppet, you would do well to know your place. Do you think you are the first person to conjure up false bravado in my presence? Hardly. You are a feeble dissident, an itty bitty fly in the ointment. Men of greater stock than you have wept at my feet. Titans have groveled for my assistance. I am the one with the power. You may have been given one of the greatest gifts in all of mankind, but it is all for naught. I am the master; you are nothing." The traveler's voice darkened, "Why do you think that is? Have you any idea the gravity of your actions? Do you realize what you are a part of?" With a sinister grin the traveler paced the room before continuing his oratory. "Of course you don't. Because that, Adam, is my crowning accomplishment. To keep the big picture hidden from you, that is. The task of twisting your gift to serve my purpose was surprisingly easy. At times I even thought you were laying it out on a platter for my enjoyment." The older man's face was now inches from Adam's. "I am the preceptor of the flesh! I am the lord and controller of fates." He whispered the last sentence, letting each syllable slide off his tongue amid his hot breath.

The sulfuric words permeated Adam's senses. His eyes stung and his nose curled in contention at the odor. Smothered by the breath's thickness, Adam gasped for air, his cheeks itching beyond relief.

The stranger stepped back. Adam quickly shuffled his way to a more comfortable distance. An eerie silence settled in around the two of them, neither one speaking as time passed.

"If you're the piper, I guess that means I need to pay." With a smug smirk Adam mustered up every ounce of youthful American pomp he possessed. He did his best to stand strong. "You play yourself up to be a god, titans bowing before you and all. You're right, it didn't occur to me that I was part of something bigger than myself. I know now. Thanks for laying it all out for me to see. But if I'm nothing, I see just what kind of master you are. You lied to bring about death. You want what doesn't belong to you. You're a murderer! A defiler, taking what's good and turning it into evil. I know exactly who you are."

The stranger gestured politely. "Apparently my reputation precedes me. Glad to make your acquaintance." "My ability is a gift. If you want a go with it, I suggest you ask the one who gave it to me if you can have a turn."

"Perhaps, little flea, that's exactly what I've done." And with that, the traveler from Adam's dream disappeared.

* * *

Many hours lapsed from the time Adam began throwing the world around like soft clay to the time he realized just what he had done. The awareness manifested in a developmental way, similar to the mourning process people experience after the loss of a loved one. The realization of his actions was present, although the grieving period had yet to begin. It was not the severely altered appearance of New York or the continent for that matter, but rather the intrusion by a neighbor that caused the ramifications of his actions to hit home. The kooky lady from down the hall tapped Adam on the shoulder.

"S'cuse me son," she spoke hesitantly, "were ya able to get back into yer breeches?"

"What?" Adam was stunned at the normalcy of the woman's question. Ever since Adam began tampering with the world, this woman talked to him as if nothing was different, like she knew he was just a young man from a small town trying to make it in a big city.

"Yer breeches, do they fit again?" The woman had a curious look on her face.

"Ma'am, you're not all there, are you?"

"I may not be from yer 'spective, but at least I didn't ruin the world, my clothes still fit just as they always did." She smiled, her eyes telling Adam that there was something more to her question, something that he was not getting.

"What? What are you saying?" Adam realized that she commented about what he had done. How did she know it was his fault? No one knew except him and Evalynn.

"Son, I've been warnin' ya 'bout reachin' yer stars for quite some time," she laughed as if it were Adam that did not understand what was happening. "Of course I know twas ya that's made a mess of things."

"Wait, what do you mean?" Adam's attention was undividedly hers.

"Ya might wanna think 'bout doin' somethin' 'bout this mess ya've made. Didn't yer mother ever teach ya to clean up after yerself?" The woman walked down what was left of the hall, adding, "I'll find my broom and give ya a hand." He contemplated what she said as he watched her walk away. Adam could not help but think that all her earlier ramblings had been some kind of warning, an alarm he had most certainly ignored.

The young man stopped to take a look around at what he had done. The buildings were demolished; the entire world was in shambles. He had launched countless bombardments of natural catastrophes and now nothing was recognizable. The measure of destruction was captured by the fact that Long Island was no longer an island. The terrestrial landscape was completely altered. A sense of responsibility came over him as he looked at the unruly reality of his performance. Disgust for himself, accompanied by the internal desire to fix what he broke, grew within his soul.

He went over to the ledge where the window looking out over the empty lot had once been, and sat down. Dangling his feet off the ledge, he leaned back onto his hands. He was determined now to heal the wounds he had slashed into the flesh of the world. It was evident that he could not take back his deeds. Adam did not understand the reason, but accepted it as truth. Sitting there, he searched for a way to make right, at least somewhat, his wrongs. If there was not a way, he made up his mind that there was only one thing to do. Remembering the words of his father, he would simply lie down in the bed he made and live in the hell he created.

Sitting in pure isolation for days, he contemplated what to do. The only distraction from analyzing his predicament was the occasional crash of a piece of metal or concrete debris falling to the street. Finally, nearly a week after the outburst that dismembered the Earth, a solution came to Adam.

Just like the old nursery rhyme, "Humpty Dumpty," Adam could not put things back the way they were. Every time he tried to correct something, he failed to accomplish his intended goal. So with that understanding in mind, he decided to simply leave everything well enough alone, to merely allow the world to begin anew, without hindering the process. Life existed before Adam; it would undoubtedly continue to do so now.

His actions left the entire planet disfigured and in ruins. It was painfully obvious that to right all the wrongs in the world, to rid the Earth of sin's plague, he would need to have much more power and wisdom then he did. He possessed a great gift, an ability so unique that he was the only person in the history of mankind on whom it was bestowed. But in the end it was indeed a gift he had squandered.

Adam's logic was leading him down a very uncomfortable path. If his power was a gift, albeit a magnificent one, then whoever had the ability to give such a gift possessed even greater power. As he came upon this epiphany it was obvious that there was nothing else to do other than get out of the way. While he possessed the ability to kill, he did not have the power to heal. No matter how hard he tried, he could not will the world into a utopia.

"It'll work!" Adam was convinced his idea was a good one. Contemplating the end result of his simplistic idea for hours, the young man came to the conclusion that doing nothing was the best he could do.

He stood up just as he had when he had released his wrath, and began to purposefully think. This time his thoughts were custodial in nature. He was intent on letting the designed system run its course, and he was confident it would. All that he had to do was, like his neighbor said, clean up his mess. Closing his eyes, he imagined that the rubble, the landfills of once-prosperous civilizations, the charred and desolate remains of man's achievements, those endeavors he had mentally molested, were all gone. He removed entire cities (or what was left of them). Vehicles, roadways, power lines, cell phone towers, it all vanished. The Earth, as far as he could tell, was once again empty of the world he had known. The people who were still alive, despite his destructive thoughts, would be left, unhindered by him, to start over, to rebuild, to live under the life-sustaining control of the one who had given him his gift, the one who had the greater power.

After wiping the slate clean, Adam thought up one last thing: a home, or rather a tomb, for him to dwell in until the end of the world. He considered himself a threat to everyone and did not wish to relive the terror he had just brought forth. Knowing that his life would last as long as the planet's, in a confident decision, the once-ordinary man chose to live it out in solitude. Adam placed a cave near a valley exactly where New York City had previously been. It was as close to the Malloy building as he could figure, only now it was a wide open uninhabited wasteland. He hid the entrance, preparing to remain alone in the confines of the rock until the day the world stopped spinning. Making an internal vow, he was determined to never think another atom-shifting thought. That was the purpose behind the seclusion. He figured if he never saw another soul, if he never interacted with the world again, then he would be less apt to succumb to the temptation to manipulate his environment.

Evalynn never crossed Adam's mind after he erupted in his violent fit of rage. Overwhelmed by his actions and eventually the desire to reconstruct his obliteration, she escaped his thoughts. Now in his self-made prison, he wallowed in the memories of his family, sulking with every thought of his past.

Chapter Twenty-One

The name of the man pointing at the map was
Eliazar. He was a mighty man and very humble.
Normally, he would never boorishly press his
opinion on his colleagues, but he was aware of the
grim realities they faced and felt that the time for
civility was over. The warrior held few
characteristics associated with nobility. His
appearance was rough, even for a soldier. He was a
tall man, standing at least a head taller than the
average Lumenite. His frame was large, bearing the
weight of a thick physique, a direct result of an
insatiable appetite and unquenchable thirst for fine
ale. He carried his weight well, though, his posture
an unyielding symbol of strength. His beard was full
and raggedy.

For Eliazar, nothing was done unless it was
thought-out and sensible, including the overgrowth
on his face. He spent most of his days in the field
surrounded by the harsh elements; the beard
shielded his face from the bite of winter winds and
the sting of hot summer dust storms. His hair was
long and unattended as well, with the exception of

one braided strand that hung from the left side of his head, just in front of his ear. Eliazar placed a bead in the braid every time he felt his life was miraculously spared. The beads were the only sign that he recognized the seriousness of his profession.

Sarcasm coupled with a haughty approach to life were Eliazar's token attributes. His quick-witted remarks and bellowing laughter in the face of danger drew attention from groundsmen and commanders alike. Eliazar thought nothing of his personal safety; he simply did what he had to do, most of the time downplaying it, as if the task was of no concern.

The King's Defenders requested the mighty warrior's service many times. The answer was always a resounding, "no." In fact, he teased the royal knights, referring to them as glory hounds and overdressed, soft-bellied boys that were nothing more than the pretty faces for those that did the king's real fighting. He made his comments in unmistakably good spirit, since most of his closest friends were Defenders and Eliazar enjoyed the respect and freedom given to them. Despite not officially belonging to the order, he went where he saw fit, and took on tasks as he deemed necessary. He was, in effect, everything they were. All he lacked was the title and the armor.

All the men in the tent had heroic stories from past battles. Most Lumen military men did. Their episodes were full of legendary bravery and miraculous victories against tremendous odds. Eliazar was no exception. His most well-known feat was when he stood alongside King Josiah's father, Charles. All the groundsmen had fled in fear, but the king and Eliazar held their position in the middle of a field of barley. The opposing force stormed them with all but a guaranteed victory. Despite the overwhelming odds, the two brave warriors cut down all the men of the advancing garrison, each in turn.

When asked to tell the story, Eliazar always laughed it off, proclaiming that all he had been trying to do was protect the field of barley in which they were standing. It never failed: he would end his narrative with an anecdote about how the harvest eventually quenched the thirst of many parched men. He would, as if on cue, raise his mug, handsomely grinning as he swallowed another swig of brew. Anyone within earshot would know Eliazar had finished his tale by the rumbling sound of laughter that followed. His adventures were welcomed stories, if for no other reason than that they always lightened the soldiers' spirits.

The men in the tent were in a heated debate over the strategy of their next maneuver. Eliazar was the only one who felt they should advance toward the Malum. He did not like the idea of sitting in camp waiting for the enemy to attack, which was the inevitable conclusion, in his mind, if they held their current position any longer.

The other men disagreed loudly, as Eliazar tried to convince them of his perspective. None of them were shy when it came to a matter as important as this.

"Eliazar, I am not going to lead my men to their deaths over one of your gut feelings! You must understand we need to bunker down and hold our position!"

Ben was the only one in the room who was a member of the King's Defenders. He was, therefore, the highest ranked officer and had the final say. He had seen many men die in the past wars. He was older and his spirit to fight had vanished long ago. No one could have told him that, of course, for his pride was full. But it was obvious that Ben was too soft to make the hard choices expected of a leader.

In his youth, Ben had been a valiant knight. The list of his famed adventures was longer than the combination of those who still fought today. The highlights were as exciting as they were impressive. The last great exploit had been as recent as the Malum war. In the beginning days of the conflict, after being ambushed, Ben killed two of the enemy so easily that the others ran off.

Before the war, he had set out to look into the death of several of the Lumen army's steeds. The stable master reported seeing a bear roaming the fields nearby. Tracking it to a nearby cave, Ben simply walked in, sword in hand and slayed the beast.

Another of Ben's legendary tales occurred when he was face-to-face with a raider in the open country of Lumen. The thief was seven-and-a-half feet tall and nearly as wide. Ben had only a club which he had taken off one of the raider's fallen comrades. The giant man bore a spear. As they fought, Ben tossed the club, and knocked the spear from the clutches of the scavenger. Recovering the weapon, Ben gave a quick blow to the knee of his opponent with the blunt end of the spear and escaped the man's grasp. When the angered giant rushed him, Ben ran him through with his own spear, catapulting the man over his head and onto the ground.

Despite all this, the war with Malum had taken its toll on the great warrior. Many of his friends had fallen in battle in the years since the war began and age itself had finally begun to catch up with him, removing him from the field of battle and cooling his once-great spirit.

"You, of all men, should understand the importance of holding fast in order to prevail," Ben told Eliazar, a blatant reference to Eliazar's famed stand.

The attempt to capitalize on Eliazar's pride, however, failed terribly. The seasoned soldier was not so easily manipulated, and everyone knew it. Under different circumstances, Ben would never have been so daring in his effort to win the debate, but he was just as confident in his decision to stay and defend as Eliazar was to advance and attack. Anger flashed from the warrior's eyes as he tried to control his temper.

"I do understand holding fast, when the situation calls for it. This is not one of those times, Ben. Do you think there is but only one way to fend off a foe? We must bring the fight to the enemy," Eliazar replied. "I would not have thought you needed to be schooled on this. If I am not mistaken, you have a certain lion's skin by which you warm yourself in the cold of winter, a blanket that never lets you forget the value of having the courage to attack when the enemy has repeatedly proven himself capable of coming in from the wild to weaken your troops."

It was at this point that the men noticed Michaelis standing in the doorway of the tent.

"Excuse me," Michaelis bowed quickly as he greeted himself, "I am Michaelis, Defender of the King. I bring a message from Gidaen."

"Gidaen sends word?"

All were silent upon hearing this news. The field officers were bound to follow the strategist's orders. This would most certainly put an end to their current squabble.

"He wishes for you to follow me north, to the mouth of Devastation Valley." Michaelis paused to let his words sink in.

"Absurd!" Ben did not believe what he was hearing. "And what, might I ask, is the plan once we have reached the valley?" Although curious, Ben was certain he knew the answer.

"And why, my young sir, should we follow your lead?" a man named Gareb asked. The question reeked of disrespect, so much so that, if the man had spoken in such a tone to an older Defender, a known veteran, all in the room would have rebuked him.

"Because, sir, I am a member of the King's Defenders, and because the three senior strategists send word that this is what our next move shall be. There is also the unavoidable fact that you are all slowly being killed off, just sitting here. Unless I am mistaken, you are in deliberation right this moment, trying to conceive a plan." Michaelis looked into the eyes of every man in the tent. "This, my friends, is that plan." The Lumen knight spoke with confidence, but deep down speaking to such great men in so direct a manner made him extremely nervous.

"May I ask, sir, what is our plan once we get to Devastation Valley?" Eliazar inquired.

"Victory."

The word did not get the response Michaelis had hoped for. The intent of the forthright and oversimplified answer was to inspire. The hearts of these men would not stir with the uttering of a single word. Michaelis realized this and instantly began to elaborate.

"Baramatheus is leading the northern camp to the valley. The report is that twenty thousand Malum are on the march."

"Twenty thousand? That is suicide. We cannot expect to defeat so high a number," Gareb blurted out in contempt.

"We can, if all the men unite. That is the plan: both this camp and the one up north will merge with the troops already positioned at Devastation Valley. If we all fight together we will be able to drive back the Malum and end this war once and for all."

Michaelis was not sure how the men were taking the news. There was a long pause and all of them wore a look of doubt on their faces.

"If we head north, the Malum brigade here will follow us. They will still be stronger than us." Ben was running the scenario through his mind.

"Yes sir, in numbers they will be, but not in heart." Michaelis saw that the men were beaten down and done considering the plan. It was only creating more questions. "We are Lumenites! We have right on our side! We will win this war! The king does not doubt that his people will be saved from the clutches of our enemy. Should you not have faith in his plan? The final battle between the children of Lumen and the Malum has come. It is time to crush Bebbel-uk's head, once and for all. We either stay put and die slowly, or band together and rid the land of this venomous adversary." Michaelis had thus told his elder audience exactly how things were. It was now up to them to decide if they were going to help or hinder his orders.

"Eliazar, it looks like you win. By default, of course." Ben smiled a bit as he spoke.

"I will take it any way I can get it if it means defeating the Malum slime." All the men laughed as the burly old soldier lifted his mug and gulped down a mouthful of beer.

Once Eliazar agreed to the orders, the other men fell in line. The mood lightened as they began to have faith in victory, a feeling that had been absent for a long time.

"Great, we need to move as fast as we can. We want our movement to catch the enemy off-guard. We do not want them to take advantage of our distraction and ambush us while we are breaking camp," Michaelis directed.

The knight was pleased he did not have to debate the strategy further. He was a dwarf in a room full of giants. Contending with their experience in matters of warfare was not an idea with which he was comfortable.

The next several days rushed by. All the soldiers were nervous as they packed. The leaders of the groundsmen delivered the new orders and plainly expected the men to do as commanded. Michaelis could see the disheartened expressions and sense the unwillingness of the men as they begrudgingly followed instructions.

The guards were on double duty. The Lumen officers were taking absolutely every precaution possible to avoid an ambush. Michaelis and Pura assisted the troops in their mundane task of rigging down tents and prepping their gear. As they did, Michaelis overheard the conversation of two groundsmen.

"I am not certain our privileged Royal Commanders even know what it is like to be in the midst of battle anymore."

"One thing is for sure, they know what it is like to watch battles from their guarded outpost, safely behind the lines."

"Yes, calling out orders while they feed their faces, watching us get slaughtered."

The men spoke with a morbidly sarcastic tone. It was obvious that most of the troops shared this sentiment. The emotions were familiar to Michaelis, the groundsmen he served with prior to his unexpected advance of rank made similar comments. Suddenly, he thought of Pura's father. He too must have felt the same way as he looked over his shoulder moments before his death and saw the commanders cleansing their pork riddled palate with Lumen's choicest wine. Michaelis' thoughts brimmed with sympathy. The only thing these men wanted was to live their lives. They did their duty honorably, although not welcomingly. The young knight decided that they all deserved to be kept in the loop. He made his way to where the group of royal officers was planning the journey north.

"Assemble the men." Michaelis was resolute in his demand.

"What? Now? If you have not noticed we are in the middle of mapping out our route. We do not have time to gather the men."

The arrival of Michaelis aroused a thick sense of pride in Gareb. An experienced and war-hardened veteran, he felt that he earned his place in the menagerie of Lumen's military leadership and that Michaelis did not measure up to his self-defined standard of admittance. Unfortunately, the only qualification he cared about was the young Lumen knight's reputation. In short, Gareb was annoyed with Michaelis and thought he was in over his head, thus he was not yet deserving of the respect given him. He most certainly did not share the same confidence that Ben, Eliazar, and the others were beginning to express.

"I need to speak to the soldiers. They deserve that much."

Michaelis did not allow Gareb's dissidence to delay his request. He walked over to where he would address the groundsmen, and waited while the word spread and the disgruntled troops assembled in front of him.

None of the officers knew what Michaelis had in mind, but all of them recognized that it was consuming valuable time. The men stood looking up at what they saw to be another royal member of the elite. The knight waited until all of them were in front of him before speaking.

"Warriors of Lumen, I wish to shed some light on the situation we are facing." It was important that Michaelis show the men he was being upfront and honest with them. He did not want them to hear his words as more rhetoric from on high. "You all have been fighting tirelessly in duty to your king and country. Trust me: your sacrifice has not fallen on blind eyes. There are people who see your valiant calling for what it is."

His audience grumbled in disbelief.

"Trust in the knowledge that your service is greatly appreciated by all the people of Lumen, from the king, to your children. Warriors of today, you follow in a long line of brave and inspiring soldiers, heroes who have time and time again served to save this nation from the terror beyond the gate. Now is no different. We face a new evil, a breed who knows not the rules of engagement, nor the mercy of a heart. The time has come. This generation will determine whether this land should remain standing or fall around us."

The men's facial expressions were changing. More and more of them gave Michaelis their undivided attention.

"It is a heavy and agonizing burden to bear. I know as well as you the cost of our service. But we must face this foe with a fire in our hearts that burns so bright that no force on Earth could possibly extinguish the ember of our resolve! Villagers of the kingdom of Lumen, remember your heritage, take hold of the memory of your fathers, and recall the lives laid down in payment for the land we call home. The cost has been high and the return low, but if you hold onto the memories of your fallen brothers we will reign victorious."

"What do you know of it, standing up there with your precious armor and your delicate clothes?" a soldier asked.

The remark did not upset Michaelis, although it shocked the other Defenders. "Much more than you would think, my friend. My father died in battle and when the call for new groundsmen came, I stepped up. I am like you, brothers. We are one in this struggle. Are you so caught up with what I wear that you cannot see the make of my heart?"

Michaelis drew his sword and held it with the same intensity as he would if he were about to charge into battle. "The king of Lumen has bestowed on me his sword, and I bear it proudly. Me, a common man, as you all are." He extended the blade, swinging it across the crowd. "I will not fail in my service to the one who raised me up for a purpose. We, the army of Lumen, shall meet the evil enemy with our king's sword.

"You all have grown bitter and cold. You curse the king for asking you to do your duty and you mock the leaders he sent to do his will. But you, my fellow soldiers, are the ones responsible for the outcome of this struggle. If you choose to wallow in disbelief, then the outcome is death. But, if with me and all your brothers, you choose to trust in the sword the king has given you, holding firm to its power, then you will see the victory celebration at the end." Michaelis was finished. He said all that he had to say. To punctuate the end of his speech, he lifted his blade higher, the sun gleamed radiantly off the lumenium.

The atmosphere was still at first. No one spoke. They were waiting to see if the young knight might say something else. When Michaelis started to walk away, the men all at once erupted with shouts of inspiration. They cheered and yelled and eventually began to chant the phrase, "Victory for our king, victory for his people."

Michaelis turned and faced the men. He was astounded at the response. The Defender managed to pump life back into the Lumen troops. He ran down into the crowd of men, chanting with them. The sight of warrior clasping warrior in glorious anticipation of victory moistened the eyes of all who witnessed it.

The men moved more quickly and in much better spirits. The entire camp was disassembled and ready to depart by nightfall, allowing the men time to rest.

Michaelis, however, could not sleep. The excitement of the day ran through his head alongside the dread of what was to come. He arose from the line of sleeping soldiers and went over to where he found a couple of other restless men, Ben and Gareb.

"Sleep comes not to you either eh, young one?" Gareb grunted while walking away.

"No. Thinking about tomorrow."

"Well I think everything will be fine, especially after seeing your performance today," Ben offered as he smiled at Michaelis.

"Have I done something to offend him?" Michaelis nodded toward Gareb.

"I imagine you just stirred his emotions." Ben was much more pleasant than he had been the first time Michaelis spoke to him. "You did a great thing today. You know that, do you not? I would call it a victory in and of itself."

"The men just needed to hear that they are not doing this for nothing," Michaelis responded humbly.

"Yes, but none of us old men have had the courage to speak to them in such a way. You are a true leader, my young friend." Ben stared into the darkness.

"We all have the same thing at stake. Why not convey that to those who are doing most of the work?"

"An excellent point, Michaelis."

"Has tomorrow's route been determined yet?"

"Everything is in order; just waiting for sunrise."

The two men talked for a while longer before they both withdrew to find some rest. The trip would be a relatively quick one. After that, the war's end would be upon them.

Chapter Twenty-Two

Baramatheus' engagement with the leaders of the northern camp occurred much differently than that of his younger counterpart's efforts in the south. Baramatheus was a well-known Defender of the king. His name was synonymous with his father's title as a member of the Council. After his arrival, all the commanders took their instruction from him, responding by immediately carrying out exactly what he ordered. Baramatheus was, of course, a man of the people. His primary concern was always the wellbeing of Lumen. Consequently, when he spoke, men listened.

He did not address the groundsmen as Michaelis did. The northern men moved south toward Devastation Valley simply because that was the order given to them. They were the same broken men they had been before the knight announced the new plan. From their perspective the relocation was merely more of the same.

The northern soldiers' journey was nearly over as Michaelis, Pura, and the others were just setting out on theirs. Upon reaching the mouth of the valley,

Baramatheus' men immediately began to unload supplies, supplementing the provisions that were already there.

They established the fortified location near a spring which the soldiers utilized for both themselves and their horses. The contrast of the life-giving water spewing from the ground in such close proximity to the superstitiously cursed site resonated, even if briefly, in the mind of every man who refreshed himself with the cool water. The valley ran to the north where Bebbel-uk's Malum fighters were already marching south. On the eastern side of the valley, a beautiful protrusion of snowy hills sparkled. If the situation had not been so bleak the view would have been hauntingly beautiful.

Baramatheus made his way to the commanders' large tent in the center of the campground, where after much hospitality, the men discussed Michaelis' strategy. All the field officers were happy to see additional troops arrive. It meant relief from duties and more importantly, communication from a different part of the land. Many of the troops were kin of some sort, so as the two groups merged, morale rose. The northern soldiers were quick to ask the questions that desperately needed answering. They wanted to know what the other men knew about the forthcoming enemy barrage. Were there really 20,000 of them moving through Devastation

Valley, and were the Lumen leaders honestly thinking about facing them here in this spot?

The valley had a discouraging history. No one, Lumen, Malum, or otherwise, wanted anything to do with it. Gidaen realized this when he ordered the deployment of Lumen fighters to the mouth of the valley. It was a decision that made him uneasy. The legend of the valley was dark and mysterious.

According to the Martinian records, in the days of antiquity, there had been a terrible release of natural disasters. Everything from tornadoes to earthquakes to volcanic eruptions covered the Earth. Where there was water, the seas had sprung up, unleashing hurricanes and tsunamis in violent spasms. Blizzards and fires had whipped across the land, numbing life and scarring the ground. Stars had fallen from the sky, colliding with the Earth in massive force. It was written in the records that the world had been cleansed with an immense accumulation of naturally-occurring anomalies of the worst degree, killing off nearly everyone who lived before the rebirth of the planet. Everything was destroyed, except for a small remnant of people, who not only survived, but were the founders of the new civilizations. They carried with them a link to the past, to the age before the destruction.

To this day the Lumen scholars and historians continued to study anything that had to do with the event. No one was certain of the true happenings, although many theories existed. Controversial debates and heated arguments were ignited over the subject on numerous occasions. The most popular explanation involved Devastation Valley. The theory differed slightly depending on who related it, but the gist was that the valley was the point of origin for all the catastrophes that decimated the world.

Throughout Lumen history, many peculiar incidents had occurred near the valley, adding to its unearthly reputation. When battles were lost near the valley, the blame always found its route to the geographic site. People whose lives were touched by mysterious events usually pointed to the valley as the explanation. They blamed a trip which took them near it or even the animals they ate, which must have migrated past it. Nearly everyone in the region had a superstition which pointed to Devastation Valley.

"Baramatheus, what does the king think? Is he confident that this defense will work?" the highest commander in the camp asked, more for his own reassurance than for any other reason.

"The king has the utmost confidence in the soldiers of Lumen." Baramatheus answered, looking straight into the valley, taking in the full panorama of the landscape.

To his right he could catch the northernmost hills of the valley. Directly north he saw what he determined to be the route of the enemy. He analyzed the lay of the land, trying to gauge the flow of the battle.

"Is there the possibility that the king will change our orders?"

"While possibilities abound it would do you well to trust that the king relies on the Defenders to do their job, and we are. We act as an arm of the king. The strategists have outlined our new tactic. I suspect that the only thing that will change our orders is time itself and that is only because time inevitably moves us forward, whether we like it or not."

"What if we are defeated?"

The question shook Baramatheus' confidence in the man, who was supposed to be the officer in charge of the camp.

"Then the days of torture and agony await us," Baramatheus bluntly replied as he turned in order to face the man before speaking again. "A man of your status should not be asking such foolish questions." Baramatheus moved right into the man's face as he spoke, his teeth gritting together. The remark had stung him sharply. For an officer of the Lumen army to ask such a thing meant only that the man had already given up hope. "I am taking over this outpost."

"Sir, I did not mean anything by my question. I only wish to know what to anticipate."

The squeamishness of the soldier was plainly agitating the knight. "I suggest you look to your king, for victory is his." Baramatheus had finished his piece. After a few moments of silence the commander, removed from his office, slowly walked away.

The terrain was not advantageous for either army. Weather was favorable, with no telltale signs of a storm to come. There could not have been any better stage for the drama to unfold. It would be a bout between men, the only variables being skill and determination. Baramatheus knew if his men had the heart, the day would be theirs.

The Malum had the numbers and the brutality to easily take the field, but the Lumen had a history bulging with accounts of glorious overcomings. All that had to happen was for the men to trust that the strategy put forth would work. For without faith in the plan, nothing would come of this attempt.

The night came and the groundsmen did their best to stay on their guard. Patrols were on lookout and special units of King's Defenders were covering the outlying areas, making it nearly impossible for any premature advance by their enemy.

Ever since word spread that the Malum were marching toward the kingdom, Gidaen and the other strategists had sent word that all Defenders should ride for the mouth of the valley. They were to aid the groundsmen in all matters. Several Defenders had stayed with the men in the north and Ben remained in the south, otherwise all were here at Devastation Valley. Each one, upon arrival, reported spotting Malum troops heading toward the camp. This verification only helped solidify the urgency of the upcoming conflict.

Baramatheus and Michaelis had left the City of the Throne with such haste that neither of them were aware that Gidaen and the strategists were traveling to the encampment as well. The king informed Gidaen that he did not intend to sit idly by as his kingdom faced its darkest hour. The top Defender agreed with the sentiment and all the elders of the order made their way to the approaching battle. Josiah stayed at the kingdom's capital to aid the city's special defense force in protecting the heart of the land from the approaching enemy, presumably poised to attack from the shoreline. He badly wanted to be on the frontline alongside Michaelis as the knight fought off the large wave of Malum, but he recognized that if the city fell, a victory at Devastation Valley would be meaningless.

So it was that he stayed behind watching as his highest military strategists rode off to war. Nicholas and the Servants of the Council had come to King Josiah and vowed to stand firm with him until the end. They would fend off the threat or lose their lives trying. It pleased Josiah to know he had such brave men around him to help deliver the land from the crushing grasp of Bebbel-uk's vile army.

The city was busy preparing for an invasion just as the valley camp was. The special guards gathered all their resources in an effort to be fully prepared.

None of them had ever fought the Malum; the opposition had never breached the security of the Lumen wall before. Their emotions were ten times more scattered than the men in the field. All they had to base their preparation on were the horrible war stories which made it back to them from outside the walls, often exaggerated in the retelling. While word of mouth was a decent method of communication, one had to filter out the gossip and elaborations.

Baramatheus was examining the supply log when a scout sent word that a large number of men were approaching from the southeast. He grinned and dispatched a company of soldiers to greet them and lead them into camp. Michaelis accomplished his first task as a Defender; he made it to the valley with a full entourage. Baramatheus was happy to know his pupil would be by his side as the fight began. He had witnessed the youth's bravery once before in the heat of battle, but now Michaelis had knowledge to accompany his courage. This notion excited the veteran, causing an extra bounce in his step as he made his way to the entrance of camp. He was also anxious to greet the company of soldiers Michaelis traveled with. They were some of the bravest and also some of the most colorful in the Lumen ranks. Bebbel-uk truly did not know what he was getting into.

Generally, when the men traveled, the groundsmen followed behind the officers and

Defenders, but as this party approached they were moving as one. They were all intermingled, walking and riding side-by-side. It actually took him a moment to spot his student among the surprisingly energetic crowd.

"Baramatheus!" Michaelis was delighted to see his mentor as well. "I see your journey went well."

Baramatheus looked around as the men passed by. "As did yours. What is going on?" The happy faces peppered throughout the unusual formation bewildered him.

"Let us get a drink and some food. I will tell you all about it."

The Royal Commanders and Defenders all moved toward the serving tent, as did some groundsmen that had been talking to Michaelis before they arrived. Michaelis let Baramatheus in on what happened at the southern camp and how the men rallied to the cause so willingly after he spoke to them. Ben, Eliazar, and even Gareb attested to the event, adding in their own personalized narration where it seemed to fit, all of which spoke well of Michaelis.

Proud is the only word to describe how Baramatheus felt. He knew that if Michaelis had the chance, he could lead the groundsmen to peace. And it looked as though he was doing just that. While the men all ate and drank, laughing and enjoying each other's company, Michaelis took the chance to ask his old friend how he managed to get over the kingdom wall.

Eliazar assumed his role as the groundsmen from all the different camps gathered to eat, and especially to drink. He entertained the men with his tales of adventures and victories, never boastful and always humble in his speech.

"I got to tell you, boys, that it was certainly by no doing of yours truly, but by a miracle, that I walked away from that confrontation with Elymas, for if the boulder had not been positioned just so by the arrangement of creation, my blade striking the earth beneath it would have made no difference. The poor conjuring soul, with all his dabbling in the spiritual realm, was blind to the immediate consequences of the physical. But enough of that. Hoist those heavy mugs. To health and heavy rocks!"

The evening was pleasant. All the men were aware of the grave situation ahead, but for once they all were able to forget about the future and enjoy the present. The brash attitude of the gritty royal soldier emboldened the men as the night carried on, giving them a strong sense of comfort in the rightness of their purpose.

That night the men all went to sleep content and more prepared for the future than they had ever been. It was as if the war were over and all that remained was to go through the motions.

Chapter Twenty-Three

The rising sun revealed two surprises. To the north, up Devastation Valley, the Malum were within sight, much closer than anyone expected. The men's sense of joy washed away very quickly as word spread that the enemy had been spotted. The other surprise was that Gidaen and the other aged Defenders had arrived. They rode into the camp just after the status of the Malum army was reported.

The men that traveled from the south with Michaelis were intermixing with the others; their attitude lifted everyone's spirits slightly. However, some did not believe the leaders truly cared about the common groundsmen. Gidaen's arrival proved that the king was behind them and that this war was everyone's concern. Still, some naysayers would not trust and could not believe that the royal blood was as fully poured into the war as that of the ordinary men. The Malum had placed fear back into the hearts of the soldiers while the arrival of the wisest, most experienced men serving the king had given them all comfort and ease. The climate of the camp was, to say the least, a strange mix of elation and fear.

After Gidaen and his comrades had a chance to rest from their journey, they called a meeting of all the field commanders and King's Defenders. When everyone assembled, Gidaen turned the table over to Baramatheus as it was he who had taken the helm of the camp up to this point. Baramatheus briefed all the leaders on the strategy and tried his best to answer their questions. A fellow Defender expressed that he was not confident in the resolve of the men. Baramatheus delivered a pungent reply to the concern, stating matter-of-factly, that if any hope of victory existed for Lumen, all the men would have to be strong, possessing a desire in their heart to fight off the Malum. A half-hearted army was worse in Baramatheus' eyes than no army at all. The officers all agreed and began discussing probable methods of getting all the groundsmen to passionately support the effort. Many pointed to what Michaelis did at the southern camp. They suggested he give a similar speech to the much larger assembly of fighters. Michaelis rejected the idea on the basis that the men would presume the message was nothing more than hollow rhetoric.

The young orator did have an idea, however, "If it seems reasonable, I suggest that we send for the leaders of each clan of groundsmen." Chatter silenced Michaelis.

The commanders and even the other Defenders did not like the slightest hint of others usurping their leadership.

Like slaves to tradition, they all shunned Michaelis' idea.

"Friends, please hear me out." The room eventually settled down. "If we ask the men from each village to raise up one of their own to lead them, side-by-side with us..." He made sure to play into the insecurity of his cohorts. "We include their leaders in the discussion and then they in turn will spread the word to their kinsmen of our plan. Let everyone own the reality of the coming conflict." The room erupted with discussion.

Ben was growing fonder of the youthful Defender every day. "It is a sound idea. I for one agree with the thinking of young Michaelis. The groundsmen will ultimately fight with us wholeheartedly or be the weak link that breaks the chain." The stable-boy-turned-Defender was wise beyond his years, an attribute which Ben appreciated very much.

After a few moments of debate, the group, still split on the idea, decided it was worth a try. Gidaen eased the pain of those who were not positive of the ramifications by reminding them that although the enemy had been spotted, they still had a day if not two before the time to bear their swords would be upon them.

Up until this point, Eliazar had been, for the most part, silent. It was not until he heard the lasting uneasiness in his colleagues' voices that he decided to speak up.

"Are you so insecure in your ability to lead, that you frown on a fresh idea which will embolden the men who bear the brunt of the sacrifice? Or is it that you are uncertain of your own ability to fight that you grumble for the sake of grumbling?"

The room silenced immediately as the crass soldier spoke his mind, the harsh words demanding the attention of all in the room.

"Do you doubt the courage of your countrymen? I am sickened by the weak-spirited men surrounding me today. Our ancestors would be just as disgusted if they were in our midst.

"I propose that if Michaelis' idea, which is worthy of an attempt, does not succeed, that we as stewards of the king's men should release any man uncertain of his desire to fight from his duty. That goes for both groundsmen and officers." Eliazar made direct eye contact with several of the Royal Commanders who had bemoaned the situation as he moved to the tent's entrance. "I can only speak for myself; I do not wish to entangle blades with the Malum next to any man who doubts his king or the integrity of the Lumen soul."

The tent flap dropped down behind Eliazar as he left. He had said his piece; he wanted nothing else to do with the squabbling of the Lumen leadership.

The word spread to all the groundsmen, and within several hours the elected leaders were reporting to the officer's tent. The village representatives stood proud as they entered the tent. When they all arrived, Michaelis and Baramatheus briefed them concerning the issue at hand. They took their time, conveying the importance of the spirit of the men.

Michaelis chose his words carefully and showed the men that the wellbeing of the land depended on this battle, that if they did not beat back the Malum, every last Lumenite would become a slave to the evil ones.

After the duo finished, they sent the villagers back to their men to inform them of what they had discussed. The two knights demanded a quick response as to the attitude of the men. It was obvious that they were worried. The soldiers received the information well, but there were some that had mixed feelings about the plan.

The men returned with what Michaelis thought was devastating news. Most of the men, nearly two-thirds of them, did not want to fight. Baramatheus graciously accepted the news and thanked the men for doing their duty to their king. After all the men reported the desire of their clans, the clamoring of words began to flow among the officers again.

In the middle of the exchange, Gidaen interrupted, "One thing is left for us to do. We need to address the groundsmen and give the option

Eliazar suggested; we need to let the wavering troops return to their families. Then we can focus on preparing the rest for the coming struggle." The warrior's eyes conveyed confidence. He could not control the heart of another man. All he could do was lead by firmly believing in the victory over the Malum.

All the royal leaders left the tent. They headed for their private quarters. The word went out that Michaelis was going to speak to the groundsmen, an announcement that caused much excitement among the troops. The ones who had heard him once before looked forward to hearing him again while the rest were intrigued by the awe generated in regard to this Defender who was once a villager. The men described him as "not of royal blood, but of royal spirit." His popularity was spreading. The mass of soldiers hurried to the meadow to listen to him speak.

Michaelis was disappointed that men wanted to abandon the cause. He could not understand why they did not realize the gravity of this battle. Trying to see the groundsmen's perspective, he recalled his first impression of his mentor: believing Baramatheus to be a coward during the Malum ambush. An inexperienced groundsman, he jumped to a conclusion before fully understanding the enemy and before he understood Baramatheus' point of view. This time was different though. He was aware of their foe and of what the vile army was capable. Michaelis certainly knew the groundsmen's outlook because he had lived it, and he knew what they thought of the current situation, and how they spoke about the war and about the men who were leading them into harm's way. He also knew what the people outside of the danger thought about the fighting. Pura had shed a very bright light on how those back home felt about the Malum and more specifically, about what it all meant for their loved ones charged with stopping the terror. With all the different views accounted for, he just could not fathom why any man would want to tuck tail and run home. Retreat was the last thing on his mind. He wanted to advance and he wanted to do it as soon as possible. Michaelis wanted every last Lumenite to be safe, and to him that meant driving the enemy as far back as humanly conceivable.

Nearly everyone was standing in the open meadow just outside the camp as Michaelis began to speak.

"Brave men of the Kingdom of Lumen, the time is at hand when the very existence of our country will be decided. I thank you all on behalf of King Josiah for your selfless service to the cause we have undergone to this day." As the words left his lips a tear dripped from his eye. He was about to give the groundsmen a way out, and he was fairly certain most of them would take it. "You all have been given the chance to express your opinions on the predicament we face. The Defenders and the commanders of all the brigades have come to the conclusion that only a willing army will have any chance at triumph against the barbaric force breathing down our neck." Michaelis swallowed to prevent his voice from cracking with despair as he continued. "So I am here to tell all of you who wish to head back to the safety of the Lumen wall, that you are free to do so." The collected mass began to stir. The combined volume of their whispers was louder than the shrill of a banshee. "No one among us will think any less of you for returning to your families. We all want to see our loved ones again." The conversations were hard for Michaelis to yell over. "So if you do not wish to face the Malum in the coming hours, go, for there will be no other chance to do so. Go with the support of your king."

The men were shocked. Never before had the king allowed such a thing. Michaelis just gave them the legal authority to desert their post. The whispering continued all night long as one by one, groundsmen began to leave. The number of men at the mouth of the valley waned with each passing hour.

The field officers tried their best to sleep, although none did. Morning came fast and when they awoke, they found the number of men that left utterly shocking. Gidaen sent out servants to take a count of the groundsmen. Upon their return, they reported that nearly 22,000 soldiers had decided to return home.

"The cursed valley is to blame for this!" Gareb observed.

"Now, now," Gidaen put in, "we all knew that if the choice was given, a great number would take it. There is no surprise in this."

"Gidaen, do you actually think we have a chance now, now that two-thirds of our men have left?"

Baramatheus interrupted with an answer to the question. "Yes, I do. The men who headed for home would not have done us any good anyway. We are just as strong as we were at this time yesterday. Nothing has changed."

"Sure, but now we have less bodies to sustain our defenses," Gareb said, the outcome of the radical decision weighing on his emotions.

"I think you mean we have fewer bodies to shield us from our own deaths." Baramatheus was past the point of pleasantries. He was disgusted that his friend and royal brother would doubt their chances of victory so quickly. "Personally, I am not in the practice of hiding behind my countrymen. Whether we have thirty thousand or three thousand, I plan on being on the frontlines with the men, leading the charge, not cowering in the back row hoping to live another day."

"Come on Bar, you know that is not what I meant." Gareb did not want his reputation tarnished by the implication of his sentiment.

"That is how it sounded to me," Eliazar chuckled as he stuffed a piece of bread in his mouth. "Look," he began with his mouth full, "it is as simple as this. The kiln is lit and right now we are passing through it. The men who left could not stand the heat; they crumbled before the temperature rose. We who are left will pass through the flame and our makeup will be shown for what it is." Eliazar shocked even himself as he reflected on what he said. "One thing is for certain: if we continue with this petty bickering and fret over the outcome, we will defeat ourselves before the chance to win has even arrived." Eliazar spoke a profound truth, and it hit home with all his comrades. He knocked back a mug full of lukewarm cider and then wiped off his beard. "Now buck up and let us show these merciless savages a thing or two about Lumen courage." Eliazar's inspiring moment was over and so he sat down next to the other officers, listening as the debate simmered down.

Chapter Twenty-Four

The Malum had been marching for days. Based on the pace at which they progressed through the valley, their enthusiasm and morale were very high. Just as Michaelis predicted, Bebbel-uk shifted the men stationed near Lumen's southern camp to fall in line with the soldiers who were marching through the valley. The size of the Malum force was nearly impossible to measure. Each individual warrior moved so sporadically that their numbers were unknown. Their formation, if they had any, was complete chaos.

The Lumen scouts estimated that there were at least 50,000 enemy soldiers in the valley. The unexpected change on the part of Lumen definitely caught the attention of Bebbel-uk, or perhaps the one he served. They saw it just the way Michaelis thought they would, as a chance for an end to the war, a chance to conquer the Lumen Kingdom at last.

News of the number of Malum spooked all the remaining groundsmen. Five to one was the ratio circulating amid the ranks. The terrifying reality was enough to frighten anyone and it worried all that were, up to this point, not concerned about the fight.

Baramatheus and Michaelis, along with Ben, Gidaen, and all the other Defenders prepared themselves by putting on their royal armor. It was a comfort to Michaelis as he slid the breastplate over his head and peered down at the behemoth posed so valiantly in the center of his chest. This would be Michaelis' first battle donning the lumenium armor that the king bestowed upon him at the ceremony at Oren's Haven.

Pura was sitting with Michaelis when Gidaen's horn blew. The two were talking about why Pura was not going to get to fight alongside Michaelis and the other soldiers. The boy was furious. He desperately wanted to help and he did not understand why he could not be on the front line, especially since the Lumen army was so outnumbered. That fact was precisely why Michaelis asked that his young friend stay back. If victory appeared to be in the hands of the Malum, Pura was to get word to the king. The boy hated the idea of sitting idly by as his friend marched off to die. He did enough of that when his father went to war. Michaelis convinced him, however, that the need would be great if indeed, the time came for a rider to head toward the kingdom gate. For if the army fell, the Malum would march straight on to the City of the Throne.

Baramatheus had put the Defender's armor on many times before. He was used to the somber aura which encased him right before war. A duality of emotion collided in the dawning moments preceding a battle. He hated and loved his vocation.

The horrifying things he did to the men he faced on the battlefield gnawed at his soul. The only thing easing the agony was the knowledge that his deeds were just. He did not ask these people to invade his home. He did not force them to draw their daggers or whip their ropes in his direction. The way he saw it, was that he was performing a duty, a duty that his king asked him to carry out. He was not brutally murdering the enemy. There was no hate or malice in his heart. He was quite simply a soldier working to protect the citizens of Lumen from harm. Baramatheus was very professional. He did not get caught up in the bigotry and prejudice like many of the other soldiers did. He was not swinging a sword of hatred, but rather of service, clearly understanding that the men on the other side of the field were very much like himself and his men. They had families and homes. They loved and they felt pain. He felt sorrow for the men he had faced in the past and he would feel the same for the Malum combatants today. Even in the midst of war, as he gripped his blade, this Lumen knight understood the need for compassion and mercy. This was how Baramatheus dealt with that which was placed in front of him and how he found peace with his actions.

The horn Gidaen signaled the troops to begin forming the battle lines. The men were prompt in their formation. All the soldiers grabbed their weapons and headed for their position.

The Malum army stopped directly in front of the camp and assembled into their own, more sporadic formation. The legion of foot soldiers were jumping around like animals, beating their chests and hollering an assortment of horrific sounds. The Lumen officers could not perceive any sort of organized assembly. Bebbel-uk's army was not accustomed to fighting in the daylight or in structured positions. They found it more efficient to use the cover of darkness and the chaotic, independent attack of the individual fighter. Lining up felt like waiting for defeat.

Michaelis and Baramatheus rode up in front of the groundsmen where they found Ben, Eliazar, Gareb, and the other Defenders and Royal Commanders all mounted up and ready. The atmosphere was uplifting. It stunned Michaelis. He expected to see worried faces, not ready and anxious expressions. Some of the men were even cracking little jokes as they waited for orders.

He had never lined up with fellow soldiers and so did not know what to expect. Any of the seasoned leaders could have told him that the day of the battle was a much different scene than the days leading up to it. It was the duty of those in charge to weigh out the options and to push for the course of action which they thought to be right. If they did not, then all the possibilities would not be fielded and a key factor of preparation might be overlooked.

The groundsmen formed by village. They stood as units among the lines, each village recognizable by its family weapon. Some of the clans used swords, some spears, a few even had bows. Not very many carried shields and only one village used the ax. In times of peace, these weapons were symbols of pride for the villagers. They were relative masters of the tool they chose to bear. None of them were as well-trained as the Royal Commanders or the King's Defenders, but with respect to each other, they were excellent with their specific weapon. Games were even played among villages to see which clan was best with its weapon. The tournaments were always very festive, not to mention extremely competitive.

As if on cue, the village units began to sing their family songs. Although the groundsmen from particular villages did not all belong to the same family, in times of war, they would sing a song representing their village's founding family. Just as the king was the head of the kingdom, each hamlet had a patriarch. On occasion, throughout history, there had been some schisms within villages over who was in charge. Generally, the end result was a split and the man who lost would move all of his kin out and into another village. In certain instances the men would team up with the thieves of the open country or the conjurers and try to inflict turmoil onto the village that had ousted him. These incidents were few and far between.

During previous wars, a Lumenite tradition developed. In the hours before battle, soldiers, nervous and restless, their veins flowing with anxiety about the inevitable event, would sit down by candlelight to write songs. These new verses were poetic lines of hope that would not only inspire the men on the field, but eventually the generations to come. It was a lost custom in recent days, primarily because the men had become so downtrodden; all they could think about was life before the war. Their bodies were drained of all inspiration as defeat seemed inevitable. But things were changing.

A young groundsman, just before dawn, quietly sat in a tattered tent. The orange flicker of a single candle danced on his round cheeks. Intensity spilled out onto the paper in the form of a beautifully simple song. This single soldier was a cross-section of the new spirit growing within all the groundsmen. They had fire in their blood; they were invigorated again. A transformation had occurred as these men were now the ones who wanted nothing more than to disrupt and destroy the Malum threat. These were the brave fighters who were intent on undoing Bebbel-uk's cruelest faculties. With a deep-seated passion in his heart, the lowly groundsman poured forth the words to sing on the field of battle as he and his compatriots swung their blades, weapons which would spill the life-enabling fluid of their foe.

As the time for battle emerged, the lyricist lined up next to his brothers in arms and began singing his words, his chest full and proud:

> "Brave and steadfast for our king,
> A groundsman's sword victorious,
> Defends against the Malum sting,
> To claim the day glorious.
>
> This cold barbaric force
> Has sworn to run its course.
> Without mercy, this evil power
> It readies for war this hour.
>
> Our numbers cannot match its might.
> The land lost and disappointed,
> If not for a Defender who came to fight,
> Whom the king himself anointed."

Hearing the melody, the men around him noticed that his tune was a song never before sung. One by one each villager stopped singing his old family songs and slowly shifted to this new one, absorbing and spreading its faith filled message. None had heard the words before, and yet the entire army was singing it within only a few short moments. The spirit and legacy of the Lumen groundsmen began to shine brighter than it had in many years. Cheers of confidence filled the valley. The men were ready to fight for their king.

"Do you hear that, my brave friend?" Baramatheus looked over at Michaelis warmly.

"Yes. What is that?" Michaelis was trying to decipher the words through the roar of voices.

"That is inspiration. That is a sign that I was right about you. I knew if given the chance, you could change the minds of our people. That, my brave friend, is their way of honoring the one that will lead us to victory. Love for the kingdom is back in their hearts, and you put it there." Baramatheus laughed as he spoke.

Michaelis was stunned. He did not think he was ready for such leadership. A sudden realization that not too long ago he was a simple stable boy flushed the color out of his skin.

"Do not worry; you will do fine," Baramatheus was chuckling through every word as he watched Michaelis' face turn white, the young man's eyes bulging with awareness.

"But just in case, if you think your stomach might reverse the natural order of consumption, do it over there." With a quick nod over his shoulder Eliazar grinned mockingly.

"Thanks for the advice," Michaelis said smiling.

All the Defenders lined up, ready for battle. They sat magnificently on top of their brilliant red-haired horses. The beasts were calm, basking in the sunlight as the crisp morning breeze whipped their manes through the air.

Michaelis straddled a plain warhorse, a humbling reminder of his inexperience.

The Malum began pounding their drums all the while jumping up and down and screaming. The sight was dreadful, accomplishing its goal of frightening the onlooking army. It was a form of mental warfare which the Malum executed with precision and fiendish delight.

Gidaen held his sword in his right hand and a horn in his left. He was nervous; it had been a long time since the aged warrior had seen the horror of battle. He took in a deep breath, filling up his lungs to their utmost capacity. And with the vigor and brilliance of a seasoned commander, he released the breath in a single burst through the horn and into the air in the form of a blaring blast that told the troops to charge forward. As the trumpet sound went out, the other officers blew their horns in response, signifying to the men that all were to advance.

This company of sounding horns was the Lumen army's own form of mental warfare, as the high and clear notes resonated through the air until they reached the ears of the enemy, alerting them of the imminent attack. Gidaen dropped the horn, letting it dangle from his neck. In the same motion he snatched up the reins of his horse and directed it toward the bloodthirsty army across the meadow. The Defenders, groundsmen, and all the commanders followed after him. The terror of war was upon them.

Chapter Twenty-Five

Michaelis was the first Lumen knight to meet the Malum army, metal-to-metal. As the flood of groundsmen rushed toward the enemy, the Malum charged, bizarrely bounding forward, each man's body flailing in unreserved chaos. The two armies met at the center of the field. The smallest fraction of time was all that separated the strike of Michaelis' blade from that of the rest of the soldiers. It was the first clash of what every Lumenite hoped would be the final battle.

Michaelis slashed in an upward motion from on top of his horse, his lumenium sword gleaming brightly in the sunlight as the Malum fighter extended his dagger, deflecting the smaller blade with ease. One would have thought that the momentum behind the Lumen blade would have sent the Malum soldier flying, but that was not the case. The Malum were so fluid in their motions that the warrior simply allowed his body to react to the overbearing power of Michaelis' swing. This first encounter forever engraved itself into Michaelis' soul, for it was almost his last. The Malum man bounced off the Defender's sword with an amazing resilience. A keen fighter, he utilized the action to gain the upper hand over his mounted opponent. While Michaelis' sword was still in the upward motion, the fanatical soldier propelled his body onto the back of Michaelis' horse and at the same time pulled the knight down onto the ground. A cloud of dust bellowed from under his body as a loud thud echoed throughout Michaelis' bones. Victorious in his maneuver, the gorilla-like warrior dismounted the horse with an exaggerated flail, landing on top of the Defender. The brutal assailant arched his back, his arms extended, a dagger in hand pointed down toward Michaelis. The Lumen warrior was about to be the Malum foot soldier's first kill in the theater of battle. Reacting quickly, the Defender threw a fatal punch, crushing the Malum man's throat. Instinctively the fighter grabbed his neck, his eyes bulging with shock as he gasped for breath. Michaelis pushed the man off of him and picked up his sword as he climbed to his feet.

Michaelis raised his sword in a show of compassion and ran the blade through the man's body, piercing the heart, thereby relieving the man of his struggle. The two fierce fighters met face-to-face as the hilt of the sword bumped up against the dying man's chest. The look on the Malum's face was one of gratitude. The spark of life vanished from his eyes quickly, causing Michaelis to shudder. Looking into the eyes of the man as he killed him forced the Lumen soldier to recall Baramatheus' view on human life. Horror filled his soul. The young Lumenite was paralyzed for a moment as the thought of what he had done clamored about his mind. Of course, this was not the first time he had taken the life of his enemy; however, the previous instance had not been so intimate. The situation before was nothing more than blind impulse. This time he was close enough to feel the man's last breath on his face.

The groundsmen seemed to be holding their own. They were invigorated and thirsty for victory. The first moments were assuredly one-sided. The Lumen army claimed many Malum lives. Their spears soared through the air and their swords gashed the flesh of their enemy. Their axes chopped through limbs like driftwood. The ease of the initial clash was unbelievable. The Lumen infantry fought like ferocious bears pinned in a corner. Their desire to survive was evident in every life-ending strike of their weapons.

In an effort to counter the tide, the Malum chiefs called out one of their cruelest and most unusual weapons, a division of men that specialized in falconry. They trained day in and day out, teaching their birds of prey, not to hunt as the traditional falconer would have, but to attack their enemy, the Lumen. The unit was comparable to the archers. They lined up behind the infantry, overlooking their fellow fighters as they charged forward to meet their destiny. These men were of the highest class within the military hierarchy of the Malum people. They had the knowledge and the patience to train their birds to deliver a distracting blow, so that the foot soldiers could gain the upper hand in the conflict. The falconers looked down at the battlefield, waiting until finally they received the command to release their birds. The winged weapons flew hard and fast before swooping down, landing on the Lumen soldiers, digging their talons into the men's skin, pecking at their faces, and removing chunks of flesh. The creatures were taught to aim for the eyes, to pluck the soldier's ability to fight right out of their skulls, to inflict the utmost agony upon their prey.

It was during this horrific moment that the brigade commanders sent in wave after wave of vicious troops. The Malum were barbaric in how they turned the tide of the battle. The owls, falcons, and hawks were extremely successful, catching the Lumenites completely off-guard. None of the Lumen fighters had ever seen such a tactic used. Bebbel-uk's falconers managed to stop the Lumenite charge, forcing the groundsmen to retreat, leaving their leaders extended and surrounded by Malum men. It was not a turn-and-run type of retreat, but rather more of an unknowing, subconscious move to safety. The overwhelming onslaught pushed the groundsmen back as they dodged the winged creatures, all the while defending themselves against deathblows of daggers and the slice of the Malum rope.

The King's Defenders and the commanders, along with very few groundsmen, stayed out in the center of the field fighting magnificently. Baramatheus and Eliazar had been close to each other when a wave of enemy warriors poured in around them. Neither of them paid much attention to how the enemy was controlling the flow of the fight. Before they knew it, they were standing side-by-side and all that they could see was the grotesque war-dress of dead body parts that the merciless Malum infantry battalions were wearing. The experienced men were holding their own. The Malum soldiers were no match for them at first and the birds were but pests, like gnats buzzing around their heads. As the evil foe stormed toward them, the two men sliced them down as if they were weeds in a garden. They even found time to critique the skill level of each opponent, in comparison to their own masterful abilities.

"To think we have been losing to these undisciplined..." Eliazar started the sentence leaving the thought open as the barrage of multiple attackers temporarily distracted him.

Baramatheus completed the sentiment: "...sloppy, ill devised attacks."

Baramatheus and Eliazar were standing back-to-back as the Malum slowly clamped down around them. The facial expressions of the two Lumenites would have led one to believe that they were enjoying themselves. Their movements complemented each other perfectly. When Baramatheus moved to his left, Eliazar defended his right. When Eliazar extended outward, Baramatheus protected his comrade's exposed stance. The two were working as if they were one. The fluidity of their fighting was nothing short of astonishing.

"Your protégé seems well-suited for his role." Eliazar remarked, attempting to change the subject of their battle distracted conversation to that of Michaelis.

"His heart is unwaveringly Lumen."

"It is apparent in his eyes that he truly believes the things he says." Eliazar dipped down, plunging his blade up and into the lower abdomen of a Malum man.

"He truly possesses the spirit of our people, and he will do great things within this land." Baramatheus leaped sideways, rolling over his partner's back, kicking his foot into the chest of an enemy combatant and driving him firmly into a group of fighters who were advancing upon the Lumen warriors' location. They continued their conversation over the clinks and clanks of lumenium striking the Malum ropes and daggers.

* * *

Pura sat on top of a horse, his saddlebags packed with enough food to get him back to the City of the Throne. He watched as the cloud of dust and feathers created by the nonstop movement of military might and the snap of flapping wings revealed a scene of death and injury. His feet barely reached the saddle's stirrups. The noble courser was a Defender's mount. Its size dwarfed the boy. The idea was that if he did indeed have to ride for Throne City, the king's men would welcome him when he arrived because they would recognize the animal. Michaelis was not too sure about the theory. He figured a boy riding by himself atop a royal horse through the raider-infested open range of Lumen would be an invitation for the unscrupulous types to get their hands on an animal of significant value. In short, Pura would be a target. Michaelis accepted the plan when he realized that without some way of validating his claim, no one would listen to an orphaned village boy wishing to speak to the king.

Pura was frightened as he watched what looked to him to be a failing Lumen army. Michaelis had instructed him to turn and ride for Throne City should he see the Malum overrunning the Lumenite position. After much hesitation, he accepted that what he was witnessing was the defeat of his countrymen, and so with tears rolling down his face, he rode in the direction Michaelis had told him. Pura came to the conclusion that he would never see his friend again. He cried as his horse raced forward. The child could barely see through the tears raining from his eyes, but it was no matter: the magnificent steed did not need guidance. The royal horse rode with great speed to a point where he could just barely hear the sounds of war before they stopped to look back at the depressing scene. Pura desperately hoped when he looked back the view would be different, a picture that would invite him to return and wait for his friend to tell him everything was all right.

* * *

All of the king's soldiers fought brilliantly. They combined the faith in their hearts with the skill they possessed, complimented by whatever weapon they wielded, to unleash the pinnacle of their capabilities. Even the groundsmen, pumped up by the inspiration Michaelis ignited within them, were able to fend off the Malum troops. It was these inexperienced villagers who bore the brunt of the Lumenite casualties. The spectacle the Malum put on with their wire ropes cut down all but a small amount of them.

Bebbel-uk's army discovered a very effective method of using their chosen weapon. Two men would take hold of the rope, one on each end, then after pulling it taut they would run into the sea of groundsmen, dismembering five or six at a time.

The result of these mass assaults was disheartening to the Lumen men. As they fought they could see their brothers-in-arms, while in mid-swing, topple over, unaware of how they had just been severed in half. This sight destroyed the remaining hope of all the Lumenites, annihilating their morale. The ultimate result of this fatal distraction favored the Malum army.

Chapter Twenty-Six

While the Lumenite army struggled against the Malum mass, Throne City prepared for a conflict of its own. King Josiah spotted the anticipated Malum party guiding their boats to the shores of the Tranquil Sea, their unpredictable movements blemishing the otherwise beautiful body of water. The king's soldiers manned their positions along the wall of the city, frightened and anxious. The Council, along with the king, had moved to the wall as well. They stood with their weapons in hand, facing the approaching enemy.

Of every city on Earth, there was none equal to the Lumen capital. Throne City, in all its splendor, was impenetrable. In the early days, before the establishment of the kingdom and yet after the line of the Lumen blood had been distinguished, many formidable foes attacked the city. None ever succeeded in their attempt. That was in the days of old, before the reign of Lumen extended to the open country, before the outer wall defined its boundary. The city was, to much of the world, a jewel to be plucked from a mine, a torch of hope burning so bright as to warrant no other response but to snuff the gleaming light. It became evident to the early generation of Lumenites that the city required fortification unlike any other.

Above all, the city's defenses included an extremely well trained unit of archers, prized for their skill. Their ability to send the sting of Lumen might beyond the security of the city's wall was unparalleled.

On this day they were perched among the ranks on the wall, ready to send their arrows into the Malum army which was edging its way toward them. Not only were Throne City's soldiers highly trained, they were also thoroughly educated in the art of defensive warfare. They had several scenario-specific contingency plans in place, in addition to their current strategy. The city was well-armed and built to withstand a wide variety of assaults. Of course, the primary focus of all the established plans was to keep the enemy outside the perimeter of the city. The centrality of this aspect was so important that it might as well have been doctrine.

The wall was specifically designed to thwart any effort to breach it.

During the construction of the city, the founders thought well enough in advance to prepare for any and all kinds of attacks. It was assembled as two separate walls, one in front of the other: the inner as the actual load-bearing structure, and the outside layer, a façade, made from a unique substance created by the Martinians called Monk's Hell. The idea behind this dual structure was to allow the outer section to burn, so that if an invading force ever tried to lay siege to the city, it could be ignited, creating an effective barrier. Monk's Hell burned extremely hot, and lasted a very long time. It was such an efficient fuel source that the flames remained confined to the wall's surface, posing no threat to the city or even the troops standing on top of it.

The Malum quickly moved up to the city's wall. Upon King Josiah's order the wall was ignited and the Lumen archers began raining down arrows, dropping the enemies at the feet of their evil brethren. Their aim was true: the arrows streamed straight toward the intended target, penetrating flesh with precision and power.

The original plan was for the Malum soldiers to be one aspect of an orchestrated attack from multiple sides. The regiments which had worked their way through the camps posted in the south and east were supposed to be aiding the breech. Bebbel-uk altered the plan when the Malum chiefs reported the Lumen soldiers rerouting to Devastation Valley. He redirected his men to meet the gathered Lumen front, which they were combating at this very moment. There was no way to inform the seafaring Malum of the change and so they were left to confront the Lumen forces alone.

The Malum fighters knew their duty and they knew that it included dying if need be. They fought tirelessly in their apparent suicide mission, until all met their death. The city guards fought with complete effectiveness, suffering neither a single death nor injury.

Celebrations on the streets of the City of the Throne were exuberant as joyous parties and marvelous feasts filled the rest of the night. King Josiah posted lookouts to the east for word from Gidaen. He then waited nervously to find out what the future held for his kingdom while the Council briefed him on possible defensive measures, should the rest of the Malum army make it to the city.

Chapter Twenty-Seven

Pura turned in the saddle, longing to see a comforting sight.

He hoped to find a reason to turn around, that perhaps the Lumenites were winning the battle. As he turned, straining his eyes to look into the distance, a falcon that had been following him away from the battlefield swooped down. The bird's talon cut through the boy's scalp, knocking Pura off the horse and onto the ground, warm blood dripping from his forehead.

The bird of prey, for the moment, was at a safe distance as it was gliding back around in order to return for another shot at the child. As Pura scurried to his feet, he caught a glimpse of the massive bird, its wings spread wide open, casting an enormous shadow that engulfed the boy as the animal dove toward him.

Pura dropped to his back again in an effort to escape the falcon's claws. Screams, both Pura's and the creature's, pierced the air the entire time the bird was ripping at his prey. The boy crawled away, all the while trying to protect his face with his hands.

The deadly bird was winning the fight, as Pura focused on trying to get away from the falcon's wrath. He inched his way across the dirt. As he jerked his body away from his feathered assailant the ground under him gave way, pulling the child downward amid the chunks of earth. Losing track of its target, the bird of prey abandoned the assault and flew off.

The impact was hard. Pura landed on his back, pain shot up from his tailbone and elbows. Dust filled the air as he slowly stood up. Frightened, he noticed that the only light coming into the cavern he was now in was from the hole he had just fallen through. After a few moments the dust settled, allowing him to see the expanse of the room.

"Hello!" His voice echoed.

How was he going to get out of the cave? The question consumed his mind. He looked back up to the sunlight as the thought of what Michaelis had told him to do rushed into his head. Pura had to get back to the surface. The Kingdom of Lumen was depending on him. He needed to warn King Josiah. The young boy leaped up, grabbing at the walls of the cave. Desperately he grasped at every possible handhold he could find. Several times the boy managed to get nearly halfway out, only to lose his grip and fall back to the cave floor.

Disheartened, he stopped to listen. He thought he heard the sounds of the battle in the distance but it was impossible to tell for sure. The urgency of climbing out of the cave continued to press on his heart. He was the kingdom's last hope. If he did not get to the king before the Malum, they would certainly conquer the land.

Pura clawed at the cave wall. It was no good: he could not gain any ground. With a sudden scream of frustration he dropped to his knees in defeat, horrible visions of what was going to become of all the Lumen people flowing through his mind as tears escaped his eyes, hitting the dirt floor.

Sobbing uncontrollably, the boy began blaming himself. Like his friend, he put the nation's burden squarely onto his own shoulders. He hated the fact that he allowed himself to get trapped in the Earth's bowels. His head hung so low that his chin rested on his chest. Whimpers reverberated off the cave walls.

It was between sobs that he heard a sound behind him. Rocks and dirt shifted, crumbling under a man's feet. Pura lifted his head. In front of him was only the triumphant wall of the cave, the light not bright enough to make out anything more. When the approaching man saw the child's head rise, he spoke.

"You are lost, I presume." The voice was old and calm.

Pura stood on his feet. His heart raced as he turned toward the sound, hoping that whoever it was would be gone by the time he looked in that direction.

"No sir, I am not." The boy looked up at the old man who was now plainly visible.

The man's clothes were strange. He was not Lumen, yet he was obviously not Malum either. Confusion began to fill Pura's mind. His dress was very basic in appearance, not like the detailed apparel of the royal Lumenites. Even the farmers had nicer clothes than the man before him.

"So…you mean to be here in this cave?" The elderly man looked down at Pura inquisitively.

"Um, no. But I know where it is that I am; at least I know where I will be when I get up there." Pura pointed toward the opening in the cave.

The old man followed his finger to the gaping hole in his roof. "Well, that's no good," he said as he gazed at the boy disappointedly.

"Sorry, I was being attacked by a nasty bird. It was by accident that I fell in here."

"Don't worry about it, son. I needed something to do anyway. I'll figure out a way to repair the hole." The cave-dweller looked at the child's face, trails from tears, amplified by dirt, running down his cheeks. "May I ask why you were crying?" The man sat down on a rock.

"I need to get to the City of the Throne to warn the king. And now I cannot because I am stuck in here." Pura looked at the man, noticing the skeletal-like shape of his bony fingers as his hand began fiddling with the hair of his beard.

The elderly man disregarded the fact that the boy had been trying to complete an important task only moments ago. "Can you tell me about this City of the Throne?"

"The city? I have never been there myself, but Michaelis says it is magnificent. Full of all sorts of wonderful things." A smile spread across the face of the youngster.

"How come you have never been there?" Curiosity fueled the man's questions. It had been a long time since he had talked with anyone.

Pura answered the inquiry politely, which enticed the aged man to ask another and then another. Pura told him about the land and the struggle to fight off the detestable Malum. He told him about Michaelis and the other Defenders. Pura answered every question patiently, all the while in the back of his mind aching to get back to his horse and ride for Throne City.

"Sir, I do not mean to be rude, but if you could show me a way out of this cave, so that I can get word to my king about the coming attack, I would greatly appreciate it." Pura's voice was weak and timid as he pleaded for the man's assistance.

"Of course, my apologies. I forgot you were in a hurry. It's just been so long since I talked to someone." The man stood up and headed away from the opening in the roof. His movement gave no indication of his advanced years.

Hesitant to leave the safety of the light, the boy stayed where he was. He was frightened. On second thought, perhaps he should not have asked for the guidance. Pura had reservations when it came to the bizarre elderly man, not knowing exactly what was out of place about him other than his clothes, and the fact that he lived in a cave in the wilderness. There was more, but the young child could not quite figure it out. Pura had not spoken to too many people outside of his village, only Michaelis and a few Lumen soldiers, but he could tell that the old man's speech was peculiar. The dialect was unusual, not so much that he could not be understood, but enough to make it a little difficult.

Another oddity was that the man was so old, yet knew nothing of the world he lived in. At first Pura figured the man just did not know about the Lumen Kingdom, since he did not live in the land and was obviously not a Lumenite. But it was more than that. The aged cave-dweller asked about things that had to do with the Malum and the rest of the world. It was strange that he would not know of any of these things.

Pura wondered if he might be some sort of Malum spy. Could it be that he was trying to sneak up on the Lumen troops? Nothing particularly pointed to this conclusion, but the youngster did not put it past the tactically unorthodox minds of the Malum.

Realizing he was walking alone, the elderly man turned back toward Pura. "I thought you wanted to get back up top? Are you going to stand there or are you going to follow me out?" It dawned on the man as he asked the question that the child was probably scared of him, given the situation and that he was moving into the darkness. "Oh. It's okay; I'm a friend." It was quite noticeable that the boy was uneasy and remembering that children were not supposed to trust strangers, the man tried to reassure the boy. "I guess I've forgotten my manners over the years. I didn't even introduce myself." The old man looked ashamed as he bent down to Pura's level. Extending his hand he said, "My name is Adam."

The boy reached upward. "Pura." The two shook hands and then Adam began leading the child out of the cave.

As they walked down what must have been a hallway, even though it was much too dark for Pura to tell, the boy noticed a bright room ahead of them. Adam went in first, followed by an awestruck Pura. The room was full of all kinds of things, most of which were very strange. Some of the items in the room, however, looked familiar in basic form, yet not like anything he had ever seen before.

"Is that a throne?" The boy looked intrigued as he stared at the most unusual seat he had ever seen.

"Just a chair." Adam realized that Pura's curiosity was piqued by the weird appearance of the unusual amenities in his isolated home.

"Where did you get all of these unique things?"

"Honestly? From my mind."

"You are a conjurer?" Pura asked, a sudden terror shooting through his body.

"No. I don't think so. What is a conjurer?" A genuine sense of naïveté was fully evident in Adam's face.

Pura was now standing as far away from Adam as he possibly could. "They are banished folks who use wicked ways to get the things they want." The boy's explanation was surprisingly accurate, although lacking in the finer details.

"Well, I suppose maybe I might have been. Although I suspect I didn't know it at the time," Adam admitted.

The description of a conjurer fit Adam Malloy perfectly. He had used his gift to get his every wish, and he had indeed banished himself to a long life of solitude. Although his intent had never been evil, the definition seemed to fit his actions well.

Anxiety paralyzed the child. Every muscle in his body froze solid as he stared fearfully in Adam's direction.

After a few moments of silence in the room, the old man spoke. "Do not fear, Pura. I gave up those ways a long time ago. I no longer use any kind of power except that which is quite normal. Besides I have never met any of these people you speak of, so I couldn't possibly be of the same ilk." Adam could tell that Pura was purposefully keeping a good distance between them. "You see, Pura, years ago I was given a gift, a gift that I abused." Silence filled the cavern. Adam had never confessed his actions before. Vocalizing the truth stirred his soul. He slowly lowered himself into the chair as he spoke. "I wasn't able to control my lustful desire to gain power and wealth, and eventually, I ruined every life around me."

Listening intently to every word, Pura surrendered to the childish curiosity within. The boy began wandering throughout the room looking at all the strange items.

Adam's face was blank, a sad emptiness glazed over his eyes. Memories of his family flowed through his heart. The life before he awoke with his gift stung. The mental picture of his life in Lakeview was as fresh now as it had been when he was still living in New York City.

Amazed at the weird items in the room, Pura walked around, taking in the sights. The cave was very simple. It was like any other cavern he might have found himself in, consisting of a stone roof, walls, and floor. There were shelves carved out of the rock walls where the Lumen boy found the stunning objects. Pura was dumbfounded as he gazed at a very small painting of several people that were dressed similar to his host. The woman was the most lavishly adorned. What he thought so peculiar was that the representation of the people was extremely lifelike. It was true that the boy was not very well-educated, but that did not matter. The image Pura was holding in his hand would shock even the greatest Lumenite artist.

"Did you use your wicked powers to trap these people?"

The innocent question took Adam by surprise. The child had been behind the chair in which Adam was sitting. At first the old man had no clue as to what Pura was referring to, but then he looked over his shoulder and began to laugh.

"No, Pura. In fact, I'm in that picture." Laughter rang out as Adam imagined what the boy must be thinking.

Pura examined the image more closely, quickly glancing back at Adam. "That cannot be. You are sitting right here."

"I am the young boy standing in front of the woman. She is my mother," Adam responded, amused at the boy's confusion.

Not understanding, Pura put the picture back onto the shelf. "Sir, I have never seen such things as you have.

Where are you from?"

Adam thought about his life and the events that transpired up to this point, and then began dictating each matter of importance to the boy. Pura lost the sense of urgency that was driving him to get to the king. Instead, he was now listening to how the world he knew came to be, intrigued by the narrative his new acquaintance was telling him. Pura had no idea if the story was true. He was not educated enough to know that Adam just answered most, if not all of the land's mysteries, mysteries that had baffled theologians and scholars for centuries. It was almost a pity that Pura had been the one to stumble upon this stranger, for if a man of higher learning had been talking to Adam, he most certainly would have asked better questions.

Adam summed up the superstitions surrounding Devastation Valley, for it was the spot where New York City once stood, the place where Adam unleashed the disastrous weather that butchered nearly every living creature on Earth.

After the story, a single question popped into Pura's mind. "How is it that you are still alive?"

The boy's imagination latched onto the fantastic account with ease, as he had no reason to doubt the aged man.

"I bound myself to the existence of the world. As long as the Earth continues on, I will live." Adam stated this fact with sadness in his eyes.

He recalled conceiving the thought that cursed him to a temporally everlasting life; he remembered it as if it were yesterday. A smirk spread across his face, with the memory of how he, in his inattention to detail, double-crossed his wishful desire. Adam failed to think about staying young forever. And so now here he was, aging as the years went by, aging, but not fading. His strength remained, his mind remained, but his physical appearance progressed through the natural course, albeit considerably slower. It was an ironic turn of fate that he had doomed himself to grow old and yet never die. Adam considered it his punishment.

Confining himself to his earthen prison, Adam refused to ever use his gift again. The outcome of the abuse of his talent clouded his reasoning. And though deep down, he knew it was his defective application of the gift that brought about so much destruction, the Lakeview native hardened his heart and refused to "think" again.

After centuries went by, in a moment of weakness, Adam had attempted to bring about a small change. To his surprise, nothing happened. He went through several experiments, each time coming up empty-handed. With nothing but time on his hands, he laid out a multitude of possible explanations as to why his ability was gone. Adam did not understand why or how. It could have been that the time for such an ability was over. Or that his neglect of the great power caused it to expire. Of all the hypotheticals, there was one that seemed the most logical. Simply put, the gift was taken away by the one who had given it to him. He did not have the slightest clue. All he knew was that it was gone.

Chapter Twenty-Eight

The battle between the Lumenites and the Malum raged on as Pura talked with Adam about the past. Michaelis, along with every other Lumen soldier, fought courageously. The level of gallantry among the warriors was phenomenal. Each and every man feverishly engaged the enemy, their minds overriding the fatigue in their muscles. The fact that the Malum fighters increasingly outnumbered them amplified the heroic air of their effort.

All that remained of the Lumen military force was a mere three hundred troops comprised mainly of commanders and Defenders. Only a handful of groundsmen survived the initial clash. The massive Malum machine had thus far won the war, relying heavily on attrition.

Michaelis was fighting side-by-side with Gidaen, both struggling to stay alive. The elderly veteran and the youthful novice were doing all they could to remain on their feet. Michaelis watched in awe as the aged Defender sliced through wave after wave of enemy combatants.

Baramatheus and Eliazar were still adding to their running tally of individual victories, but their energy was beginning to fade. Ben, Gareb, and the other officers were barely holding their own. However, the remaining groundsmen were showing no acceptance of failure. Of all the men still breathing, these were the soldiers bound and determined to come away from the battle as victors. They were not succumbing to the insurmountable weight crushing down upon them, refusing to give in to their opponents. What fueled their combat-battered bodies was the intense power of their faith in the king and the one he sent to lead the way to victory. This small remaining group of ordinary farmers, carpenters, mill workers, and innkeepers slammed through the Malum wall with pure adrenaline pumping through their veins. Every muscle was strained to the breaking point as they struggled to keep fighting, displaying a prowess that even the Malum had to respect.

Bebbel-uk's army most certainly perceived these fighters as well-trained professionals, a deduction solely based on their fierce presence. Spit flung from the groundsmen's lips as their teeth gnashed, their bodies nearly exceeding their physical limits. Blood poured out of the open wounds that covered their flesh. The agony only added to their drive to accomplish the task laid before them. Focused, nothing stood in their way. It was as if their eyes had been engulfed in fire and the only way to extinguish the flame was to lock their gaze onto their next foe.

But all this was for naught. The Malum army outnumbered the Lumenites. Bebbel-uk's men kept coming.

"Gidaen, we must do something." Michaelis was exhausted, his blade heavy in his hand.

"My young friend, I am afraid it is all but over now." The sound of defeat rang out in Gidaen's voice and his efforts were wavering as the Malum kept coming.

"No. I am still on my feet, as are you. We must push on until death, or triumph!" The passion in Michaelis' voice echoed in Gidaen's heart.

"I fear death is more likely at this point," said Gidaen. "It is only a matter of time before the last of us falls. The sun is low. If the Malum do not claim victory before nightfall they will certainly use the cover of darkness to hasten it along before dawn."

"We can still fight, even in the darkness. The Malum will not overcome us." As the words left his lips and as his lumenium sword met yet another Malum weapon, Michaelis was reminded of Oren the Ablaze, not the artwork he saw upon the walls of Oren's Haven, but the legend the Martinians had taught him when he was training in the monastery. "Gidaen, do you recall Oren's legend?"

"Of course."

"It was his wit and his weapons that saved his life." Gidaen thrust his sword into an attacker's stomach. "Indeed. Had he not had Chakkah he would not have been able to get close enough to the livyatan to strike its eye."

"Exactly! The light reflecting off his lumenium blade blinded the beast, enabling Oren to make the condition permanent with the tip of Chakkah." Michaelis paused long enough to throw a punch. "But even before that, Oren used Monk's Hell to stay alive, right?"

"Ah, right you are." Gidaen recalled the whole of Oren's encounter with the livyatan. "He and his companion, the scribe who recorded the event, managed to survive as long as they did by tossing lit canisters of Monk's Hell at the devilish dragon."

"And how much of it do you suppose we have throughout the camp?" Michaelis asked.

"An abundance. Each Lumen camp is supplied with enough to support the needs of the men: campfires, torches, even the candles are made out of it. When you and Baramatheus brought the five camps together you brought together five times the supply."

Gidaen made eye contact with Michaelis for but a brief moment before the younger Defender said, "Call the men."

Gidaen placed the horn hanging from his neck into his mouth, all the while deflecting attacks. He exhaled into the Lumen horn in a pattern that signaled the men to converge on his location.

Due to the chaotic warfare of the Malum, the Lumen soldiers were isolated from one another. They were fighting in pockets of two or three, each group completely cut off from the other. The blast of the horn rose above the shrill cries of death letting them know they were not alone, that others were still alive and fighting.

Upon hearing the sound, three hundred men erupted with the might of thirty thousand. Malum after Malum dropped at the feet of the mighty Lumen knights. The small but powerful group of groundsmen sprang forth with even more luster, ax, spear, and sword in hand, barreling through the mass of Malum as if they were running through a wheat field in order to find their way to the source of the signal.

* * *

When the horn sounded, Baramatheus and Eliazar were fighting the many Malum soldiers that surrounded them. The falcons dove from above while the rope masters moved in from all sides. As the two men fought to reach Gidaen, they became isolated from one another.

Baramatheus lunged toward the enemy with the same spirit he had shown throughout the entire battle, unaware that he had been cut off from Eliazar. His armor shone in the sea of hides worn by the Malum around him. He was severely outnumbered. As the knight buried his blade into the heart of a Malum warrior, a sharp pain raced across his ankles. Instantly he dropped to his knees. The fighting near him stopped. The horde of Malum soldiers separated as one of their chiefs, standing like a mountain among foothills, stepped forward, his metal rope dangling from his hand. Obviously one of Bebbel-uk's captains, the man stood with better posture and dignity than the rest of the fighters. The deep slash across the back of Baramatheus' ankles left him motionless. There was no chance of escape, and worse, there was no way to fight. His injury left him stranded on his knees at the mercy of the Malum chief approaching him.

The warrior was smiling ear-to-ear, apparently recognizing Baramatheus' rank. Before the Malum leader reached the knight, he stopped and made a mocking motion with his hands, his fingers popping into the air with bursts of energy as if to describe the wide-eyed expression on Baramatheus' face. The contempt for the defenseless soldier caused the men nearby to erupt into laughter. Standing several feet in front of Baramatheus, the man looked straight into the Lumenite's eyes and said something in his native tongue, causing the company of Malum combatants to begin jumping and yelling with excitement.

Baramatheus knew that he was being made a spectacle. He could imagine that the soldier was using him as a means of inspiration, an example, describing what happened to those who tried to stop the will of Bebbel-uk and she whom the Malum king served.

The chief's face bore many more scars than his underlings'. On his brow was what Baramatheus perceived to be a sunrise, a design consisting of a half-circle which began above one eye, extending over to the other. On top of the curved line was a series of slash marks which ascended up the man's forehead. The symbol appeared incomplete: there was room for several more lines on one side of the curved line while the other side was full, leaving the depiction asymmetrical. The Malum fighter reared his arm back, his glistening rope lying in preparation to end the life of the prized Defender.

The Lumen knight mustered his strength, extended his lumenium sword, pointing it toward the sky, and shouted, "For the king of Lumen!" His words rang out passionately, his face showing fearless readiness and his eyes revealing the courage that dwelled in his heart.

The Malum chief swung his razor-sharp rope forward in a downward motion, the flexible wire wrapping around the Lumen knight's wrists several times before the chief snapped the line tight, quickly slicing off Baramatheus' hands, causing the lumenium blade along with his severed appendages to fall to the ground. Screaming in pain, the courageous warrior retracted his arms in response to the dismemberment. His teeth gritted together, spit flying from between them with each intense breath. He stared at his sword lying flat on the boot-trampled earth, his right hand still grasping the weapon's handle.

The Malum war-chief picked up the Defender's blade, peeling off the lifeless flesh, finger by finger. He then began playing with the iconic tool for a moment, tossing it back and forth between his hands in an effort to illustrate to Baramatheus exactly what he could no longer do. Malum fighters were not accustomed to the use of swords, a fact made evident by the chief's clumsy handling of the weapon.

Inspecting it, he eyed the engravings on the hilt of the beautiful instrument. The sadistic soldier took a step back, the sword firmly grasped, the bloody rope hanging from his belt. The mass of Malum fighters surrounding Baramatheus cackled and screamed in adoration of their leader. The intensity of what was to come drowned out the noise as the two veteran soldiers stared intently upon one another. The Malum man lifted up the lumenium blade and pointed it at Baramatheus. The end had arrived for the brave knight. He looked fixedly into his enemy's eyes, almost challenging the man to do his worst.

"Live by the sword, die by the sword." His voice was unwavering. Baramatheus was at peace.

He had served his king and believed in Josiah and Michaelis and that the spirit of the two men would drive back Bebbel-uk. He knew in his heart that the kingdom would withstand the threat.

The Malum chief began the motion that would end the Defender's life. To Baramatheus, every second seemed like hours. It felt as if an eternity passed before the blade reached him. The gleaming lumenium edge cut through the brisk air until the metal met the warm flesh of the soldier's neck.

Baramatheus executed his service to the king with honor, dignity, and valor. His actions glorified the kingdom he loved. Throughout the years the knight had had the opportunity to do much in the name of his king, the greatest task being the role he played in Michaelis' anointing. Baramatheus would forever live on in the thoughts of the Lumen soldiers who shed blood with him on this day, as well as in the hearts of all the people of the land. Without a doubt the man lived a life which shone as a beacon to a generation of hope-deprived Lumenites.

* * *

While the remaining Lumenites made their way to Gidaen and Michaelis, the strategist and his young counterpart worked out the details of the latter's plan.

"Sound the retreat on my signal."

"Retreat?"

Michaelis smiled. "Will they follow?"

"No."

"Then we will have time for our assault."

Michaelis recalled his first and only battle as a groundsman, the night he met Baramatheus and, against his counsel, charged the Malum who had attacked his camp. "The Malum own the night. They are accustomed to fighting under the cover of darkness. They are, however, not use to us fighting at night. In the darkness they attack, but lest they lose the element of surprise they do not chase, right?"

"True."

"Then, as soon as the sun sets we flee into the darkness, each of us in a different direction."

Gidaen was shocked to hear Michaelis say such a thing.

"Flee?"

"Yes. With any hope the Malum will hold their position giving us the opportunity to prepare our final assault."

"Which will involve our supply of Monk's Hell?"

"Exactly. Monk's Hell and the luminescence of the Defenders' lumenium armaments." Michaelis paused to think through his plan. "Certainly the Malum will perceive our scattering as a retreat, considering their numbers, momentum, and the setting of the sun. Instead of retreating we will gather as much Monk's Hell and lumenium as we can. If we divide up the lumenium, a group of men can stage it along the east and west, up above the valley…"

"To give the impression of reinforcements approaching on the flanks—as if a double envelopment," declared Gidaen with enthusiasm.

"Yes. And not just any reinforcements, but Defenders."

"Superb! A few torches placed by the lumenium and it will all light up like the stars. You have the mind of a strategist, young man."

Michaelis grinned and then relayed the conclusion to his plan.

* * *

When the glow of the sun receded the Lumen warriors dispersed, each man running as if to save his life. The Malum force was infused with a sense of victory, standing their ground and scavenging through the dead Lumenites at their feet.

Michaelis and Gidaen relayed the plan to the men, each leading a group, one to the east and one to the west, to stage the ruse. The conditions could not have been better: the darkness, the angle of the enemy's perception, the torches and amount of lumenium, even a false sense of confidence on the part of the Malum. As soon as Bebbel-uk observed the gleaming lumenium he commanded what remained of his army to attack. This sent his men in two opposite directions.

"Here they come!" yelled a groundsman.

"Good. Now quick, back to the valley floor." Gidaen guided his men around the oncoming enemy and through the dark.

While some of the men had followed Michaelis, and others Gidaen, a third detachment remained hidden as near as possible to the battlefield without being seen. Once the Malum took the bait and left the area they began positioning the bulk of the Monk's Hell so as to create a barrier between the divided Malum men. As the Malum fighters reached the outside edges of the valley, the reunited Lumen force ignited the wall and then all together, charged east. With complete control of the battlefield they focused on annihilating one half of the remaining Malum army, fighting their way back up to the eastern rim of Devastation Valley.

The unexpected Lumenite movements dizzied Bebbel-uk. He sent his western force east, but the firewall slowed their advance. By the time they maneuvered around the flaming obstacle, Michaelis and the Lumenites had defeated the eastern Malum and were prepared to meet the last of their enemy who now found themselves caught between the Monk's Hell and a fierce Lumen front.

Eventually the enemy was no more than a memory. Nearly all the Malum lay slain. Only a few escaped, running as fast as possible toward Acerbus. No one pursued them, if for no other reason than that they were exhausted; they had pushed their bodies to the very brink. After they had time to rest, the Lumenites would organize a strategy to go and root out the remnants of their former oppressors. For now they reveled in the knowledge that the Lumen land was safe. Gidaen sent out a group of men to comb the battlefield for survivors. They would give aid to anyone they found, regardless of allegiance. At this point, which side of the battle one had served on did not matter.

During the course of the battle, Bebbel-uk's warriors had managed to push the Lumenites into their camp. Ironically, the Lumenites died at the very spring which had, only hours before, provided them with the ability to establish their position in anticipation of the Malum. Now, having fought valiantly the men lay limp in the flowing streams coming from the spring. The life-giving water swirled around their bodies, gently absorbing their blood, embracing their death, as it trickled past.

"Has anyone seen Bar?" Michaelis asked as he meandered among the men.

The answer was a cold "no." Every man was tired and needed time to replay the struggles of the day in his mind. Michaelis searched all over the field for his mentor, anxiety escalating as time passed without any trace of his dear friend. Panic doused his face until he found Baramatheus' body lying among a mound of Malum men.

"No! Not you, not you. Please no!" Michaelis rushed to the lifeless body. Tears dripped from his eyes as his voice cracked in despair.

"He died righteously, Michaelis." Eliazar was sitting on a rock next to Baramatheus when the young Defender spotted his teacher's disfigured form.

"Of everyone, he should have survived this fight." Tears rolled down Michaelis' cheeks while his fisted hand rested on his friend's breastplate.

"We all go at our own time. It is not for us to decide. All we can do is fight the best we know how. But when the day comes, there is no stopping it." No one ever expected it, but Eliazar had a very firm grasp on the deep philosophical realities of life. The commander rose to his feet, as if in respect for the deceased.

"Maybe so, but this man was the best. He deserved better than to die at the hands of this wretched evil." A very youthful anger echoed from Michaelis' lips.

"You suggest that Baramatheus somehow earned a better exit than any of these other men. My friend, that is not how it works. Bar knew the risks of the life he chose. We all live out our days in this world and when it is over, it is over. Most of the time there is no glorious ending. It is brutal. It is sad. And usually, it is quickly forgotten." Rubbing his beard, Eliazar cleared his throat. "None of us deserve anything, son. Remember that." A brief pause caught Michaelis' attention and he looked up at the weathered veteran standing above him. "We do the things we do because we believe, not for any other reason."

Michaelis turned his head back toward Baramatheus' body. The words Eliazar spoke were true, and he knew it.

"Now come. Seeing all the poultry flying about today has made me hungry. I have been waiting all day to eat." The attempt to save face was transparent. "I will be a laughing-stock if people find out I survived the battle only to die of an empty stomach." Eliazar reached down toward Michaelis, helping him to his feet. The two soldiers gathered the Defender's armor and said a quick prayer. They then turned and walked back to the center of camp.

Michaelis had another friend whose whereabouts were unknown. Pura was nowhere to be found. The Defender came to the conclusion that the boy had seen the Malum overtaking the Lumen troops and rode for the city. Since Gidaen was heading for the City of the Throne to deliver the news of the victory to King Josiah, Michaelis asked that he keep an eye out for the child, emphasizing the fact that he would be easy prey to any raiders who might spot him.

The post-battle chores were tedious and not for the faint of heart. Over the next few days the men gathered the bodies of their fallen comrades. It was a Lumen custom to never leave a soldier on the battlefield. They would bring them back to their homes and bury them properly, in the tradition of their village or, if they were royalty, in the fashion reserved for the nobles. Everyone pitched in to separate the bodies into groups which were determined by the direction they would be taken. Michaelis stopped and watched. Disturbed, he noticed how even though things had changed on the battlefield, they were reverting back to the old ways now that the threat was over. Groundsmen had become equal to Defenders as everyone fought for the same cause, but now that the fighting was over they were all going back to how things were before. The idea of certain men receiving a more prestigious burial than others, solely based on their status in life, infuriated him.

"Stop! What are you doing? Those men died for the same cause as these men," Michaelis yelled, getting the attention of the men working. "Hear me now! All these men will be given a royal funeral in the City of the Throne. They will be buried alongside Baramatheus and their families will receive the same gratitude for their sacrifice as that of the King's Defenders. Do you not see that we are all a part of this kingdom? We all breathe and bleed in the same fashion! All these soldiers, despite rank, died, allowing us to return to our land and live a peace-filled life. They all will be taken to Throne City; put them all together." Michaelis half-expected Gareb or one of the other royal men to step forward and dispute his statement, but no one did. All were in agreement.

Ben approached the young Defender without saying a word. It had been a long day with a heavy price. Many brothers, fathers, friends, and companions paid the price for freedom. In a gesture reminiscent of Michaelis' fallen mentor, Ben placed his hand upon the village knight's shoulder. Michaelis was right. It was not only the Malum who were defeated. The distinction of class was also overcome. The battle of Devastation Valley proved to be a dual victory: freedom from darkness and equal status for all the children of Lumen.

Chapter Twenty-Nine

Adam answered all of Pura's questions, and the boy answered to the best of his knowledge, all the questions Adam asked of him. A great deal of time had passed from the day Adam thought up the terrible destruction of the world to the present. Imagination proved to be a valuable tool for Pura as he concentrated on the events leading up to the current point in time. Most certainly his childlike ability to believe and make-believe aided his picturing of Adam's narration of the past.

After Adam unleashed death on the planet, depression took over his mind as he wrestled with what he had done. In the blink of an eye, the youthful small-town boy had managed to annihilate nearly all of the Earth's population, including his very own family back in Lakeview. In the days following the cataclysm, survivors built makeshift shelters. They lived in constant fear, unaware of whether or not there would be a second wave of unexpected attacks sent forth. Some gathered, while others wandered. Everyone searched for hope, for meaning. For the survivors, however, it was a new beginning.

Adam, operating with limited knowledge of his gift, forgot a key function of it. When he first showed Evalynn his power, he performed a tangible alteration right before her eyes, changing her blouse, but when he altered other events, such as the tunnel collapse, no one was aware of the change. This was because his mental modification required adjusting that which occurred prior to the incident, something he did not do after exercising his apocalyptic thoughts.

Because of this oversight, the fresh world which came about remained connected to the old. His actions became nothing more than another event in the history of mankind. Of course, there was no way for the few inhabitants of the world to know that the events stemmed from misguided ambitions. Humanity dealt with the reality at hand in the same way it always did: by faithfully applying truth to gain understanding.

It did not take long for people to start teaching their children about their history. Tales of the old world spread with romantic fervor. Adam eventually forgot the self-hate which had consumed him and relished the opportunity to witness the reforming of life. Hypnotized by the scene of regeneration which unfolded before him, Adam did not think he would ever become lonely, but eventually the life of isolation he vowed to live weighed on him and depression engulfed him once again.

Leaving the cave, Adam traveled away from what the Lumenites called Devastation Valley, wandering the land with no purpose other than to keep moving. He walked far from where the Lumen land was, traversing the Earth for curiosity's sake. Along the way, he watched the rise and fall of many kingdoms, always from a silent distance.

It was while hiking across a treacherously harsh region of wilderness that Evalynn popped into his mind. He had completely forgotten about his female companion and that she too should be alive since not only had he bound his life to that of the Earth, but he had also tied Evalynn's to it as well. From that moment on, as the aging man trekked through the forests and deserts of the reborn planet, he had one objective: to find the woman he had so terribly wronged. Millennia passed as Adam hunted for Evalynn, never finding her.

One day, as Adam took in his surroundings, he recognized that he was back in the area of his cave. The quest to find Evalynn ended as he rested in his cavernous dwelling. He convinced himself that somehow she had escaped the curse he bestowed on himself. At as much peace as he would ever be, the ancient man decided to simply exist, no goal, no purpose, merely quietly existing, because he had to.

Pura and Adam talked for hours when the boy realized his distraction and that he must get on to the king. Adam understood and with a comforting grace invited the youngster to return if he ever found himself nearby.

Adam missed interacting with another human being. He missed knowing about all the things that were going on in the world, even if it was a world foreign to him. He was used to the things of his time, not the workings of a world of chivalry and gallantry. It was exciting to listen to Pura's perspective concerning the history of Lumen.

Pura and Adam went to the entrance of the cave which the elder had made undetectable. The old man guided Pura in the direction of where he fell off his horse. With any luck the royal mount would still be there.

After they parted ways, Pura ran as fast as he could to find the steed, which was patiently lying by the hole in which the boy had fallen, waiting to see if he would come out. When Pura spotted him, he called out its name and the horse stood up, ready to ride for the throne.

"Amicus! Amicus, you are here. Excellent!" Pura exclaimed.

The horse knelt down, aiding the boy in his effort to climb onto its back. Once soundly in the saddle, Pura grabbed the reins and steered the horse toward the city. As the horse trotted off, the absence of disorderly clanking metal slowly dawned on Pura. He turned to double-check the battlefield, finding a shocking scene as he brought the courser to a stop.

"Whoa, boy."

The view stunned the child. The battle was over. He did not see any birds in the sky and there was no stirring up of dust. The queer thing was that there was not a massive Malum army in the field. All he could see were a couple hundred men moving about crimson layers of contorted bodies. Curiosity got the best of him. He should have been riding for King Josiah, but the question in the boy's mind forced him to get closer in order to see what was happening.

Pura rode as close as he dared and then dismounted so that he could sneak over to a ledge. There, he was near enough to almost make out the words the men below were saying. The language was Lumen. The darkened evening sky made it hard for him to make out what the men looked like, but he was fairly certain it was groundsmen who were talking. It was not until the setting sun hit the light of a Defender's lumenium armor that Pura was confident that the soldiers were his kinsmen. As if on cue, when the sun hit the armor, Pura shot up onto his feet, racing back to Amicus.

"They are Lumen! They are Lumen!"

The boy's arms were waving with excitement. He was thrilled. He figured if the Lumen army won, certainly Michaelis was alive. Leaping on to Amicus' back the boy raced as fast as he could down to the men.

A groundsman took him to Michaelis and the two friends greeted each other as if it had been years since they parted ways.

"Pura, what are you doing here? I thought you had ridden for the City of the Throne?" Michaelis was glad he had not.

"I started to." Pura looked around, frightened by the reality of the scene about him. When he was on the ledge above, he had not noticed all the bodies still lying scattered in the muddy soil, if not Lumen soldiers, then Malum.

"Why did you turn back? Are you alright?" Michaelis took Pura into a tent to escape the terrors of war and to examine the wound on his head.

Pura told Michaelis the entire story of what happened to him as he had tried to ride for the kingdom's gate. Michaelis listened with open ears, trying to grasp all that the boy was saying. The knight promised that on their journey home they would look for the cave and then called for someone to tend to the cut on Pura's head. After it was cleaned and dressed, Michaelis prepared a place for the boy to sleep. From the sound of it, the child had just as long a day as the rest of the men. The army was setting out for the City of the Throne at daybreak, Pura would need his strength.

Under normal circumstances the twelve-year-old orphan's mind would have been racing with fanciful thoughts concerning his trip to the most magnificent city in the kingdom, a place where everyone was of noble birth, even the servants. But on this night all Pura could think about was his conversation with Adam. He had learned a lot, most of which he could not accurately remember. What intrigued him more than anything was not that the man was thousands of years old. It was not even the ancient items in his cave. No, the most fascinating thing to Pura was that Adam had never interacted with another Lumenite before. The young child was amazed that he had taught the old man so many things, that he had been the first person to talk to a man older than the known world. Pura taught Adam things he had barely learned himself. The thought of teaching the man about the kingdom sparked such interest in the boy's mind that all he could think about was talking to his new friend again. Night dragged on for Pura, lying there, waiting for the sun to come up and for the men to rig down camp so that they could begin their trip toward Adam's cave.

The pink glow of the sun rising was met with glad hearts. All the men were thankful, in a way only a soldier could understand, to be leaving the site of such brutality. They had survived their darkest hour and were prepared to go home with the knowledge that they did their job and that their families were safe.

Pura, on the other hand, was ready to return to his odd friend, Adam. He hardly slept at all and yet was still more energetic than any of the triumphant soldiers. Michaelis was just as eager to meet Adam as Pura was to guide him there, even though he had his suspicions about who the stranger was. The Lumen knight supposed that he was a conjurer who had found a victim to prey upon. Michaelis wanted to see for himself the items his young friend described.

It was a relatively short ride to the ledge where Pura thought Adam's cave should be, compared to the long road back to Throne City, a trip awaiting them after this quick detour. Pura led Michaelis, Eliazar, and a couple of the groundsmen to where he swore the mouth of the cave was. All that was there were sandstone cliffs. The boy ran his hands along the earth walls, desperately looking for where the old man had said goodbye to him the day before. Certain he was in the right spot, his eyes began to tear up as he realized how it looked to the men with him. Michaelis had seemed uncertain of his story from the moment the boy told him about Adam and the cave. Surely Pura's older friend doubted the validity of what happened to the child.

"It was right here! There was an opening in the rock, right here," Pura said, looking at the yellowish-tan rocks as if they were playing tricks on him.

They were.

Adam designed his home to provide a life of solitude, painstakingly hiding the entrance. When the ancient man mentally constructed it, seclusion was the primary goal.

Pura's excitement and the sense of urgency which consumed him when he left the cave was no help. If he had taken the time to look at his surroundings, he might be able to see the door now that he was back.

Adam stood just inside the opening where he could hear the boy's saddened voice trying to convince his older companions that he was not making up his story. Adam hated not helping his young friend. All he had to do was walk out and reveal himself. It was an odd thing, Adam's hiding. When he heard the group of men approaching, he actually hurried to the door to greet Pura. It was not until he had seen the types of men the boy was with that he decided to hide. He was afraid of what the soldiers might do. They were youthful, the oldest a tender babe compared to Adam and they all were carrying weapons. Adam thought Pura had misunderstood; he must have thought the old man was going to hurt him. The elderly man had tried to tell the Lumen lad that he no longer was a bad person. Since he did not know Pura's motive for bringing the soldiers, he decided not to take any chances.

"Pura, it is okay. Maybe this is the wrong ledge. Is it possible you were disoriented when you left the cave?

Maybe it is that ridgeline over there. You hit your head pretty hard, you know?"

"No. I know it was here. It was. I know it was." The child's voice tapered off until it turned into a whisper and then plain breath, his lips moving in silence.

Pura turned, disappointed and defeated. After several confused moments, the young boy headed in the direction of the rest of the men, who had begun to make their way toward Lumen.

Michaelis jumped off of his horse, scanning the rocks for any signs of an opening. "Pura, we can look some more."

The only thing separating Michaelis from Adam was rock the width of a man. The rock felt and appeared to be solid from the Lumenite's vantage point. Michaelis looked over his shoulder and saw that Pura had already made it to the bottom of the hill. The boy's head hung low as he kicked the rocks under his feet, pouting as children do when they do not get their way. Michaelis mounted up and the group of soldiers made their way down after Pura.

"Poor kid just wanted to believe it so badly that he actually dragged us out on this wild goose chase. Must have been a heck of a fall." Eliazar's voice carried a sense of sympathy.

Adam shrank back into his cave. He had done it again. Even without using his gift, Adam managed to upset the course of things, at least in the heart of the boy who had so pleasantly left the day before. The disgust he felt was gut-wrenching. He hated himself for not stepping out, for not having the courage to fix a wrong, even a little one such as this. The boy would more than likely get over the sadness he felt at the moment and would carry on without remembering the letdown. But Adam would not.

Chapter Thirty

Gidaen arrived at the City of the Throne to find a grand welcome. He had sent a rider ahead of his envoy to prepare the king for their arrival. When they reached the city entrance, King Josiah, Nicholas, the rest of the Council, along with Martinian monks, and a slew of other concerned and hopeful citizens, were all there to hear what news the group had brought. The smile on Gidaen's face as he greeted his king was answer enough for the young ruler to know the day was theirs.

"So, the Malum have been defeated?" Josiah sounded more like an inquisitive teenager than the king but he did not care. His only concern was the wellbeing of his land and the condition of his soldiers.

"Yes, all but a few Malum were killed on the field at the mouth of Devastation Valley." Gidaen paused. "My Lord, we did suffer many casualties." His smile vanished as he reported the death toll to the Lumen leader.

The men retreated to a private hall where the Defenders could brief the king in detail on all that happened during the battle. King Josiah sat as Gidaen told him of the events at Devastation Valley, missing no detail from Michaelis' arrival in the southern camp to final, miraculous victory. By the end of the debriefing the king was so ecstatic that he could hardly contain his emotions. He had trusted Baramatheus, defying tradition and the advice of the Council, and it had proved to be the deciding factor in the war.

Dismissing the Defenders, the king remained in his seat for quite a while, pondering what action to take next. It was during this period of deliberation that the young king had a revolutionary idea.

King Josiah summoned the Council to discuss the probable ramifications of what had transpired at Devastation Valley. Specifically, he wanted to hear their perspective concerning the leveling of men brought about by Michaelis. As the Council shared their thoughts, he kept to himself an idea brewing within his head, an idea which would more than likely upset several of the Servants. Some of them had expressed their dislike of the change already taking place, a change revolving around Michaelis and the events in Devastation Valley. It threatened their security. If all the people of the kingdom were treated as nobility, then how would the system continue to function? Would royal farmers still want to tend their fields? Would the peasants still carry out their day-to-day vocations if they were equal to the royal bloodlines of the City of the Throne?

Nicholas, in a very wise and caring way, illustrated that the ramifications would not be so deleterious. He assured them that all that would happen would be an expansion of how the inner city currently operated. They knew that the royal bakers, maids, guards, blacksmiths, and carpenters, among others, already performed their societal roles despite their noble titles. Nicholas not only condoned the knight's actions but applauded the wisdom in what Michaelis had initiated.

The king, too, could see the benefits of living in such a land. He did not feel that any of his people should be held at a lower level than another. Of course, he recognized the reality that not all could have the same standard of life as those who lived in Throne City. Comprehending that within time the country would prosper like never before nullified this unavoidable truth. In a kingdom of royal citizens, nothing could stop the people from doing well for themselves, for their neighbor, and ultimately, for the entire kingdom of Lumen.

With these thoughts in mind, the king amended the laws to fit this new ideal. He wanted it made so, and he wanted it done by the time the remaining troops made it back to the city. He sent out a decree that anyone born of Lumen descent would be recognized as royalty. Every man would be as a prince in the land of his father. The people would live for their king and Josiah would live for his people. The king graciously gave all the citizens of

Lumen an unwarranted gift. The gift to live as noble men, men who were equals among their brothers, not because they deserved to be so, but because of the love King Josiah held for them. When Michaelis returned, another idea would be set forth that would exemplify these new laws.

* * *

Michaelis tried consoling Pura for almost the entire journey, but the boy wanted none of it. The two rode side-by-side mounted atop red-haired horses, Pura on Amicus, while Michaelis directed Baramatheus' old steed. The company moved slowly, weighed down as they were by the men they carried and drained by the exhausting struggle they had been through. The excitement of victory had worn off along the way, and now the men were simply making their way to a new place. They did not know what to expect; all of them had been away from the kingdom for a long time. Most had never even seen the City of the Throne, and yet there they were headed. For what reason, they knew not.

Michaelis had told them that things were changing—that they fought like equals, and would live as equals—but who was he to make such claims? Yes, he was a Defender of the King, but that did not grant him the power to establish new laws. Most of the groundsmen did not allow their hopes to rise too high. They would wait and see what happened when they arrived in the city.

Michaelis offered a sympathetic explanation in an attempt to cheer up his young friend. "Is it possible Pura, that when the ground gave way under your feet, you hit your head harder than you thought? Maybe you were unconscious until the battle was over and…"

"I did not make it up. Wait! The hole! Michaelis, I got into the cave from the ground falling from under me!" Pura had life back in his eyes. He was energized. "We can go back and I will show you that I did not dream it or imagine it or whatever you think I am doing." Pura was pulling on his horse to turn around.

"Okay, but we are almost to the city. We cannot go back. The king is waiting to see us." Michaelis kept Pura's horse from turning.

"Yes and there is a fine pub at the north end of the city which has Drahregian ale," Eliazar stated, attempting to provide further reasoning for why they must stay the course.

Pura understood the necessity of getting to the city. He understood the reality of how far they had traveled and that the other men wanted to be done with their morbid task of carrying their fallen brothers to their final resting place. Pura let the excitement in his heart flicker out. He dropped the issue, keeping the desire to go back to himself.

As the convoy pressed on, Eliazar talked about the city's entertainment, its food and, of course, where to get the best beer. Michaelis on the other hand, kept his eyes forward, looking for the first sign of the River Ax and the bridge which crossed it, resting at the gate of the city.

It was not too long after their conversation that Michaelis saw the city gate. A Lumen spotter alerted the king of the group's approach just as he had when Gidaen and the others had come.

The looks of astonishment, disbelief and awe on the faces of the groundsmen, and even Pura, as the men approached the massive behemoth statues with the fire blazing on top of them were priceless. The river was magnificent, shimmering as bright as a knight's glistening armor. The men were stunned that they could see the fish swimming in the water so clearly.

Upon their arrival at the city, they were greeted with joyous festivities. Horns sounded in jubilation while the soldiers made their way in, the people welcomed them all with true gratitude for what they had done. It was not just the Defenders and commanders who received the greeting; the groundsmen did as well. Flower petals rained down onto the men from above as the line of troops passed under windows. The atmosphere resembled that of a parade, a parade in honor of the brave Lumenite men of the land. What Michaelis had told them somehow was becoming true. They were as equals in this marvelous city.

An entourage led the group up to a square filled with decorations and musicians loudly playing songs of victory. The entire army filed into the wide open area, celebrating with their hosts. Michaelis smiled, watching the men's faces as the wave of Lumenites controlled the direction of their movement. It was all new to him as well. At the square, Michaelis noticed Gidaen standing above the crowd on a stage usually reserved for street plays. Hurrying, the young warrior made his way up to him. Hugging his friend, Gidaen explained to the knight that he had informed the king of the victory. Precisely at that moment, a symphony of horns blared an announcement and the music stopped. All the hustle and bustle of the happy return ground to a halt instantly as the eyes of the crowd searched for the king. He approached from the far side of the stage where Gidaen and Michaelis had been standing. The two men naturally dropped down a couple of steps to show the king his rightful respect.

"Citizens of the Lumen Kingdom! All of you, with the exception of these who have just arrived, have by now heard of the decree I sent forth. I will repeat it out of respect for the heroes of Devastation Valley." The king proudly announced that they were all equally noblemen of Lumen, concluding his statement with a huge grin, at which time the throng of people erupted, cheering wildly.

Josiah stepped down to one of the groundsmen and grabbed his hand. "Thank you for your service. May the rest of your life be full of joy and peace." The king looked directly at the man, genuinely meaning every word.

The common groundsman began to weep as the words fell upon his ears. Michaelis had told them that things were changing, and they had indeed.

The king then ascended back to the stage so that everyone could see him. "Michaelis, I know of your actions. I know that if not for your love for this land and your fellow man, all would have been lost." The king looked down at the villager he had anointed. "It is an honor for me to offer this kingdom to you." The crowd began to whisper; no one understood what the king meant. "It would be the greatest of privileges to extend to you… a seat beside me in the Hall of the Throne."

The whispers grew louder and louder as the shock of what the king had just said echoed through the minds of all who were present. King Josiah had given his throne to Michaelis. It was Lumen law that if a king did not have an heir, he could appoint one. This had never actually occurred in the history of the land. The stunning thing was that the king was still so young. It was not as if he did not have many years left in which to marry. The king freely offered the rule of the Lumen land over to a man outside of royal bloodlines.

Cheers erupted from the crowd as the king placed his hand on the shoulder of his new prince. The celebration continued and the festivities lasted long into the night. The king proclaimed the day a holiday and the people rejoiced without worry of the days to come. Peace had arrived. The threat of the Malum was no more.

Word spread fast concerning the changes in the country. All villagers throughout Lumen had a new hope. Peasants would no longer march off to die, but would work in the fields and shops near their homes. Children would once again grow up knowing their fathers. It was as if a cloud had lifted from the troubled land.

Michaelis had the dreadful task of informing Nicholas of Baramatheus' passing. The fallen soldier's father did not fret over his son's death. He was just as secure in his son's passing as the warrior had been. Baramatheus chose a life of service in a function that put him at risk. Nicholas understood serving for a greater good better than most. He too had spent his entire life serving the kingdom, albeit in a different manner. He was confident in his son's final actions, positive that he had died honorably and with saving faith in the Lumen teaching. Although he was not aware of the exact details, he was certain that Baramatheus had died the same way he had lived: valiantly.

Nicholas, from that moment on, took Michaelis under his wing. He would look after the young man just as if he were his own son.

Eliazar found his pub after the celebrations simmered down. He and several of the groundsmen remained there for what seemed like days, the old commander educating the soldiers on the ways of the city and its people.

Gidaen and the other strategists began conceiving plans for trips into the Malum Mountains, to find Acerbus and Bebbel-uk, in an attempt to finish off the threat before it could cultivate new strength. Ben assisted them and was welcomed to their ranks through a formal ceremony, retiring from the field and vowing to keep the groundsmen's best interests at heart.

Pura was the only one who felt as if he lost, not gained, something. His youthful mind remained fixed on Adam.

Pura tried to forget about the things in the cave, the little picture of people, the chair... everything. He tried to wash away the memory of the strangely-dressed man who claimed to have destroyed the world. Thoughts of the experience just would not leave the boy's brain. Pura believed Adam and wanted to believe him so much that he could not, no matter how hard he tried, forget the man in the cave, the old Adam. The more Pura pondered the situation and what Adam had told him, the more he was sure the elderly man was telling him the truth.

It was funny that as the kingdom had progressed in a wonderful way, this little child's thoughts were trapped near a dismal, grisly battlefield. Lumen, with all its splendor and joy was secondary to Pura. All things being equal he should have been worry-free, yet his mind was buried in a damp, dark cave where the complex and horrible tales of the world took precedence.

Chapter Thirty-One

Ben approached the Council's meeting hall with a heavy heart. In the midst of the joyous season he had the task of formulating a strategy to mount an assault in the Malum Mountains in order to eliminate the threat of the remaining enemy, an endeavor perilous at best. The Council sat enthroned along with King Josiah and Michaelis. Confidence and cheer filled the room. Seeing the merry mood of his comrades, Ben felt a sense of reassurance.

"King Josiah, Michaelis, and loyal servants of the Council. The Defenders have, as you know, been plotting a battle plan to enter the Malum Mountains with the primary purpose of rooting out and annihilating the remaining combatants of Bebbel-uk. With great reservations we have conceived a strategy which, if nothing else, would at least give our men a chance for survival. As you all are aware, the mountain range is itself a formidable foe." Ben's resolute words caused a respectful silence to fall upon the Council chamber.

"You have our attention. Explain please." The Council was anxious to hear what he had to say.

"We are going to put together a small group of volunteers, a group which will consist primarily of Defenders. We decided against sending out a full garrison of soldiers due to the difficult terrain and harsh conditions of the mountain range. A limited number of men will be able to move with greater ease and stealth."

"Ben, have the Defenders taken into consideration that there may well be an entire army still preparing for battle at Acerbus?" Nicholas inquired.

"Yes, of course, the possibilities are endless. There could be any array of things awaiting our men as they embark upon this mission. That is why we are going to send only our bravest and most skilled warriors," Ben said, looking directly at Michaelis as he finished his statement.

"Ben," Michaelis asked, "do you have any volunteers yet?" The knight was eager to finally remove the threat to his land. He desperately longed for his people to enjoy the peace of mind which would accompany the dismantling of the Malum threat once and for all.

"No. Before we start recruiting, the Council needs to approve our strategy."

"Upon the endorsement of the Council, I would like to request to lead this proposed mission," Michaelis stated.

Once Michaelis announced his wish to lead the group, the Council wasted no time approving the mission. A sense of surety filled the room. Michaelis had led the army against great odds before; he most certainly could do it again.

"Thank you." Ben knew the ease with which Michaelis could muster support for the group.

Men would line up behind the young heir, going wherever he asked without hesitation. He was the cornerstone. With it known that he was leading the mission, all other matters of importance could be arranged. After receiving the go ahead from the Council, Ben set out to gather supplies for all the troops who would be accompanying Michaelis, while the princely Defender put his attention to gathering recruits.

In the mind of Michaelis, he needed only one man to be brought aboard in order for the task to succeed. All others would help, but Eliazar was essential. When asked, the champion of the battlefield jumped at the opportunity. He knew that the toughest of Lumenites were the few who could handle the hazards of the Malum Mountains, and he ached for an opportunity to add this task to his portfolio of sterling deeds. As far as Eliazar was concerned the mission had been conceived especially for him.

A few brief moments elapsed between the time Michaelis asked for the rugged Royal Commander's enlistment and the time he had the full complement of men. Hardy warriors rallied around the grand icon of Lumen might no matter where he was. The resilient soldiers surrounding Eliazar were the bravest veterans of the Battle of Devastation Valley, commanders and groundsmen alike. When they learned that Michaelis and Eliazar were setting out to take on the remaining Malum, they all clamored for the right to be included. So many men stepped forward that Michaelis had to turn some away. He was satisfied with his team, consisting of ten of Lumen's finest, not counting himself or Eliazar.

While the men prepared to depart, Michaelis went to find Pura. He had promised the boy that they would return to look for the strange cave-dweller. Now would be the time. The route that would take them to the Malum Mountains was the same they had taken from the battle.

"Pura, are you in here?" Michaelis peered around the opening of the Defender's stable. If there was one place the boy would be, this was it.

"Over here." Pura stood, brushing down Amicus.

"Do you think you could show me where to find the cave your friend lives in?" Michaelis teased the boy a little, knowing that Pura would be ecstatic to go back.

"Are you joking? I know I can!" Pura's face lit up.

"We leave at dawn." Michaelis smiled as he left the stables.

In the morning there was not a soul around as the party departed the city. It was not like when they had arrived. No celebration, no excited crowd, only the sound of the early morning birds singing as the sun rose steadily in a color-filled sky.

The men's spirits were high. They were still drunk with the joy of the new era. The reality that they were heading into the belly of the Malum Mountains had not yet gripped their hearts and minds. Full of victorious optimism, the soldiers would not face the mental burden of their task until the peaks revealed themselves on the horizon.

Michaelis and Pura talked the entire morning about Adam and his claim. The elder of the two was still very skeptical. What a declaration! A nearly immortal man from a highly advanced civilization had not only destroyed the world, but had done so with his mind, and now lives all alone in a cave?

"What is it, Michaelis?" Eliazar spotted the look on the Defender's face.

"Oh, I was thinking about what this Adam person told Pura, that he destroyed the world long ago. It is such a ridiculous claim."

"I guess that depends on if he did or not." Eliazar was exposing his wisdom again, which caught Michaelis off guard.

"You do not think he actually did, do you?" Astonished, Michaelis shook his head in bewilderment.

"Why not? After all, we know the Earth was decimated somehow. Why rule it out? Other than the Martinian records, we have no idea what happened. Perhaps Adam is the key to understanding a big chunk of our history. Based on Pura's recollection of his claim, there is nothing which contradicts what we already know."

"That is true. I guess I just figured the destruction to be the result of a power far greater than that of a man."

"Michaelis," Eliazar's tone dipped in an expression of disappointment, "it is said that all things happen according to God's will, but that is not to say man is absent in the playing out of that will. We have a role, every decision we make has a consequence, and those consequences can have major ramifications. If you can accept, as the Martinians teach, that the One who made the Earth once lived on it, why is it so hard to accept that the man who destroyed it is still living on it?"

"I suppose a carpenter can live in the house he built. It just seems so incredible." Michaelis' words remained in his head for a while as they made their journey toward Devastation Valley.

At the end of the day the group set up camp near the edge of a wooded hilltop, using the trees as a natural windbreak. While the other men lay down to sleep, Michaelis made his way into the clearing. With the stars overhead, he thought about the day's discussion. The young man had never pondered such things. Distress came over him as he imagined who Adam could be. The more he thought about it, the more he hoped they would find him tomorrow.

If the man existed, he could answer a lot of the questions beginning to brew in Michaelis' mind.

The next morning was dim, the clouds blocking out the sun. It did not take long for the Lumenite soldiers to get back on the move. Once they reached the crest of the hill, they easily spotted the valley. A stinging discomfort coupled with the pride of winning the battle stirred among the small ensemble of men. It had not been that long ago that they fought against tremendous odds, straining to claim the day. Each man remembered friends they had lost while at the same time thinking of the families back home whom they had saved. It was Eliazar who lightened the mood by singing one of his favorite tavern songs. Smiles and laughter spread among them again as they all joined in, horribly butchering the already unmelodic song.

For the rest of the day as the men headed toward the valley, lighthearted conversations and exaggerated accounts of the battle filled the air. The tall tales of legendary heroes began taking hold of the day—the kind of inspiring anecdotes Eliazar was famous for—the type which drew men into a life full of adventure and discovery.

Chapter Thirty-Two

The wind was blowing hard; gray clouds moved across the sky. Adam sat in his chair, his eyes closed and his breath slow and steady. Off-key singing ricocheted through his ears, gradually waking the old man. As his eyes opened he could hear the higher-pitched tone of a child. Remaining still, Adam listened carefully, trying to visualize exactly from where outside the sounds were coming. The scene was unfolding in front of his cave.

Only Michaelis and Pura had gone up the ridge to where the boy said they could find the entrance. The rest of the soldiers stayed behind, singing song after splendid song.

"I still cannot see it. I swear it was near here." Pura scurried across the ledge looking for a way into the earth.

Adam refused to cower in the security of his home; he would not continue living in the same error-filled cycle.

Approaching the door, he heard a man's voice.

"You were going to take me to where you fell in."

"Ah, yes! It was over here." Pura scrambled up the steep ledge, fist-sized rocks tumbling down from underneath his feet.

Adam could hear Pura move up right beside the cave's entrance. He stepped out of the hidden door right as the boy passed by it.

"Pura." The soft voice of a scared old man called out.

Uncertain of what was to come next, Adam stayed close to the opening, his hand resting on the earth-formed frame.

"Adam! Michaelis, over here, I have found him!" Excited, Pura slid back down. "I knew it. I knew I could find you."

By the time Pura reached Adam's side, Michaelis was standing at the top of the ledge. The initial sight of the Defender surely intimidated Adam. The knight stood in the wind, his hair waved like a banner, his cloak snapping to one side of his body, revealing his sword and armor. As Michaelis made his way down to where Pura and Adam stood, the boy began to introduce the two men.

"Michaelis, this is Adam." He did not get very far before Michaelis took over.

"I am Michaelis, Defender of the King, heir to the Lumen Throne."

"Hello, I'm Adam Malloy." That was all he could think to say, not knowing how to make small talk with someone from an entirely different time and culture.

After a lengthy pause the older man invited the two Lumenites inside. He figured Pura had told his friend all about him and that Michaelis probably wanted to hear his historical account. It did not take long for Michaelis to become a believer in what Adam claimed to have done. The objects inside the cave were compelling. The royal Defender acted the same way that Pura had when he had first laid his eyes on the things in Adam's home, fondling and eyeing every artifact within his reach.

Adam slowly explained everything he had told Pura, expounding on certain details as Michaelis asked. He pulled no punches in his recitation of the past. Astonished, the Lumenite sat, hanging on every word he spoke.

"To sum it up, I don't know why or how I was given this cursed gift. I do know that I squandered it though. I was unable to control the temptation, unwilling to restrain from the lustful desires in my heart, giving into every whim of my imagination."

Michaelis held the clock in his hand. "How do you, as the doer of miracles, not understand the method of your actions?"

"I could never wrap my mind around the complexities of the ability. I have spent ages trying to sort out the answer. All I have are theories, and they're not that convincing." Adam said.

"A mystery beyond our understanding." Michaelis looked down at Adam's clock. "A powerful gift."

"But why would I be the only one with this extended ability?" questioned Adam.

"Were you? The oldest of ancient records preserved by the Martinians are historical accounts that predate even you. I have read with my own eyes of men that were able to control and even rule over nature. Every child in Lumen could recite these events to you." Michaelis stared into Adam's eyes. "Perhaps, friend, you refused to see the truth about your gift and what it was meant for, even though it was right in front of you the whole time."

Several minutes passed in complete silence. "Adam, will you come back with us to Throne City?" Michaelis knew the Martinians would have many questions for the ancient human, as well as many answers for him.

A smile spread from ear to ear across Pura's face.

Adam thought for a moment before answering. "It would be an honor." After all this time, loneliness would not be the old man's only friend.

"Great! We will stop on our way back, which will give you time to gather up your belongings," said Michaelis.

"I don't have much to pack, but that will be fine. Where, if I might ask, are you going?"

"We must finish the fight the Malum started. We are headed for Acerbus. What Bebbel-uk and his mistress have in store for us will determine when we will return."

"Bebbel-uk, he is the leader of the Malum, their king?" Adam asked.

"Yes, he is the Malum Emperor. As far as their leader, not solely. He serves the will of Her."

"Her? Who is Her?" The old man's voice cracked with anxiety.

"The epitome of evil. She is said to be so unnaturally beautiful, so striking, that many claim she is from another realm. With her beauty she controls the actions of men, manipulating them to bend to her will." That was all Michaelis knew of her. That was all anyone really knew of her.

"Unnatural? Not another realm, another time. Evalynn," Adam said in a whisper. "I must go with you!" He placed his hand on Michaelis' shoulder. "I have to go with you."

Adam was sure the woman was Evalynn. Who else would be described in such a way? He had made her perfect in every possible aspect, unnaturally beautiful. But how was it that she still possessed her beauty? The old man had scoured the Earth in search for her. He could not pass up the opportunity to find out if this woman Michaelis spoke of was truly her.

No more needed to be said. Three reasons convinced the Defender to allow an addition to the party. One was that Michaelis could see the eagerness in Adam's eyes. The second was that the ancient man's immortality might be an asset to the Lumenites. And finally, if the woman Adam called

Evalynn was Bebbel-uk's mistress, having someone along who knew her would be most beneficial.

As they rode, Michaelis explained to Eliazar and several of the men within earshot who Adam was. The battered war veteran laughed, saying nothing. Adam rode with Pura upon Amicus. The two talked as if they had known each other for a lifetime, which was refreshing for Adam. Holding a conversation with someone so young and full of a zeal for life, someone ready to see and experience everything possible, was a pleasant change from his isolated lifestyle. It had been a very long time since the old timer had felt any emotions similar to that of his counterpart. For centuries, life for him had been nothing more than a prison.

Pura could not get enough of the stories; he begged for more episodes from the futuristic past. The boy would ask about something and as Adam attempted to answer it the look upon Pura's face would become shrouded with confusion. Simple things that Adam took for granted bewildered his audience. No one from Lumen could grasp cars and their quick speed or fast-food restaurants where the meal was so unhealthy that to eat it did more harm than good. The concept was foreign to a people free of artificial sweeteners and laboratory produced preservatives. The mentioning of TVs, computers, airplanes, satellites, and space shuttles all prompted thoughts of sorcery; magic arts which trapped people in boxes, or allowed people to fly.

The travelers had enjoyed good weather so far. Although overcast, no rain had yet come. The wind had been the only hindrance and that had stopped soon after they left the cave. As they approached the mountains, their surroundings began to change. Green meadows slipped away, overtaken by rigid rocks and tumbleweeds. The top layer of earth moved with the wind, wisping back and forth. Dust stirred up with each step of the horses. Ditches cut through the ground where streams had once flowed. Dry lakebeds were nothing more than lulls at the base of the mountainous titans. The men could not help but feel unprepared for what was to come. They had not even reached the Malum territory and the terrain was already quenching their courage.

"A bit parched, ay?" Eliazar said, mainly to shatter the uncomfortable silence. The pall of quietude only added to the land's eerie persona.

None of the group had ever been this close to the Malum region. The journey forward was uncharted territory for all.

Wanting to be fully rested before they entered the mountains, they made camp at the foothills. The area was desolate, lacking any naturally suitable location, but the Lumenites made do. Sleep came hard as everyone was on edge, aware of the vast possibilities of what they might encounter. Adam sat by the fire, Michaelis and Eliazar across from him.

"Please Adam, tell us about the woman you call Evalynn. Does she have the talent as you did, to alter the world?" Michaelis asked, knowing that any information would help them if the time ever came to face her.

"No. She helped me, but only by suggestion. She never possessed the ability." The old man stared into the fire, his eyes shimmering in the light. "I don't suspect that her power stems only from her appearance." The two warriors could tell Adam was at that very moment trying to decipher how Evalynn managed her domination of an entire race of people. "I was never able to find her. I looked all over the Earth. Where did she go?" The ancient man was more thinking aloud than talking to the Lumenites. "Gentlemen, I do not know how she has become so powerful. The last I knew, she was a ruined young woman full of hatred for me, a hatred she undoubtedly has nurtured."

The fire eventually burned out, the heat and light it gave off fading into the night. All three men never moved, their minds endlessly working to discover the answer as to the nature of the enemy whom they were about to face. The glowing embers flickered from time to time as the wind passed through the camp. So preoccupied by their thoughts, they did not seem to notice the sun beginning to rise. It was a new day, a day which would prove to be packed full of surprises.

Chapter Thirty-Three

Not showing any sign of fatigue despite his being up all night, Eliazar was the first to begin the trek into the canyon which was the mouth to the mountains. All the Lumenite soldiers carried their supplies in the satchels provided by Ben and the King's Defenders. From this point on, unfortunately, they were on foot. Expecting narrow ridges and almost impassible inclines, the terrain would be much too rough for the horses. This was the Malum's home; they were experts at traversing the rocky cliffs, which meant Michaelis' men were at a disadvantage. Mobility was of the utmost importance.

"Leave what you can do without. If you think it will slow us down, leave it." Michaelis removed his breastplate and dropped it to the ground as he followed behind Eliazar. "Pura, stay close to my side."

The sun was beginning to shine in front of the brave band of soldiers, casting dramatically long shadows in a sporadic fashion across their path. Aware of the legend of the Malum Mountains, nerves tightened almost unbearably. The shadows of hawks flying high overhead instantly became demonic ghosts sneaking about. Pebbles gently settling down the mountainside morphed into the presence of ghoulish fiends. Imaginations began wildly creating evidence supporting the myths.

The first thing Eliazar noticed was the temperature. It was still early morning and yet it felt like midday. The air was dry, no moisture to help cool the hikers, but it was beyond just that. With a sneaking suspicion, the commander placed his hand upon a large rock, only to retract it.

"Whoa!" Shaking his hand a little, Eliazar turned back toward Michaelis, noticing the sweat pouring down his comrade's brow. Quickly glancing at the rest of the soldiers, he began to move up the ridgeline. "Hurry! We have to get to the top of this canyon as fast as possible!" With that, his movement turned into full-fledged running.

"What is it? What is the..." Michaelis was keeping pace with his friend, the others directly behind him.

"The canyon. It is a furnace. If we do not get out of here before the sun is straight overhead, we will roast." Eliazar's labored breathing chopped his explanation into bits.

To the amazement of the Lumenites, Adam kept up with the group just fine. He moved as if he were in his twenties, certainly not like an elderly man.

It was a long way to the top of where the walls of the canyon would no longer be reflecting the heat of the sun against one another. The path was steadily getting steeper and steeper. Everyone pushed hard, their legs burning from the inside, pain shooting throughout their lower limbs. The Lumenites' steps became heavier as the grade grew greater, sloppier as well; exhaustion began to overcome the soldiers. The path gradually altered. Running room became scarce. Small rocks were getting larger and larger, eventually becoming boulders. Until now the boulders were far enough apart to weave through them, but the farther into the mountain they went, the closer together the monoliths grew. Before the men realized the problem that was hindering their progress, it was upon them, forcing them to climb up and over each stone barrier.

Pura maneuvered the obstacles the best, leaping with relative ease from one to another like stepping stones in a small stream. The agile boy had youth on his side. His bones were flexible and his movements nimble. As for the others, they were left reaching out to each other for help, using their companions' bodyweight as an anchor they scaled the massive rocks.

"We cannot possibly make it!" a commander bringing up the rear exclaimed.

"Hold your tongue, Didymus!" Eliazar snapped.

"We cannot get to the peak of the mountain before... it is impossible!"

"We do not have to. All we have to do is get out of this caldron. We are almost there." Michaelis' encouragement helped for only a moment, and then the commander fell victim to his own pessimism, succumbing to the sun.

He did not say anything else. As the group made their way up the mountain, the man's motions slowed. He continued moving, only with no heart behind his movements. His body was climbing but his will had stopped. One-by-one, everyone pulled themselves over the final rocky edge, tumbling to the ground to rest. Michaelis noticed that they were one man short. Speeding to the crest of the canyon, terror struck his soul.

"Didymus!" The Royal Commander was lying face down, his arms draped up the rock in front of him.

As Michaelis started down the ledge, a voice called out to him.

"Michaelis, there is no time!" Eliazar was pointing down at the body. "Look, smoke!" The boulder the man lay on was so hot his flesh was burning.

Frantic to find a way down, Michaelis' eyes scanned the terrain. It did seem hopeless. Even if he was able to get down, the chances of getting back up carrying Didymus were slim.

"The satchels! Tie the ropes together. I need a long rope." Michaelis headed away from the canyon, away from the frying man.

"It is too late." Eliazar barely got the words out.

As fast as he could go, the Defender barreled down the hill. His stride was long and powerful. Right before he reached the edge of the canyon where Eliazar and the others were standing he leaped forward, hurling himself through the sky, his legs still running and his arms bent in front of his body. The men looked on, stunned.

"The satchels!" Eliazar screamed.

Michaelis soared above the ground, bracing for the impending impact. Violently he collided with the stacked balls of compressed earth, his body tumbling end over end, his energized momentum stopping suddenly against a wall of rock. Unconscious, the daring Defender's body lay limp on the scorching hot earth.

Eliazar stared down into the simmer pot, waiting to see some sign of life, the wavy heat mirage distorting his view. After a few moments, Michaelis achingly began picking himself up. Scrapes and bruises covered his limbs. Blood dripped down his cheek from a gash on his forehead. Willing himself to move, he turned over Didymus. The man's flesh was singed, black from the burns. Throwing him over his shoulder, Michaelis shuffled to get strong footholds, creeping up the mountain. He did not carry him far before a rope dropped right in front of him. Grabbing the lifeline in one hand while holding firmly onto Didymus, Michaelis began ascending the canyon wall, all the men on the other end pulling as fast and as hard as they could.

Eliazar clutched the Defender's arm, helping him up the last few steps of the way. A groundsman took Didymus, lowering him down to the ground.

"What were you thinking, my brave friend?" Eliazar asked as he looked over Michaelis' wounds.

Pura and Adam knelt by his side waiting to hear that he was okay, the old man astonished by the supremely selfless act he had witnessed. Even when he had possessed the ability to, he had never done anything as great as what he had just seen.

"It is never, never too late," Michaelis spoke, his words drained of volume.

"Well, I am glad I could inspire you to heroism." Eliazar rose to his feet. "You will survive," he said as he began tending to Didymus.

The comment, which was just as much medicine as anything else the gruff commander could have administered, left a groggy smile on Michaelis' face.

The rock had severely burned Didymus. His face, unrecognizable. Eliazar did everything he could to ease the man's pain, but without the proper medicine there was only so much he could do. The injured soldier would simply have to deal with the agony. The group waited while the wounded man slept. His body needed all the rest it could get as it worked feverishly to heal its injuries.

The journey ahead of them looked more welcoming than what they had just come through.

A short hike up from their location was what looked to be a game trail. It led along a plateau and disappeared onto the other side. Several of the men volunteered to go ahead and scout the area, but Michaelis suggested they all were safer if they stayed together.

By midafternoon, Didymus was awake. With some help he was up and as ready to go as he possibly could be. The game trail was easily manageable. For the most part, it was level and wide enough for a man to walk on. It was when they arrived at the previously hidden section of the path that the passage became difficult. The reason for the path's apparent disappearance was that the ground split. The trail ended. A gap almost ten feet wide separated the natural road. On the other side of the chasm, five feet higher, was more than likely the spring point for whatever creature used the walkway.

"Now what?" Adam asked calmly.

"Well, everyone cannot jump like our fearless leader." Eliazar shifted his shoulders, his bones cracking with relief.

"But we all can go around." Pura was pointing down the edge. "That looks like where the two sides meet."

"Good eye." Michaelis squeezed his friend's shoulder as he passed, leading the way. The others rubbed his head or patted him on the back, as if he were a pet, in the precise manner children despise.

Getting to the other side took much more of the day than they had suspected, since they were farther away than they first estimated. It turned out that on the other side, the path disappeared. There was an obvious trampled-down area where the animals jumped, but nothing else. With Eliazar in the front, the Lumenites made their way deep into the heart of the mountains, all the time looking for signs of the Malum. The farther in they went, the more tense they became. With no sign of their enemy, they worried about being caught off-guard.

The men climbed well above the tree-line where the air was thin. Foliage of any sort was absent from the scenery at this elevation. The environment was nothing but pointy gray rocks. So sharp were the rocks, that when Pura stumbled, catching himself with his hand, one sliced open his palm. With every step, clots of earth clattered against each other, alerting anyone who cared to listen that they were coming.

After what seemed to take forever, the group came upon the first sign of Malum civilization. On the rocky hillside a single pole ascended into the sky. The sharp gray rocks were stacked along its base for support. At the top of the pole was a long skinny strip of purple cloth. More than likely the banner served several purposes. Of course, one was being a landmark for the Malum. Also it was an excellent indicator of wind direction, giving the residents of these mountains some hint as to weather patterns. Based on these presumptions, a Malum village was probably within line of sight to the pole. Eliazar stopped the group and they all slowly squatted down to make themselves less conspicuous.

"I imagine the beasts live down in that valley." Eliazar was pointing across his body toward the southeast.

"I will sneak over to the ridge line and see what is down there." Pura started toward the direction of the ridge, but did not get far as Eliazar clutched his sleeve, stopping him immediately.

"You will not be able to get low enough once you are over there. Unless, of course, you are willing to be gutted like a fish. I am certain there is something down there. We need to backtrack and move around from the other direction."

There was no telling whether the terrain on the other side would be any more accommodating, but it was worth a try. The Lumenites were in enemy territory. Every action needed to be exercised with extreme caution.

It did not take very long for the men to circle around, they were all alert to their surroundings, listening and watching for any indications of the enemy. The other side of the area proved to be much more accessible and was a good vantage point as they peered down the mountain. The sight surprised them all, for what they found was no mere Malum village, but Acerbus itself.

The first thing they noticed, besides the civil functions happening around the city, was the obvious embrace of evil. Everywhere they looked they could see the practice of dark arts, shopkeepers demonstrating the uses of different materials for conjuring specific spirits for specific purposes. An entertainer was on a stage having a conversation with what could only be described as a demonic force. Soldiers were going in and coming out of what was the equivalent of a Lumenite sanctuary. An old Malum man was out in front of it chanting some sort of spell as he dropped an odd powder from his fingers which caused small flames to spring up quickly as it hit the ground. Malum music, with its foreign meter, polluted the air, sending chills through the Lumenites' veins. The way the sunset was lighting the fortress only added to the aura of uneasiness engulfing Acerbus.

"I can even smell the evil," Eliazar said with a disgusted look on his face. "These people cling to the world of the dead. No wonder they are so repulsive."

"What do you think? That looks like where we will find Bebbel-uk." Michaelis was pointing to the apparent palace deep inside the city.

The castle was built up against the wall of the canyon, its size massive in comparison to every other building in Acerbus.

"It is a long way if we have to try to go through that unholy city." The veteran soldier began looking around desperately, hoping to find an alternate route.

"Pura. If that is what a conjurer is," Adam paused, "I was never like that." Terror crossed the old man's face.

"From what I hear, you did things worse than they can imagine." Eliazar, in his ever so blunt way, expressed once again his wisdom. "Perhaps they exist because of what you did."

"True. Very true." Adam's guilt pounded in his chest.

"We will scale the cliffs." Eliazar motioned toward an unpleasant route leading to the palace.

"If we all go we will most definitely stand out. Anyone who happens to look that way will spot us." Michaelis was running the options through his mind. "El, you and I will go, the rest of you wait here. If something happens, head back to Throne City and report what we have found so the Defenders can plan an attack."

"I'm going with you," Adam said sternly.

"Sorry, Adam, I do not think you will be able to make it."

"Don't be misled by my appearance. I still have the energy of my youth. And remember I can't die. I could at the very least be a witness to what is in there if something happens to you two."

Michaelis looked to Eliazar in a silent search for wisdom. The expression he found on his friend's face indicated that the ancient man had a good point.

"Done. The three of us will go. Pura, tend to Didymus. We will be back soon." Michaelis was being optimistic for the boy's sake, downplaying the cold, hard reality of what might happen. After all, he was about to go into the belly of the beast.

Chapter Thirty-Four

Getting into the palace was no easy task. Traversing the cliff without being detected was a slow and grueling process. They were overtly aware of the ramifications of finding a wrong foothold or grabbing onto an unsecure ledge. The smallest bit of debris tumbling down the face of the formation could alert the Malum soldiers below.

The advantage to this route was that they bypassed all but one of the palace's securities. Only two guards stood in front of the entrance next to the rock face that the three men used to gain access. Eliazar made light work of them, dumping their bodies over a nearby ledge into a clump of thistles some fifty feet below.

Inside the Malum's stronghold the men moved with somewhat more ease. Now their concern was the people within the building. The hallway was a long barrel vault amplifying each and every sound immensely, allowing the three intruders to hear the sounds of guards heading in their direction with ample time to react, but also allowing the guards to hear their movement if they did not move silently.

The building's interior was as one might expect, dark and damp. Candles placed into alcoves lit their path; their positioning was just far enough away from each other that shadows crawled about the ceiling, walls, and floor. In addition, the temperature of the castle was noticeably cooler than outside, a welcomed relief considering the incident with the mountain's furnace. Streams of water trickled down the roughly finished walls from somewhere above the ceiling, leaving behind red and yellow accents from the mineral deposits all along the hallways. Combined with the dim candlelight the faint colors were unsettling, giving an eerie, deadly sense to the place.

"I do believe we are in the mountain," Adam whispered.

The Malum had built the palace straight into the mountain range. A labyrinth of passages with rooms sprouting off filled the cavernous keep. After walking a good distance in, the men found that they were gradually descending an ever so slight slope. The deeper they went, the steeper the decline became, and the more cave-like the hallway appeared. Unattended dirt replaced the cut stone of the flooring. The round shape of towering columns bracing the ceiling turned into thick snags of wood. Various tools adorned the nooks and crannies as if workers were in the middle of the arduous task of expanding the tunnels.

Ahead of the trio sounds of rushing water gurgled, growing louder the farther they went. Before they knew it, there were no longer candles illuminating their path. The only source of light gleamed from an opening immediately in front of them. They stopped and waited for a moment, being careful not to be noticed. In the opening, shadows danced as the light flickered about. Using the darkness to conceal their movement, the men gradually approached the doorway.

Now closer, they could make out the sounds of voices. Although still muffled by the loud rushing of the water, the voices were loud enough for the men to discern that whoever was speaking was doing so in the Malum tongue. The dialogue was heavily one-sided, with the voice of a woman clearly dominating.

Michaelis led the way as the three of them quietly, but quickly, slipped through the entrance. It opened up to a cavern larger than the entire surface city of Acerbus. Most of the area was under construction. Workers were busy moving stones and digging in the dirt, their tools clanking and smacking against the earthen walls.

The water noise they heard was coming from a massive underground river. It looked as if the men were trying to divert its flow. A gorge was in place that would be filled up once the new path was complete.

"What are they doing?" asked Adam as softly as he could manage.

"If I had to guess, I would say they are building a very elaborate throne room," Michaelis answered.

Adam looked a little harder. "I don't understand. What makes you say that?"

"Look up there." Michaelis pointed as he spoke.

The voices the Lumenites and their new acquaintance had heard were coming from above, the apparent focus of the room. A throne sat on an enormous rock slab, high above the construction area. An intricately designed serpentine stairway carved into the bedrock led up to it. There were seven faces carved into the back of it, four on the outside and three on the inside. The four outer faces each bore a single horn which extended out dramatically while the three inner faces all sprouted two horns.

Sitting with an authoritative demeanor upon the throne was a woman. She wore a blood-red dress with purple lace draped over her face. Jewelry adorned every possible inch of her body, necklaces of gold, pearl, and various other gems hanging from her neck. She sat watching the workers, periodically sipping from a golden goblet gracefully resting in her left hand. Reclining next to her was a man nearly stripped of all clothing. Grotesque ritualistic scars covered his entire body. Without doubt, the man was Bebbel-uk. The woman's right hand rested on his head, her fingers gently massaging his bald scalp. Behind the throne was a pair of enormous, stone fire pits, flames blazing. The orange glow cast by the fire drenched the depraved couple in a monstrous light, warping their features into something hideous.

Eliazar, Michaelis, and Adam climbed up to a well-hidden spot behind a large wooden beam supporting the rock ceiling. As they reached it, the woman stood up and started speaking to the workers. She lifted the veil which concealed her face, revealing her legendary beauty.

"Evalynn," whispered Adam, his eyes widening. She looked exactly the same as she had so long ago, exactly as he had formed her.

At that moment he remembered a detail about his thought that had made them immortal, he remembered how breathtaking she looked sitting across the table from him in the restaurant, he remembered how she sat there nibbling on her desert, how her face had captivated him and how he had thought about her beauty never ever fading. Driven by lust he had thought about her appearance while completely overlooking himself.

"More like the Scarlet Harlot if you ask me." Eliazar's raspy voice echoed off the walls loudly.

Evalynn snapped her head toward where the three men were hiding, simultaneously barking a command to her minions. The Malum men stopped what they were doing and raced toward the intruders.

Without hesitation, Michaelis and Eliazar jumped out from behind the beam, swords in hand, ready to fend off the bounding force that was fast approaching. Adam slowly stepped out after them, hypnotized by the creation of his youth.

"Evalynn?" Adam called out to her inquiringly.

An expression of curiosity sprang to her face. "Adam Malloy?"

A moment passed as the two of them stared into each other's eyes. The trance broke as the woman burst into a fit of cackling laughter. "You look horrible." Evalynn watched her ancient friend walk toward her. "Seize him!"

Hearing those words, Michaelis dashed to Adam's side, his sword ready to slice through anyone wishing to take hold of Adam. A herd of Malum workers were in full sprint, charging the Lumenite warrior, when Evalynn called out.

"Stop! A Lumenite, I presume?" The empress did not wait for an answer. "Do you know who you are protecting? He is death, the ultimate plague, a disease of destruction who holds only his whimsical, self-indulgent wants close to his heart." Passion poured out of her mouth as she described the Adam she had known.

"Perhaps that is what he was. But he has put aside his errors." Michaelis spoke without letting his guard down.

"Do you not know that he is the cause of the death of so many of your people? He is why the world is the way it is." Evalynn began to descend from her throne, Bebbel-uk falling into place right behind her.

Michaelis stepped to a more defensible position. "From my perspective you are the one responsible for the death of my people. You are the one who has ordered the invasion of my land. You are the one calling on evil spirits to do your bidding."

"How naïve. Do you not understand that I wouldn't even be here if it wasn't for that old bag of bones beside you? He made me this way. He tore away any happiness that used to be inside me. He unleashed death like a pack of rabid dogs. He killed everyone I loved. In fact, he killed everyone everybody loved. He is the root of death. I am only a branch of his seed." Anger was festering within the Malum mother. Her eyes beaming hate toward Adam.

"Call him what you want. You chose to wage war with the Lumen Kingdom. That was your choice, not his." Michaelis kept his eyes fixed on the Malum men.

"You're absolutely right. I have made my choice. A long time ago I chose to align myself with the one who could give me power and I chose to use that power to hunt down the man next to you. How ironic that after all this effort, he just walked into my home. Adam, you're not the only person who can manipulate the wonders of the world. You're not alone." The angry woman moved closer to Adam.

In the Malum language she began spitting out words that were so rhythmic they flowed like poetry. Adam stepped backwards as she pressed closer.

Michaelis and Eliazar looked at each other with bewildered expressions. As Evalynn approached, the flow of the river began to slow down. Each step eased the rate of the water until finally it was perfectly still as Evalynn stood directly in front of Adam. Appearing just as gorgeous as Adam remembered, the woman leaned in next to his ear.

"You should have let him guide you." The woman took a step backwards. "He's helped me." A smile crossed Evalynn's face. She was referring to the man from Adam's dream, the one who wanted Adam's gift.

"Evalynn, he is only using you. You know that, don't you?" Adam's voice was frantic.

"No. I would say I am using him. He has taught me how to conjure his world in service of my purpose. Who do you think showed these people how to be so strong, how to possess such otherworldly skill? Me. I revealed the techniques of calling upon unsettled spirits in order to conquer this world." Evalynn twirled around in a playful parody of innocence. "This world sprang forth from your destruction and now it belongs to me."

"Evalynn, can't you see that there are other forces at work? The things you are doing in this world and to these people are not at all original. As the years have gone by I have done nothing but ponder the reason behind everything I did. Do you know what I have come to believe? I was given a gift for a specific purpose. It wasn't to alter the world for good or for bad according to my terms. It was simply given to me to illustrate an already completed work, a more important work. You see, the manner in which things have occurred has been different, but the outcome remains the same. Good still ultimately prevails and your source of power still inevitably loses. Nothing is new. It can't be changed, because the end result has already been determined; it is finished. And it was finished long before I manipulated anything." The old man ached to convince the woman of what he was trying to say.

Once again speaking in the rhythmic Malum language, Evalynn crossed her arms confidently and watched as a mist seeped out of the ground in front of Adam. The moisture was warm as it crawled up the old man's legs. Reaching his shoulders, the cloud began pulling Adam against the wooden beam behind him. Seeing that Adam was being controlled, Michaelis grabbed him in an effort to free him, but without success.

"You are no match for the forces I possess." Evalynn laughed lightly.

"What are you doing to him?" Michaelis struggled to help Adam off the beam.

Adam's head dropped down. His strength left him, flushed away, leaving only a tingly sensation behind as his inner body suddenly caught up to the age of his outer body.

"Bringing him the pain I have felt for ages." The woman spoke more poetic lyrics as she walked up to Adam. "Do you want to know what I have done?" She waited a moment to watch the look on his face. "I have just removed your curse. You should thank me. I have made it possible for you to die as the old man you are. You no longer possess the ability to live forever." Looking over, she pointed at Michaelis, sounds of the Malum mysticism spewing from her lips. "Your dear friend here will now be the one to live as long as the planet we are on. He will have the opportunity to witness the annihilation of his people and the desolation of his land. He will watch from his shackles as I destroy all the good in this world. I will block out all light in this wretched world you've created. And I will do it all in the name of Adam Malloy. Rest assured that your legacy will not die with you. Everyone in this world will feel pain just as everyone from our world did."

Michaelis felt nothing unusual. He listened as the Malum queen spoke of her plans for his country. Behind him Bebbel-uk and the group of Malum workers who had been in front of him rushed forward. The Lumen knight did not have time to react. Before he knew it he had been disarmed and restrained.

Eliazar was facing off against the rest of the Malum workers, his weapon extended, ready for anything. He was focused on the threat in front of him, never taking his eyes off his opponents as he listened to the scene unfolding behind him. At the same time the Malum men overtook Michaelis, those before Eliazar attempted to subdue him. The fight was on. All at once the Malum charged the commander's position. With ease he deflected them, his blade swinging with systematic precision. As he fought, Adam began to speak. Mustering all the strength left in his body Adam looked up at the woman he had once longed for.

"How careful were you? Manipulation is a funny thing. Somehow, no matter what we try to change, it always seems to have a way of running the course already set out." He spoke strongly, but with a slight crackle in his voice. "Don't you think it is a little strange that despite all the destruction I caused, the planet still managed to support life? And isn't it funny that the way people act today is so similar to what we knew from our world? Everyone is still torn by the same evil preoccupations which infected those from our time. I didn't have the power to change the outcome, only the way in which the outcome was achieved. Do you understand I was granted a gift? I didn't create the gift. There's a difference." His voice was getting weaker as he spoke. "We make our choices, but the end result is already known. And trust me, Evalynn, that end will not be with you achieving the plans planted in your mind by he that wanders about the Earth." Adam looked at Michaelis. "I think perhaps the end rested with someone else, and those who follow the way he established." A subtle smile drooped from Adam's face as he let his head rest.

Evalynn followed Adam's gaze, glaring at Michaelis, understanding her former companion's words to be an endorsement of the Lumen people over and against her own. She struggled to control the anger that was growing in her heart.

"Bring him here." She commanded as she lifted Adam's head. "We'll see about that." With Michaelis in front of her, the woman ordered her servants to bind Adam and Michaelis together, facing one another, and then bring them to the river's edge. "You don't think I will succeed in my task? Given that I'm the one with all the power now, that I'm the one in control, perhaps you should've thought about your friends and whether or not you were careful not to provoke me with your words. But then again you've never been one to consider how the consequences of your choices affect others." As she spoke, Bebbel-uk pushed the two into the river. The last of her words reached their ears just before their heads sank below the water.

She smiled menacingly before amending her plans for Michaelis, "I suppose he'll forever be in shackles, so to speak, however, he'll find it difficult to watch the annihilation of his land while spending eternity under water. Oh well, such is life."

The two men sank to the bottom of the river ever so slowly, bubbles gradually rising past them as air pockets within their clothing gave way to gushes of water. The cool liquid danced about the duo, causing their hair to drift according to the current. Dim rays of light breaking through the surface highlighted their faces, revealing each man's emotional state.

At first Michaelis tried with all his might to swim for the surface, but with Adam tied to him his efforts were fruitless. Adam had barely been able to hold up his head, let alone swim. The old Adam was nothing more than an anchor weighing the two men down. As they drifted downward, they looked into one another's eyes, Michaelis' showing hope and determination. He was as focused as he had been on the battlefield, intent on making it through the day. Adam's eyes on the other hand, revealed a somber peace, a longing for the situation to hurry, to run its course so that he could be freed from his torment. Although his heart and mind wanted eternal rest, his body did not. A burst of energy shot throughout the man just as they hit the riverbed. Franticly he jerked about, struggling desperately to live. It was instinct. He had wished for death so many times, but when it was upon him his flesh chose to fight to live.

As the ancient man gave his last attempt to hold on, Michaelis accepted what was happening. The two bodies peacefully settled among the river rocks as Adam Malloy's lungs filled with water, his softly thumping heart beating for the last time. Michaelis noticed that as death received his counterpart's limp body, it became still and more buoyant. Several moments went by before the Lumen warrior started to shimmy his body in an attempt to escape his bindings. Seconds later he successfully managed to work his way out from under the rope. Free, Michaelis looked at Adam's empty body briefly, making sure the old man was dead before swimming to the surface. A loud gasp of air bellowed from his mouth as he broke through the water's surface.

Evalynn and her laughing entourage were startled as the Lumenite erupted from the river, their mouths and eyes wide open.

"What? No!" Evalynn shrieked.

Michaelis pulled himself up onto the shore, coughing. Eliazar, still fighting the Malum, began to chuckle hysterically at the sight of his young leader.

Furious, Evalynn picked up the Defender's lumenium sword, wrenching it back, preparing to swing it as her foe climbed to his feet.

"Michaelis, look out!" Eliazar now focused more on Michaelis' situation than his own.

Upon the warning Michaelis dropped down to one knee, tumbling forward under the slash of his own sword. When he turned, rising to his feet, Evalynn was already lunging toward him again. This time she had the blade aimed straight at him, ready to run the man through. Michaelis tried to dodge the attack, but wet and still disoriented, he was not able to move quickly enough. The weapon pierced him between the ribs, slicing all the way through his body until the hilt of the sword pressed firmly against his skin. Evalynn did not allow the fact that she had no more blade hinder her rage induced desire. Using the momentum she had gained, the woman slammed Michaelis up against the beam of wood to which Adam had so recently been restrained. Realizing the Defender was pinned against the wood she backed up, a look of satisfaction washing over her face.

"Stay." She demanded.

Michaelis was amazed. He did not feel as though he were dying. It was then that he recalled what the Malum mistress had said to Adam. She had transferred the old man's immortal status to him. When she had said it, Michaelis had not truly believed that she possessed the power to do such a thing. But as he looked down at the handle of his sword protruding from his body, he realized what was happening.

"Who says I won't succeed in achieving my goals?" Evalynn asked, giggling as she did so.

"I do." Michaelis began pulling the sword out of his gut. "It looks as though death has been defeated, again." A loud grunt followed as he fell from the wood. "Have you already forgotten that I am no longer contained by mortality? From this point on, no matter what you try to do," Michaelis rose to his feet, "you lose. I will be here, in your way, crushing the head of all your attempts to kill my people. As they realize that you are no longer a threat, your war efforts will become less effective. When your people see that they no longer have the upper hand, they will begin to ask themselves what is happening. And as they witness the Lumen Kingdom growing stronger, they too will realize that you cannot help them. And eventually they will turn on you. They will scream for your head and curse the day they chose to follow you. Understand this. You and your ilk have no more power. You simply exist. The war between Malum and Lumen is finished." There was such strength in his rich words that the Malum who were attacking Eliazar stopped in mid-swing and began to listen.

"You're forgetting something, Lumenite. I bestowed upon you your immortality and I can remove it as well. I have an army of spirits under my command. The prince of this world has entrusted me with legions. This world is mine. I do as I wish! The Malum people are my people and they do as I command. The men obey my will and wage war upon whom I declare." Evalynn began mumbling in the Malum tongue.

Running for the entrance of the cavern Michaelis shouted, "Wage your war! The people of Lumen stand at the ready. The victory will always be ours."

Eliazar followed his lead. The Malum men stood motionless, waiting to see what was going to happen next.

"What are we going to do with Evil-Lynn?" Eliazar asked.

"She wants to rule the Earth. I say we let her sit on her throne in peace." Michaelis looked at his older friend and winked, "until the day the Earth stops spinning."

Watching the two Lumenites escaping, Evalynn ordered the Malum workers to seize them. As the two soldiers ascended up and out of the cavernous castle, they used their weapons to chop down each beam holding the mountainous ceiling at bay; first Eliazar and then Michaelis, each one addressing the opposite side of the tunnel. Nearly halfway out, the hall began crumbling behind them, a mass of earth dumping into the manmade void, burying the Malum men who were in pursuit of the fleeing pair. The two cut down every gnarled chunk of wood until they reached the columns of stone. Debris rocketed out of the hallway as Michaelis and Eliazar slowed their pace.

"Wow! That actually worked," Eliazar said, confirming that the spontaneous plan was a good one.

"Did you ever really have a doubt?"

"Honestly? Yes. I did not completely cut the third brace in. It must have been a hardwood, perhaps a Chatti Oak." Eliazar grunted at the near miss.

Under their feet the earth rumbled, thundering from the mountain's collapse.

Eliazar's eyebrow shot up in curiosity. "So, do you really think she is in league with the prince of this world?"

"I have no doubt." Michaelis put his hand on Eliazar's shoulder as the two headed out of the grisly palace.

"I could really go for a tall stein of fine ale right about now," the veteran said after spitting out some dust that had accumulated inside his mouth.

Michaelis laughed at his comrade's desire to keep everything simple. Simple. That is precisely what things were now. Michaelis thought of Adam's words, how in the grand scheme of things the end had already been decided, that the evil in the world would inevitably be defeated, even at times when it seemed to be reigning victorious. It was bothersome that so many questions would forever go unanswered, so many pieces of the past forever lost along with Adam, the ancient man from a previous age.

"Eliazar, what do you suppose Adam meant when he said his gift was given to illustrate an already completed work?"

"That sounds like a question for a Martinian," the commander said, twisting his head in order to crack his neck into position.

"Without knowing the old man's past, we can only speculate. I will say this, my friend. If Adam was an example or an illustration as he called it, I think it is safe to say he was only part of it."

The men made their way back to where Pura and the other Lumenite soldiers were waiting. Once reunited, the band of warriors departed the mountains with haste.

For Michaelis the trip back to the familiar territory of the Lumen lands was full of many thoughts as he reflected on the old man and his relationship to him. Baffled by far-reaching thoughts that he did not fully understand, he began to focus on a truth he did. He knew for sure that the Lumen people were strong and possessed all that was needed for continual victory over evil. Who knew when the next threat would present itself? Would it be Evalynn's doing? It did not matter. It was a new day for the Lumenites, a day of triumph.

Acknowledgments

Thank you, Jessica, for being my constant support and encouragement. Thanks for reading this first legend over and over and over again and for letting me geek out about my made-up world, and for not thinking me too big a dork when I did. Thank you Jonas and Bethany for stoking my imagination in play. I will always cherish our days as Defenders, sword fighting in the house. The memory traps me in the delightful world of childhood. May I never escape.

Josh and Kasandra Radke, thank you for believing in this project and helping me resurrect it and my love of writing from the tomb of uncertainty. Thanks Eric Postma for sharing your talent as editor. The Lumen Kingdom is better for all your work. Sam, Christopher, Paul, Mary, Lisa, Ray, and Jessica, thank you for your time and thoughtful feedback. I owe each of you a deep debt of gratitude. Edward Riojas, I can only hope my words measure up to your art. Thank you for an amazing cover.

And finally, thank you, dear reader, for embarking on this adventure with me. May the Light of the Lumen Legends illumine your life. The truth is knowable. It's the light that shines in the darkness, and the darkness has not overcome it.

About the Author

Tyrel Bramwell is a pastor and author. He offers readers a worldview that is packed with imagination, yet rooted in the knowable and absolute truth. He has a bachelor's degree from Concordia University, Michigan and his master of divinity degree from Concordia Theological Seminary, Indiana. When he is not shepherding or telling stories he is busy being husband to his wife and father to his two children.

Visit him at moragunfighter.com